'For God's sake, lean against me,' he growled in her ear. **'I'm going to drop you at this rate.'**

She gritted her teeth, refusing to give in, to relax against him, every nerve-ending in her body fighting him, refusing to acknowledge the tantalising closeness of his touch. The muscles along her spine strained with the effort. She sighed with relief as he threw her up onto his horse, then tensed once more as he jumped up behind her.

'Fighting me will merely slow us down,' Lussac pointed out slowly. 'Do you really want those…whoever they are…to catch up with you?'

Who did she prefer? she wondered. The soldiers hired by her father and uncle at great expense to bring her back home, or this knight at her back, handsome and dangerous, whose very nearness spiked her body into ever-increasing spirals of desire? With Lussac behind her, solid thighs cradling the soft roundness of her hips, his arms pressed heavily against her shoulders, Katerina questioned whether she was in even greater danger than she had been before.

AUTHOR NOTE

My story of Lussac and Katerina was inspired by the tales of travelling entertainers who toured the country in Medieval times. I wanted to capture those long, glittering evenings by candlelight, the audience gasping in delight at the daring feats of the acrobats, or roaring with laughter at the jesters' antics.

With her amazing skills, Katerina unwittingly becomes the person everyone desires to see, despite her wanting to hide from a past that threatens to catch up with her every day.

For the history buffs among you, the invasion of Queen Isabella of England in 1326 on the Suffolk shores provides the historical context and brings our hero, Lussac, to England. Fed up with the constant philandering and mismanagement of the country by her husband the King, Isabella raises an army to overthrow him. She succeeds in a world controlled by men, where women are very much regarded as second-class citizens—no mean feat!

I hope the Queen's bravery and strength of character are reflected in my heroine, Katerina, who has to fight, with Lussac's help, against her own impossible situation. And I hope you enjoy the story!

THE KNIGHT'S FUGITIVE LADY

Meriel Fuller

This is a work of fiction. Names, characters, places, locations and incidents are purely fictional and bear no relationship to any real life individuals, living or dead, or to any actual places, business establishments, locations, events or incidents. Any resemblance is entirely coincidental.

First published in Great Britain 2013
by Mills & Boon, an imprint of Harlequin (UK) Limited,
Large Print edition 2014
Harlequin (UK) Limited, Eton House, 18-24 Paradise Road,
Richmond, Surrey TW9 1SR

© 2013 Meriel Fuller

ISBN: 978 0 263 23962 1

Harlequin (UK) Limited's policy is to use papers that are natural, renewable and recyclable products and made from wood grown in sustainable forests. The logging and manufacturing processes conform to the legal environmental regulations of the country of origin.

Printed and bound in Great Britain
by CPI Antony Rowe, Chippenham, Wiltshire

Meriel Fuller lives in a quiet corner of rural Devon, England, with her husband and two children. Her early career was in advertising, with a bit of creative writing on the side. Now, with a family to look after, writing has become her passion… A keen interest in literature, the arts and history, particularly the early medieval period, makes writing historical novels a pleasure. The Devon countryside, a landscape rich in medieval sites, holds many clues to the past and has made her research a special treat.

Previous novels by the same author:

CONQUEST BRIDE
THE DAMSEL'S DEFIANCE
THE WARRIOR'S PRINCESS BRIDE
CAPTURED BY THE WARRIOR
HER BATTLE-SCARRED KNIGHT

**Did you know that some of these novels are also available as eBooks?
Visit www.millsandboon.co.uk**

To my children, Fin and Verity.

Chapter One

East coast England—September 1326

'Success?' Waleran called up, softly, inching forwards on his stomach.

From the top of the slope, Katerina smiled down at her friend, mouth curving generously in her pale, heart-shaped face, and held up her heavy satchel. 'Success,' she answered, tucking her catapult back into the bag. She moved down through the trees, the drab colours of her boy's clothes blending in with the surrounding vegetation, loose, flapping garments that camouflaged her true sex. Her stomach growled at the prospect of eating roast rabbit for breakfast; the last time she had eaten meat had been three days ago. Since then, they had been ekeing out the last dusty contents of a sack of oats, watered down and cooked to make a sloppy gruel.

John would be pleased with them; the rabbit was fat enough to feed at least half the circus troupe.

'Come, let's go.' Waleran pulled his thin, wiry frame upwards, heavy dew darkening his patched tunic.

'It's still early.' Katerina cocked her head on one side, grinning; her grey eyes sparkled. The sun peeked above the horizon, a crack of golden light firing the white birch trunks, touching the wisps of tawny hair that poked out from beneath her hood. She patted the bulge in her bag. 'These rabbits will feed only half of us.'

Waleran shifted uncomfortably, hunching his shoulders. 'I don't want to risk it, Katerina. Even at this hour, the Earl's men could be about; I don't want to be caught poaching.'

Katerina snorted. 'And when have we ever been caught? I doubt he'll miss a couple of rabbits from his vast estates.'

'Why not return to the camp along the beach?' Waleran suggested. 'At least the fish are free.'

'All right, Waleran—' Katerina tucked her arm through his '—we'll do it your way this morning. Roast rabbit and fish, what could be better?' She lifted small hands to pull her hood more firmly forwards, obscuring the brilliant colour of her hair.

An amused look crossed Waleran's narrow features. 'Have you forgotten?' He stared pointedly at their linked arms. 'Two boys, arm in arm, would certainly draw attention.'

'Oh!' Katerina clapped a hand to her mouth. Her laughter echoed out, sweet and clear, amongst the trees, against the slight breeze dislodging the occasional leaf from the branches spanned above their heads. 'Forgive me, I forget sometimes.'

'It's for your own safety, Katerina.' Waleran grinned at her, his gaze soft. Who could have known? he thought, as they walked through the forest, lapsed into a friendly silence, calf-length boots scuffing through the fallen leaves, kicking up the desiccated papery shapes. The daughter of a lord, no less, now sunk to the level of a common acrobat. None of the other entertainers, the jugglers and the jesters, the other acrobats, not one of them in the troupe had a clue about who she was, where she came from. All she wanted was a place to hide, to disappear.

Nearer the shore, the woodland trees grew sparser; the sound of waves breaking against shingle, then sucking back to lurch themselves forwards once more, reached their ears. The bent pines on the edge of the forest turned to scrubby blackthorn, bramble patches sprawling across shifting sands. The wind blew in from the east, keen and nippy, straight from the vast plains of the northern countries and Katerina hugged her arms about herself, against its cruel bite knifing painfully through her threadbare tunic, her worn chemise. Eyes watering against the wind, she turned towards the expanse of river estuary, salt marshes bisected by deep, muddy creeks, an immense sweep of mudflats, peppered with scores of pale-grey birds, yellow beaks bright against the dun-coloured mud.

Descending towards the salt marsh, they began to pick their way across, heading for the beach, the suck and crash of waves that landed on the shore in a boiling froth of foam. To their left, shallow cliffs, grass-topped, began to rise: sandy, amber-coloured flanks striated with clay. The wind snatched at Katerina's cloak as they rounded the base of the cliff into the next bay, Waleran walking a little in front of her, playing the role of her protector, as always. He stopped suddenly, abruptly, staggering back, swinging one arm back to stop Katerina.

'What…?' she blurted out, confused by his unexpected halt.

And then she saw.

Further up the coast, bathed in the pinky-orange glow of morning, a fleet of maybe thirty ships clustered to the shore, coloured square sails flapping in the wind. Horses, muscled, shiny warhorses, their eyes rolling in fright at the prospect of entering the water, were being led down wooden ramps, pulled by their bridles through the foaming surf to the shore. Men, hundreds of men dressed in glittering chainmail, helmets obscuring their features, swarmed over the sides of the ship, running through the shallow sea to gather on the beach. Already, some had mounted up, swinging their horses about with a look of intent, orders shouted in a harsh guttural language.

'Lord in Heaven!' breathed Waleran. 'Who are they?'

In the rising sun, the metallic shields of the soldiers shot back the light; it was difficult to decipher the colours. Heart thumping, Katerina screwed up her eyes, forced herself to focus on one shield only. Dark-blue background, gold fleur-de-lys. A gold crown above. Her stomach dropped, hollowed out in panic, and her legs began to shake.

'It's the Queen, Waleran,' she managed to judder out. 'Queen Isabella…of England.' She touched a hand to her face, unsure, confused. 'But I don't understand. Those are not English knights…'

Waleran paled. He grabbed her hand. 'This bodes ill, Katerina. We must run…and run fast, away from this place. It's not safe.'

Heeding the wavering panic in Waleran's voice,

the warning, Katerina spun on her heel, leaping the ditch behind them with the easy agility of a deer, her tunic's loose hem fluttering out over slim legs encased in woollen braies. Waleran paused, assessing the creek's wide gap, wondering if he would make it.

'Got you!' a gruff voice echoed in his ear.

Something, someone, hauled roughly at his belt, dragged him unceremoniously backwards. All he could see was Katerina's expression, white and stricken on the other side, the safe side of the creek, her mouth falling open in horror at whoever was behind him. Fear crawled in his gut; he had no intention of turning around.

A group of four or five soldiers clustered around her friend, the oldest and burliest of the group holding on to Waleran. There was no doubt as to their identity: gold fleur-de-lys glinted dully on their dark-blue cloaks and on their shields. Steel helmets obscured their faces, shining silver, the rest of their bodies clad in chainmail.

'What's in the bag, boy?' The lead soldier indicated Katerina's satchel, his eyes glinting out, narrow and mean, from the shadowed confines of his helmet.

'Let my friend go and I tell you,' Katerina replied. An angry helplessness swept over her as she watched Waleran's futile struggles within the soldier's burly grip. There was little point in her going to him; she hadn't the physical strength to wrest him away, but every instinct in her body wanted to do it, to go there.

The soldier's features darkened; he shook Waleran, but kept his eyes on Katerina. 'Don't play games with me, lad. You're in no position to bargain. I ask you again, what's in the bag?' His voice was threatening.

One of the other soldiers, a younger one, shuffled uneasily. 'Hey, Bomal, take it easy. We weren't sent out to torture the locals, remember?'

'Keep out of it!' Bomal snarled back. Katerina lifted one hand self-consciously, making certain that her hood was pulled over her fine features. If they worked out she was a woman, the situation could develop into something far more serious for her.

The soldier set his head to one side, waiting for her answer.

'A couple of rabbits,' she relented, finally, remembering to keep her voice pitched low.

'Been poaching on the lord's land, eh?' the soldier jeered at her. 'Hand them over, then.'

Despite the spurt of fear in her veins and Waleran's soft brown eyes imploring her, beseeching her to follow the soldier's instructions, her fingers clutched more firmly around the bag-strap.

'Let my friend go and then I'll chuck over the bag.'

The soldier scowled, pulling a short knife from a leather scabbard attached to his belt. The steel blade glinted, the light bouncing off the shiny metal. He held the blade to Waleran's throat.

'What do I need to do to convince you?' he shouted over to her.

Katerina was convinced. Body quaking with fear, she threw the bag over. Sheathing his knife, the soldier caught the bundle in his meaty fingers. 'Thanks very much, young squire,' he addressed her, his tone mocking, false. 'And now you, young man—' he kept a firm grip on Waleran's upper sleeve '—you're coming with us. We need someone to lead us to the nearest village.'

'Let him go!' Katerina's voice rose perilously close to a screech. Stop playing with us! she wanted to shout out loud. We are nothing, nobody. We are just humble travellers, trying to earn a living, trying to find a morsel of food to fill our stomachs from one day to the next. And now these fat-bellied soldiers had stolen them, stolen the rabbits that they had spent all morning trying to catch. They couldn't, they wouldn't get away with this!

She watched dismally as Waleran was boosted up into the saddle behind the youngest-looking soldier, endeavouring to smile at her friend as he looked back at her, eyes pitiful. She refused to succumb to helplessness, to a wavering vulnerability that threatened to encroach her, to weaken her. A few stupid soldiers wouldn't beat her! Without a doubt, she would find the means to outwit them.

'Don't worry, Waleran,' she whispered, as the horses' glossy rumps retreated, heading northwards to a dark stretch of trees. 'I will come for you.'

Lussac, Count of Belbigny, leaned his elbows against the wooden rail of the forecastle and watched, through narrowed turquoise eyes, as the last of the soldiers, a jumbled mix of hired mercenaries and exiled English lords, made their way to the shore, dutifully following their Queen. Some were fortunate enough to clamber into the few rowboats brought with them across the North Sea from Hainault; others were not so lucky, splashing and stumbling in their heavy armour through the knee-deep waves, raucous curses splitting the morning air. Behind him, taut stay ropes now released, the huge square sail hung limp, ineffectual, beneath the crow's nest, flapping dismally in the breeze. It had taken two days to sail from the Flanders coast, two long days and nights of churning seas, and an unexpected storm that had thrown the ships off course. Their exact location was unknown; it could be anywhere on the east coast of England north of the wide mouth of the river that led to London.

'Lussac, come now, you are the last!' A shout from one of the row-boats drawn alongside the high-sided wooden cog hailed him. He peered over the side, straight chestnut hair falling over his tanned forehead, trying to locate the owner of the familiar voice who shouted to him from the shadows of the vessel.

'Come on, man! Do you want to go back? The ships will leave directly.'

Lussac smiled tersely, a muscle leaping in the shadowed hollow of his cheek. He had no intention of going back. After four years of battling the demons, of never being able to rid himself of the black bile that clagged his heart, King Charles of France, his friend, had offered him a life-line, a way out. When Queen Isabella, Charles's younger sister, had announced her intention to overthrow her husband, King Edward II of England, by way of an invasion commanded by Roger Mortimer, Charles had suggested that Lussac travelled on the ships to England, to seek revenge and heal his tattered soul.

Lussac had agreed readily to Charles's proposition. The passing years had failed to wash away the pain, to dull his memory. The scenes burst into his brain again and again, as if they had happened yesterday, vivid colours etched with dreadful clarity: the pall of smoke rising above his home, the charred rafters collapsing around him in plumes of hot ash. And the running, the breathless sprinting up the steps to find his family... The slipping time seemed only to intensify his feelings of loss, of desperation, of anger. Revenge burned, deep in his solar plexus, coursing through his veins like a sour, bitter liquid; he could taste it on his tongue. Around the bare skin of his wrist, the leather cuff wrapped tight, chafed at his skin, reminding him. Scooped up from the scene of the crime, the only clue to the identity of the English knight who had killed his family.

Ignoring the rope ladder, Lussac placed one lean, muscled hand on the side of the ship and jumped down into the rowboat, planting his feet out to steady himself against the inevitable rocking from his weight. His substantial frame tilted the smaller vessel from side to side, threatening to tip them both into the sea.

'Careful! You'll have us over, fooling around like that!' Philippe clutched at the oars as they threatened to slide, pulling them back into the row-locks.

'Philippe?' Lussac sprawled opposite his friend, tilting his head in a quizzical look. He stretched out his long legs, encased in the fine silver mesh of chainmail. The sturdy boots that covered his calves were made of thick Spanish leather and stained with sea-water, each toe carrying a wavering line of white, drying salt. 'Am I'm seeing things? A nobleman rowing a boat?'

Philippe grimaced, pushing a strand of fair hair out of his eyes. Sweat plastered his fleshy face, mottled cheeks flushed with a greasy sheen. He wore no helmet and the hood of his chainmail hauberk gathered at the back of his neck.

'Do you think I have a choice?' he hissed, although they were still some considerable distance from the shore. He wrangled tetchily with an oar, trying to angle it so he could manoeuvre them away from the ship. 'I don't think the Queen has any idea who I am! Me! Philippe, Comte de Garsan! She ordered me to come and fetch you, like I was some low-born soldier! All the others are running around, trying to make her comfortable! Look, they've even constructed a tent for her, already.'

'And a fire, too,' Lussac commented drily. The smoke rose, billowing up from the white-grey shingle, fanning out against the low, ochre-coloured cliffs that lined the shore. 'Let's hope the smoke doesn't draw any unwanted attention; we have no idea whether we are in a safe area or not.'

'I said that!' Philippe jabbed the air triumphantly, the woollen tunic that covered his chainmail pulling tautly across his rounded stomach. 'I told them the exact same thing. But would they listen? Nay, says Mortimer, our Queen is freezing and her ladies are cold after such a horrendous journey and we need to warm them. Christ, I swear that man will do anything for that woman. I know that they want to keep their adultery a secret, but honestly, it's plain for anyone to see!' He turned his attention back to his friend, noting the familiar, bleak look in Lussac's eyes, the shadowed expression. 'Not that any of this concerns you.'

Lussac shrugged his shoulders, mouth tightening. Philippe was correct. The fact that Queen Isabella had fallen in love with Roger Mortimer, her campaign commander, mattered little. Nothing concerned him. Nothing, that was, except finding the man who killed his family. But the Queen's campaign to overthrow her husband provided him with the means to travel to England, and for that, he was grateful.

'Do you want me to row?' Lussac offered. Beyond the deep shadow cast by the ship, the surface of the sea sparkled, as if studded with diamonds.

'Gladly,' Philippe said, wiping his forehead. 'It took me an age to reach you.'

The two men swapped places, Lussac gripping the oars, dipping the blades rhythmically, easily, in the water. Strings of water glittered down from the pale wood. Philippe sighed, leaning back in the boat, closing his eyes and tipping his face up to the tepid heat of the September sun. The light danced off the water, shining, blinding; with a strange, keening cry, a raft of sea-birds curved in one sinuous movement towards the bouncing sea, before jerking away at the last moment, inexplicably, to head off in a different direction.

Philippe opened his eyes. 'Thank Christ the weather has taken a turn for the better. I couldn't imagine sleeping under canvas in the likes of that storm we went through.'

'I suspect the Queen will call in some favours,' Lussac replied, twisting around to see how near to the shore they were. 'I'm sure she has no intention of sleeping under canvas either.'

Soon they were in the long swathes of white

surf, shingle crunching and grinding along the bottom of the boat. Drawing the oars in to rest along the sides of the boat, Lussac climbed out into the shallow water, Philippe grumbling behind him about wet feet. The water soaked through their calf-length boots, their chainmail chausses, but Lussac scarcely noticed. He was used to harsh conditions, to being wet and damp and cold, being camped out for days and days in winter, fighting in the borderlands between the English-held Gascony and France. Fighting, battling—they were his *modus operandi;* without them, he would simply cease to be.

'Ah, Lussac!' Mortimer approached, his gait awkward across the sloping shingle. He was a tall, thin man with a rigid, angular frame and everything about him, from his jet-black hair, his brown eyes, to his grey tunic and black flapping cloak, was dark, crow-like. He slapped Lussac congenially on the back, his head making a strange bobbing motion into his shoulders.

'How are the women faring?' Lussac asked, the briefest of smiles on his face. Many of the Queen's ladies had suffered on the journey, the rolling, heavy sea taking its toll on their stomachs.

Mortimer rolled his eyes. 'Not good. Isabella's complaining about being hungry; they all are, in fact. Honestly, when you look at the way they're carrying on, you'd think we were out on some day trip, not invading England.'

'How much food do we have?'

'The bread is soaked through with sea-water… and the milk has turned. We only brought enough provisions for the journey.' His eyes swept the cliffs in desperation, as if they would provide the answer to their dire food situation. 'Our compass bearing, when we set off from Flanders, should have brought us within sight of the Earl of Norfolk's castle and estates. He supports the Queen and will give us board and lodging—'

'The storm blew us off course,' Philippe chipped in. He understood Queen Isabella's predicament, for his own stomach growled in sympathy.

Mortimer's gaze slipped over to the short, stocky man at Lussac's side, his expression blank, diffident, before switching his attention back to Lussac. 'As the first soldiers came ashore with their horses, I sent them out as a search party, to find out where we are, to find some food. But they seem to be taking for ever!'

Lussac glanced at the soldiers huddled together in large, sprawling groups on the gently shelving beach, waiting. They were tired and hungry, and in no position to push forwards, to march any long distances. The few horses belonging to the nobles stood behind the Queen's tent, tails fanning out in the breeze. He had no wish to sit and wait with them, to chew over the tedious details of the journey, to stare dully at the sea. Or to think.

'I will go and look for them. They can't have gone far.'

'Nay, you can't do that!' Mortimer looked horrified. Lussac was the same rank as himself and, beyond that, he was close friends with the King of France. They had grown up together, trained together; it simply wouldn't do to send such a high-ranking nobleman out on a simple scouting expedition. His gaze switched to Philippe. Maybe…?

'I want to go,' Lussac explained. How could he explain the constant nagging restlessness coursing through his big frame, the inability to sit still and reflect, to stare at a bird in flight, or watch the waves crash on to the shingle? Nay, that might be for other men, but not for him. Not now. If he allowed his mind to think too much, then the full horror of the past came back to him, filling his head with images and pictures he would prefer to forget. Better to keep active, to throw himself into every battle and skirmish when the opportunities arose, rather than sit around and brood. Never that.

Chapter Two

L ussac kicked the heels of his stout leather boots into his horse's side, urging the animal away from the beach. After the cramped, restrictive conditions on board ship, it felt good to be moving again. He stretched his legs out against the stirrups, the taut muscles in his thighs and calves relishing the movement as the saddle-leather creaked beneath his tall, muscular frame. As his horse climbed to the top of the narrow path that led up the low cliffs, the whole sweep of this hostile country spread out before him. To his left, through a patchy area of tidal creeks, the wide, flat ribbon of a river made its slow, meandering course towards the sea. Before him, a gently sloping area of rough grass dissolved into woodland up to his right. The place was deserted.

But then his gaze swung back, sharply. What had he seen? What has his mind registered that his eyes had not? A trace of colour, blotched on the horizon? He kicked his horse on, suspecting he might find the soldiers he was looking for. The animal cantered across the uneven plain, Lussac hunkered low in the saddle. As he approached, he realised it was one soldier, sitting on the bleached ground at the edge of the tussocky marshland, his head bowed. A dark-blue patch of colour in this pale, glittery, everlasting landscape. He had removed his helmet and his thick, sandy-coloured hair riffled in the slight breeze. Galloping across to him, Lussac reined his horse brusquely, jumping down almost in the same movement.

'You, soldier, tell me what happened!'

The boy looked dazed, drugged even, as if he had woken from a dream. Seeing Lussac, recognising his authority, he placed one hand behind him and tried to push himself to his feet, but dizziness overwhelmed him and he fell back.

'Stay where you are, boy,' Lussac ordered, impatiently. 'What happened to you?' Behind him, his horse shifted constantly, as if aware of his master's irritation, hooves pawing the ground.

'An angel came,' the boy murmured.

'And she hit you on the head?' Lussac mocked. The boy had obviously been unconscious, judging from his addled speech. What did he think he was saying?

'Aye, she hit me on the head. And she took my horse.'

Lussac snorted in disbelief. The boy was clearly talking nonsense. 'Can you not remember what *really* happened?' he tried once more.

'I tell you no lie, my lord, I promise you.' The young soldier rubbed the back of his head, tentatively. A searing, uncomfortable ache was spreading through his skull. 'I was following the others, at the back. And then, all of a sudden, I was pulled from my horse, backwards. *She* pulled me from my horse.'

'She?'

'An angel, I swear to you. Her face…like a pearl, gleaming it was. Beautiful. She was beautiful. I must have knocked myself out when I fell, despite wearing this…' he gestured towards his helmet '…and she leaned over me, told me I would be all right.'

'Did she indeed.' Lussac didn't believe one word of it. A face like a pearl? The lad was delusional, suffering from the after-effects of hitting his head, or he was deliberately making the whole story up to cover his own embarrassment at having his horse stolen. He had probably fallen off his animal of his own accord and the horse had run off, following the others.

'The other soldiers—did they see any of this?'

The lad had the grace to look faintly embarrassed. 'I'm sorry, my lord, I was lagging behind, and they didn't realise. I'm…I'm not used to riding with all this heavy armour.'

'You'll get used to it,' Lussac replied tartly. 'Which direction did they take? Can you remember that, at least?'

The boy lifted his arm, pointed towards the cloud of dark-green trees to the north. 'That way, they went towards the forest.' He lowered his arm, fixing Lussac with a resolute stare. 'And the angel followed them.'

'On your horse.' Lussac threw the lad a tight smile as he swung himself back into the saddle. The leather creaked as he leaned forwards, gathering the reins, the split side-seam of his tunic falling open to reveal long legs encased in shining chainmail.

'On my horse,' the soldier repeated, staring up at him. 'I know you don't believe me, my lord, but it's true. An angel stole my horse.'

Irritation clenched at Lussac's gut as he raised one arm to push away a low, overhanging branch at the entrance to the forest. Where had Isabella found these mercenaries to fight on her behalf—in the madhouse? The only saving grace was that they had all gone in the same direction—north—Mortimer's men, and the 'stolen' horse.

The forest was quiet, still, the thick belt of trees diffusing the power of the wind that had raced across the flat river plain. Sunlight, diluted, subdued, flickered down to the sandy mud of the forest floor. The half-light was easy on the eye, a welcome relief after the stark, searing light of the beach, the sunlight bouncing harshly off the sea. Lussac inhaled, deeply, rolling his shoulders back to ease the tension in his muscles, a clean, fresh scent rising from the ground as his horse's hooves ground into the pine needles strewn across the track. The smell yanked him back, back to the southern pine forests of his youth, those carefree days when he had ridden bareback through the trees, laughing and joking with his friends, when he had swam in the cool lakes and eaten fresh walnuts from the trees, in those idyllic days, when he had had a family to go home to.

There was no one there now. His family home was empty, half-burned to the ground. His mother and father and sister were dead, dead from smoke inhalation, their prone bodies clasping, reaching out to each other to die on the floor of the locked solar. Where he had found them.

A sudden sweep of wind brought down a shower of leaves, beech leaves, spinning around his helmet like burnished feathers, adding to the undulating carpet of dark-green pine needles across the ground, jolting him back to the present, to the quiet stillness of the forest.

A sound—a single sound carried towards him on the breeze.

The jangle of a bridle. Amidst the startled shriek of a blackbird, the sough of the wind high in the tree canopy, and the slow whisper of leaves dropping to the ground, he heard it. And heard it again. He spurred his horse on, pushing the animal from a trot to a canter, hooves flying over the soft ground, in pursuit of that delicate sound. The sound of an angel? He smiled, but the smile failed to reach the steely turquoise depths of his eyes.

Fortunately for Katerina, only one clear track was discernible through the trees: the only path that could possibly have been taken by those brutish soldiers. She prayed Waleran wasn't too frightened and would realise that she had every intention of rescuing him. As he had rescued her. The other members of the circus troupe joked about Waleran and her being joined at the hip, and maybe it was true. Her friend since childhood, he had taught her the tricks and turns which, at that time, she had never realised she would come to rely on. Waleran had offered her freedom and she had seized it as a drowning man grips on to a floating raft.

Following the path with an easy trot, she held her seat comfortably in the rigid, upright saddle, fingers slack around the bridle. Every now and again, the horse would shake his head violently, mane fanning out like a chicken's-tail feathers, the bit between his teeth jangling. It was almost as if he were protesting at having a woman on his back! But all the head shaking and eye rolling didn't worry her; she had grown up around horses and could handle them without fuss, however temperamental they wished to be.

Katerina could have moved faster; the track was wide enough, but she had no wish to barge straight into those thugs. Nay, she would have to be more cunning, for they would overpower her in a moment and the element of surprise would be lost. She intended to spring Waleran from their clutches by a far more subversive method. At this precise moment she had no idea what exactly that method was. Caught in her musing, she failed to hear the thump of galloping hooves until they were almost upon her.

'You've got a bloody nerve!' A low, powerful voice struck her in the back.

Panic shot through her, hot, visceral, sucking the strength from her limbs. Instinctively she crouched forwards, as if expecting a blow, at the same time digging her heels sharply into the horse's sides to speed him away from any attack. Seizing the reins, she felt her hands shake with fear, adrenalin hurtling at breakneck speed around her body.

'Oh, no, you don't!' From behind, two massive arms clamped viciously around her shoulders, wrenching her slight weight up and off the horse. The treacherous animal moved away from under her and she was left dangling in mid-air, her attacker, unseen, at her back. Almost immediately she began to struggle, to kick her legs this way and that, feet flailing, trying to make her attacker drop her, trying to twist her body out of that hateful grasp. Fear spurred her on, forcing her to fight, for her freedom, for her life. Would these strangers kill you, for stealing a horse? She had no wish to find out. Katerina thrashed out, heels catching back into the soft flank of his horse, as she used all the muscles in her body to throw it to and fro, trying to break the fearsome grip.

'Let go of me!' she shrieked, her voice rising with hysterical anger. She had to force him to drop her and then she could run. She was fast, she could outrun any man. Her captor's arms were like iron bands around her upper body, squeezing the air from her lungs, but his bare hands, lean and sinewy, were inches from her chin, fingers linked. Bare. Skin. Inches from her mouth. Inches from her teeth. She bent her head down and sank her little white teeth into the fleshy part of his hand, between thumb and forefinger. Drew blood.

'Why, you little…!' For a tiny moment, the moment that she expected, his grip eased by a fraction. This slight loosening was enough, all she needed to wriggle violently from his grasp, to slip from those brawny arms, to hit the leaf-strewn forest floor and take off. And then she ran, ran with every last ounce of strength in her frame, away from the path, snaking through the densely packed trees with her light, dancing step. The horse would be unable to follow and the lumbering soldier, slowed by his cumbersome armour, would simply give up. He would never catch her now.

Lussac plunged from his horse, angry now. The little brat had bitten him! And now the bobbing hood and coarse-woven tunic disappearing through the trees mocked his sword and shield, his armour, the trappings of war. The varmint obviously thought he had the means to outwit *him,* Lussac. Just wait until he clamped his hands once more around his scrawny little neck! The wretch might think he was nippy on his feet, but Lussac was much, much faster. The advantage of greater muscle power and longer legs. He kept his eye focused on the dun-coloured tunic darting through the solid trunks, his long strides powering through the piled drifts of fallen leaves, scattering them. The silvery skin of his chainmail glittered in the faint sunlight. Yard by yard, he gained on the thief, steadily, inexorably, until he was a mere body's length away.

As he launched himself full-length through the air, he could hear the boy's breath, ragged, quick, before he crashed down against the narrow back, bringing him down, flat, hard, beneath him. A muffled squeak of shock escaped his quarry before his face was buried in the leaf litter of the forest floor. Let the scamp try to escape now!

For one horrible moment, Katerina lay stunned, groping in the threatening blackness, her mind struggling with the details of what had just happened to her. A tremendous weight pressed down on her back; her mouth, and nose and eyes were full of dead leaves, wet and musty against her skin.

Hot tears of anger flooded from her eyes at the dreadful realisation: she had been caught, after all. Panic rose in her chest, an unstoppable surge; the force of the impact had pressed all the air from her lungs. Now she found it impossible to lift her head! Stretched out before her, her arms, her fingers, flailed against the earth, trying to find purchase, struggling to push her body away from the muffling, constricting ground, to find some air, to breathe.

Then suddenly, the weight lifted. She was flipped over, unceremoniously, on to her back.

Immediately she launched upwards into a sitting position, spitting bits of decaying leaf mould from her mouth. Her eyes blurred with tears; she was unable to focus clearly on her attacker, a huge shadowy outline against the trees. 'How dare you!' she spluttered, drawing her knees up close to her chest. 'How dare you treat me so!' In anger, in humiliation, she whacked both palms against the earth, as a child would.

Standing over the thief, legs astride, and ready to snag a sleeve or a bunch of tunic should the boy decide to run once more, Lussac stared in astonishment. The hood of the lad's tunic had fallen back, revealing a mass of amber hair, a curious colour, bronze flecked with gold. The long locks had been plaited tightly, pinned up, but a few loose strands drifted down, shining threads lying across the rough tunic. Huge, silver-coloured eyes glared at him, hostile, mutinous. Outraged.

He had found the soldier's angel.

Temporarily winded, her anger simmering, Katerina dashed the hot tears from her eyes to clear her vision, hands smarting from where she had whacked them on the ground. Her fingers touched the fallen hood and she yanked it viciously into place, hoping her attacker hadn't noticed. The voluminous cloth settled comfortably around her head once more. Keeping her gaze down, she studied the piles of leaves beneath her feet, the torn hem of her braies, threads hanging, drawing the air back into her lungs, steadying her erratic breathing. One soldier, one measly soldier, had managed to catch her, to bring her down, she thought. How had she managed to let that happen?

She tilted her head upwards, carefully. And she had her answer.

A man, a knight, towered above her, his large frame encased in chainmail, silver-meshed, glittering. Although he stood very still, she sensed every muscle in his body was poised, alert, ready to bear down on her once more, should she choose to run. And she wanted to run; every nerve-ending in her body was telling her to flee, to hare off into the woods again. But it was madness to think she could ever outpace a man like this. He would catch her every time. Below the shadow of his steel-grey helmet, a wide mouth was set in a firm, dangerous line. His broad shoulders were encased by the sweep of his dark-blue tunic, which fell to his knees. Gold fleur-de-lys had been embroidered down the length of cloth. So, he was one of them, one of the soldiers on the beach.

Her confidence leached from her, sank into the ground beneath her hips. Exhaustion swept through her small frame; she wanted to turn, lie on her side and howl in the face of such physical masculine strength. To give up. But, no, she told herself sternly, Katerina of Dauntsey never gave up. Bunching her hands into small fists at her sides, she drew her spine up to its full length. She didn't trust herself to stand, not yet. Shock had weakened her legs; at this precise moment, they possessed all the strength of wet, flapping cloth.

'What have you done with him?' she demanded, with as low a voice as she could muster. 'Where have you taken him?'

'Get up.' The soldier ignored her question, nudging her leg with one toe of his scuffed boot.

In response, her mouth set tight with annoyance;

she wrestled with the notion of remaining where she was.

'Do it.'

His brusque tone forced her to shuffle her legs awkwardly beneath her, tipping her body to one side so she could lever herself to her feet. Although his eyes were hidden, she felt the power of his gaze upon her and she flushed, humiliated that he could control her like this. Resentment boiled within her. Standing upright, she kept her head rigidly lowered, then swayed as a faint wooziness spiralled through her head.

A large hand wrapped around her upper arm, steadying her.

'What the hell do you think you're playing at?'

'I could ask the same of you,' she spat back, viciously, drawing her elbow down sharply to shake off his grip. His hand stayed, clamped firmly to her arm. Hostility shimmered in her eyes, darkening them to sparkling granite. 'You attacked me, wrenched me from my horse and then pursued me, bringing me down like a common vagrant! How dare you!' Her rage had made her forget that she was supposed to be speaking with a boy's voice; she growled the last three words out, in an effort to keep up the semblance of masculinity.

Gritty leaf-matter, like flecks of peat, stuck to

the alabaster smoothness of her cheek. She wiped her face angrily, with a brisk shake of her head. Perched on her tip-toes, edgy, volatile, she reminded him of a nervous cat, ready to spring, or take off, at any moment.

'You are a common vagrant,' Lussac pronounced slowly. 'You stole a horse.' He studied the face beneath the hood, the hint of rippling, amber-coloured hair. Did she really believe she could hide the fact she was a woman?

'I wasn't going to keep it!' she flashed back at him. 'It was your soldiers, ignorant brutes, who took my friend! What was I supposed to do?'

Her wavering tone, one moment high and shrewish, the next almost growling when she remembered her charade, made him want to laugh. The corners of his mouth twitched upwards. She obviously believed he thought she was a boy. And to be fair, seeing her ride that stolen horse like the devil himself, then pursuing her through the woods on foot, he had truly believed she was. But now, the game was up.

He ripped the hood back from her face.

'Nay!' she howled out loud, reaching up and back to grab the collapsing folds, gathering in soft layers around the base of her neck.

'Leave it,' he barked, reaching up to pull off his

helmet. A shock of chestnut hair sprung out around his head, a few strands falling over his tanned forehead. 'You're not fooling anybody. Any idiot can see that you're a maid.' He cast a disparaging eye over her diminutive frame, the patched, baggy tunic disguising any curves that she might possess. 'Although there's not much of you.'

'Enough of me to steal a horse, though,' she retorted, unthinking, then met the astonishing turquoise scorch of his eyes and immediately regretted her words. Her toes curled, preventing an involuntary stagger backwards. She ducked her gaze, unwilling to meet that bold, determined stare, the colour of the sea on a cold, frosty day, and fixed instead on a neutral spot on his tunic.

'Tread carefully, maid. You are too bold with your words.' His speech flooded over her, a dark warning. 'In my country the punishment for thieves is severe.' Who did this maid think she was, to address him so? From the look of her, she was a low-born wench, no more, with the lean, hungry look of someone who didn't have enough to eat. Yet her voice, when she spoke normally, held the modulated tones of a noblewoman, albeit one who was truculent, confrontational.

At his words, her heart clenched with fear, her large grey eyes widening as she stared up again at his rigid, tanned features. Her skin paled, a sprinkle of tiny freckles standing out across her small, tip-tilted nose. A pulse beat frantically in the shadowed hollow of her neck. She took one large step backwards, so she stood beyond the sweep of one of his long, muscular arms. Would he punish her for what she had done? Would he drag her back to the beach, cast her on her knees before the Queen?

She had no intention of waiting around to find out.

Chapter Three

Fear, laced with anger, a volatile combination, spurred her on. The athleticism in her body would provide her only defence against this man; she prayed it would be enough. As she sprung to her left, a quicksilver movement, she acknowledged the snaking reflex of his arm in the corner of her vision. She flinched away, evading his outstretched fingers. She had two advantages: she was small and she was light; he was not. Within a moment, she had plunged into the undergrowth, reaching her hands up to grab, then pull herself up on to a low branch. With all her training, the task proved easy; the muscles in her arms and legs were strong, practised. A sense of bravado, of success, drove her on; that horrible, arrogant man would be too heavy to climb this tree, this spindly birch with its frail, waving branches, with its few silvery, elegant leaves still clinging.

Below, a branch cracked beneath his weight. Scrambling upwards, Katerina smirked to herself. He would never catch her now. She stopped, scissoring her legs to secure her position on the thin branch, and peered down.

He was climbing. Undeterred by the broken branch, he had tried another, more secure, and was heading her way, threatening the safety of her high perch. His glossy chestnut head moved inexorably closer.

'Go away!' she shouted down. 'You have your horse back, take it, and be gone! I have done nothing wrong!'

He reached up and, before she had time to draw her foot away, his hand grabbed the toe of her boot. She jerked her leg upwards, roughly, to dislodge his grip, but instead, the boot slid from her foot and came off in his hand. Cursing, he threw the leather to the ground, then seized her dangling ankle before she had time to whip it away, fingers digging into the fine bones. She wore no stockings; her skin was pearly-cold, icy beneath his touch.

'Give up.'

'Never. I'd rather die.'

'Then remind me to kill you personally.' His response was dry, sarcastic. 'But first you need to come out of this tree.'

Warmth flowed from his fingertips into the marble coldness of her ankle, her leg; her belly shivered. She tried to ignore the odd, fluttery sensation and concentrate instead on how to extricate herself from the situation. Her choices had been severely curtailed.

'You need to come out of this tree,' he said. 'Now.' Truly, he couldn't remember meeting a maid quite as stubborn as this! And the way she had climbed the tree had been remarkable; he had watched the lithe body pull up and up the branches, bright hair glinting, every movement graceful and precise. Strong. More than anything else, he had noticed that. The strength held that small frame.

But he was stronger.

Lussac yanked on the fragile ankle, none too gently. He had dallied far too long in these woods, chasing this she-devil, this hostile, tree-climbing wood-sprite. He was wasting time on her—he should be searching for the other soldiers, curse them, and then return to the beach. The day had almost reached its zenith and Mortimer would be thinking about finding a suitable location for his Queen to spend her first night in England.

His yank effectively dislodged her and she fell into his arms, a screaming, spitting bundle of femininity. Her constant noise, her yells of outrage, clamoured in his ears, reverberating. Her hands flew out to rake against his face, as he clutched her awkwardly around her waist, the other hand grabbing at a branch, fighting to keep their combined balance.

'Stop that! You'll have us both down!' His order cut into her, sharp.

'Get your hands off me! I don't care!' she shouted back, the peerless skin of her face mere inches from his. He caught the sweetness of her breath, the indignant flash of her smoke-grey eyes, the delicate rosebud curve of her upper lip. Desire burst through him: hot, powerful…and unwanted.

One of her flailing legs made impact with his shin, jabbing painfully above the thickness of his boot, dousing the unexpected flare of feeling. His grip tightened about her as she struggled, mean little fists coming forwards to pummel his chest, to push and strain against his greater strength. Desperate to escape him, to escape that dangerous, deepening blue of his eyes, Katerina flung her weight backwards, hoping to dislodge the iron manacles of his arms in the risky manoeuvre. Her only wish was to release herself from the imprisoning clutch of his arms; if she hurt herself, then so be it.

He didn't let go.

They fell together, a coiling, thrashing bundle, through the whispering leaves, the pale branches. He clung like a limpet, his big body curved resolutely around hers, trapping her arms, her legs, in a vice-like grip. A moment before she hit the pile of leaves, before she smacked her head on the solid lump of dead wood hidden beneath, she screamed out in frustration, a vent of sheer fury at her inability to dislodge this insufferable man.

His tremendous weight knocked the breath from her body as pain began to spread around the back of her skull. His thick arms and legs formed a cage around her, strangely comforting as the forest dimmed before her eyes. The trees and leaves lost colour, becoming shadows, black and white on the edge of her vision, the birdsong faded, then nothing.

'Now what are you going to do?' Lussac murmured. Beneath the curving wing of her coppery hair, her ear was pink with cold. He could see the soft, downy hairs on the lobe. He couldn't remember the last time he had lain next to a woman and found it such a pleasurable experience. Despite the maid's leanness, the smooth curve of her hip nestled comfortably into his stomach and through the flexible chainmail of his sleeve the rounded curve of her breast pressed, softly.

No answer.

He shifted, propping himself up on one elbow, so he could see her face. Her eyelids had shuttered down, spiky black lashes fanning the chalky whiteness of her cheeks. The stupid chit had knocked herself out. Sitting up, he ran practised hands over her head, ignoring the silken coolness of her hair, finding the lump at the base of her skull, the bleeding cut. She moaned softly as he lifted her head; guilt spiked through him. He laid the back of his hand across her satin cheek; her breath sifted over his fingers. He had done this, he had provoked it—why hadn't he left her alone? But the sheer unusualness of the maid had goaded him, made him curious, made him pursue her when he should have walked away.

'Come on, woman, wake up.' Placing two hands on her shoulders, he shook her gently. All of a sudden, he yearned for the spitting, fighting termagant who had fallen from the tree with him, not this limp, lifeless doll.

'Need any help with that one, my lord?'

Rising to one knee, Lussac twisted around at the guttural tone, hands flying instinctively to the jewelled hilt of his sword, ready to attack.

A group of soldiers, on horseback, had found a pathway through the undergrowth. Isabella's soldiers. He sheathed his sword, rose to his feet in one swift movement.

'I see you managed to deal with the other one.' Bomal, the oldest in the group, nodded in the direction of the silent, fallen figure. 'A right pair of deviant characters, stealing rabbits from right under the Earl's nose!'

'Pair?' Lussac asked, frowning. Surely there wasn't another one like her? Every bone in his body wanted to turn around and see her eyes opening, to see her lift her head. He clenched his fists, resisting the urge.

'Aye, that's correct, my lord. We caught the other lad, forced him to take us to the nearest village, then let him go. We found enough food there.' Bomal grinned, showing crooked, stained teeth, then frowned. 'Should we have let him go? He was poaching rabbits, after all.'

'Nay, it's not our concern,' Lussac replied curtly.

'That one was the worst, anyway.' Bomal nodded in the direction of Katerina's limp figure beyond Lussac's broad shoulder. 'He must have pinched young John's horse as well; we found it wandering in the woods. The utter cheek of the lad! He deserves a good walloping if nothing more...' Dismounting, he started to head towards the figure.

'Nay.' Lussac stopped Bomal's forward gait, his gloved hand snaking around the soldier's stocky forearm. 'Nay. You go back to the camp and pick up John on the way. I'll deal with this one.'

'As you wish, my lord.' Bomal eyed him suspiciously. 'Make sure you rough him up good and proper.'

Lussac stood in the small clearing, watching the squat, stocky soldier mount up, and the rest of the group kick the flanks of their horses to funnel away through the trees, leading the horse that the maid behind him had stolen. He could see his own horse some distance away, through the serried trunks, cropping idly at the spindly grass.

Why had he not mounted up and gone back with them?

He stared down at his hands, flexing his fingers. The stretched skin between his thumb and forefinger still bore a trickle of blood, the imprint of teeth marks. Why was he staying to see if this spitting wildcat came back to her senses? A wildcat who sent needles of desire, oddly, spiking through his broad frame. He had no wish to think about her, no wish to talk with her. He needed to recall why he had come to this country, not engage in cat-like brawls with foolish maids.

It was guilt. Pure, unadulterated guilt. He wasn't in the habit of using his strength against women, overpowering them; it felt wrong, unnatural. He tried to tell himself that the maid had got what she deserved, with her constant attempts to escape him, to best him. Why had she not given up? Why had she persisted? Either she was very, very stupid, or very, very brave. Whichever it was, he hated to think of where her outlandish behaviour would land her next.

He turned around. In a puddle of filtered light, the maid was sitting up on a mattress of shining leaves, a ray of sunlight firing her hair to a dazzling gold, a jewel-like beacon that snagged his gaze. Lussac breathed out: one long, measured breath of relief. Striding over to her, he picked up her boot where it had fallen.

'Here.' Lussac shoved the boot across her field of vision.

Feeling his shadow move across her, Katerina jerked her head back, a faint sickening sensation lilting through her skull. She willed herself to remain calm. As she reached up, the baggy sleeve of her tunic falling back to reveal her thin wrist, she snatched the boot from him, shoving her bare toes back into the unwieldy leather. Tilting her head back once more, she fixed him with a bold, defiant stare.

'What have your thugs done with Waleran?' Her voice cracked slightly, eyes darkening to stormy grey.

'Who?'

Katerina folded her arms tightly across her belly, drawing in a deep, unsteady breath. What was this knight planning to do with her? 'Waleran.' She raised her voice in consternation. 'My friend, Waleran. The one your soldiers kidnapped… My God, they might have killed him by now!'

In response, he hunkered down beside her, his big body surprisingly graceful, balancing easily on his heels. 'No, he's safe. They let him go.'

She reeled back at his presence, fighting the peculiar wavering sensations in her stomach. Had the knock on her head affected her more than she thought? A heady mix of wood-smoke, the briny tang of the sea swept over her: the scent of him. His eyes, chips of sapphire, blazed out from his lean, tanned face. Shifting uncomfortably beneath his stark, steady gaze, she wiggled her hips to try to inch away from him, backwards, acutely conscious of her helplessness.

'How do I know what you say is true?' she blurted out. 'How can I trust what you say?'

'You can't.' He shrugged his shoulders, his dry, clipped tone cutting across her emotional outburst.

'So, if your soldiers let Waleran go, you'll let me go as well, then,' Katerina reasoned, clutching at her opportunity to escape, and scrambling, too quickly, on to her feet. Her head dipped and swayed, and she clutched at the back of her head, suddenly.

Lussac placed one hand on her shoulder, steadying her, watching the slight colour drain from her face. He cleared his throat, unsure what to say. Beneath her pewter gaze he felt strangely tongue-tied, awkward. 'Go easy now, maid,' he said gruffly. 'You've had a nasty fall.' Beneath his muscular fingers, her bones were bird-like, delicate.

'No thanks to you,' she retorted, rolling her shoulder back angrily to release his grip. 'And take your hands off me; I have no need of your help.' The silvery skin of his chainmail wavered and shimmered in front of her eyes. Narrowing her gaze, she focused on one of the gold fleur-de-lys emblazoned across his chest.

'Let me take you home,' he offered, ignoring her rudeness. 'Do you live around here?'

'No, there's no need for that!' Her words gabbled

out in a rush of protest. The last thing she wanted was to spend any more time in this man's company! She backed away from him, shaking her head. 'It's not far; you needn't concern yourself.'

'Oh, I'm not concerned,' he replied mildly. 'But I can't leave you here, a maid alone, in the forest.' He eyed her stumbling retreat with curiosity. Her look of horror. Did she not realise how vulnerable she was?

'Believe me...' she fixed the knight with what she hoped was a convincing expression '...I will be absolutely fine without your help. Dressed like this, no one will give me a second glance.'

He glanced at the tightly braided mass of bronze hair around her head, the delicate curve of her lips, her pale, luminous skin, and frowned. Even with her hood up, her fine features were exposed for all to see. And although her tunic was baggy and hid the true outline of her shape, the braies served only to highlight the slenderness of her calves. If Bomal or any of his soldiers had worked out she was a woman, then the outcome of this morning would have been very different for her.

'I doubt that very much,' he replied. 'Come on. We're wasting time here.' He glanced up at the sun, striking a diagonal shaft through the whispering trees. The dappled light filtered down, casting shadows across the carved, sculptured planes of his face, firing the glossy strands of his dark-brown hair.

'Don't you have somewhere else you need to be?' Katerina glared pointedly at his dark-blue tunic, the golden fleur-de-lys.

'Yes,' he said bluntly. 'And you're holding me up.' He crossed his arms across the broad planes of his chest, head tipped slightly to one side, waiting.

Her heart lurched. She couldn't go with him, wouldn't go! She had no wish for this stranger, this foreign knight with his hard, flinty features, to know any more about her life than was necessary. It was enough that he had caught her red-handed, but to take her back to the camp, to see where she lived? Nay, that was inconceivable. Positioning her feet more firmly on the ground, Katerina wound her arms snugly across her chest, sticking her chin proudly in the air.

At her defiant gesture, Lussac laughed out loud, a rippling, throaty sound. His teeth were white against the tan of his face. 'So, we have a stand-off,' he declared. Would she stamp her feet, like his sister used to do when she couldn't gain her own way? The laughter died within him at the sudden thought, then shrivelled up, like a burnt crisp of parchment rising from the fire. Sadness, a shard of glass, pierced his heart.

'I haven't got time for this,' he said, stern now, long boots covering the ground with a fast power-ful stride. 'I am not going to hurt you. Even you, with your foolish ways, must surely know when you are beaten. Let's go.' Snaring her sleeve, he tugged her towards the place where his horse tore at the scant grass.

'I don't want to go with you,' Katerina protested, her heels deliberately dragging through the fallen leaves. 'I've told you, I will be fine.'

'And I've told you that I will take you home, to a place where you will be safe.' He rounded on her. Through the frayed sleeve of her tunic, the warmth from his fingers penetrated her cold forearm, scis-soring erratically up to her chest, tumbling her heart with unexpected emotion.

A place where she would be safe. His words banged around the confines of her head. When was the last time she had felt safe? When her mother had been alive? The camp where she lived now provided a refuge, a hiding place, but it was not safe. Even now, she kept her wits about her, hug-ging her secrets tight to her chest, guarding her privacy. Who knew when or where her father's hired spies would catch up with her?

'All right, you can let go now, I'll come with you.' Katerina sighed reluctantly. She wasn't a fool and this man was not about to be convinced of her safety. She suspected he would stand there all day like a statue, following her every move until she agreed to let him take her home.

His fingers fell from her arm as they reached his horse. She waited as he swept up his helmet and attached it to the back of the saddle, before gathering up the loose reins. He grinned suddenly; her expression was one of utter dismay.

'Whoever would have thought it?' he said. 'A woman wanting to roam around alone, with no one to keep her safe. You must be seriously lacking up there...' he tapped the side of his skull derisively '...if you think you'll survive unscathed. A man would have you down on that ground with your undergarments off before you even had time to think, or scream.' He turned abruptly, heading for the track that ran towards the outskirts of the forest.

Fuming, her pale face flushed with embarrassment at the rough, unsettling image he painted, Katerina stumbled after him. Tears threatened at the corners of her eyes and she dashed them away. Horrible, horrible man! Who was this stranger who had intruded so abruptly, so violently into her life?

Who shot massive holes through her hard-won sense of security? Hating him, she trudged in his wake, eyes burning resentment.

He hadn't even turned around to see if she were following. He knew he had won.

Chapter Four

Beneath a vast bowl of cerulean sky, Lussac marched along, covering the ground with quick, long-legged strides. On the outskirts of his peripheral vision, he could see the bright blaze of the maid's hair as she followed him, the wisps of amber silk curling out from beneath her hood. He knew he was walking too fast for her, but refused to curb his pace—let the chit suffer a little, for wasting his time, for giving him the run-around in the forest. But despite his speed, she seemed to have little difficulty in keeping up with him, her steps light and dancing across the stiff, dry grass.

The back of Katerina's head ached as she squinted grumpily at the man's broad back, his shoulders silhouetted against the sky. They were clear of the trees now, tracking back towards the coast, working their way alongside an immense flat area of tidal creeks and rivulets, a grid of shining ribbons empty of water now, but covered at high tide. Against her better judgement, she had given him scant details of the camp's location, based at the Earl of Norfolk's castle where they were due to perform the following night. Anything to be rid of him!

Lussac stopped, surveying the horizon. The shore and river estuary were to the east, the forest at his back to the north. The strong breeze from the east riffled the straight hair across his forehead, tousling the strands. The strong noon light cast shadows beneath his high cheek-bones, giving him a devilish appearance.

An icy shudder seized Katerina's bones. She hunkered further down into her tunic, yanking her hood more securely around her head. The breeze sneaked beneath the sagging, extended hem, flowing up across her belly, her chest.

'Are you cold?' he said. Lifting one hand, he rubbed it against the back of his neck; the weight of his chainmail pressed against his fingers. He was certain that beneath her loose tunic she wore nothing but a thin chemise, and her feet had been bare, he remembered. And despite the sun, the breeze from the sea drove fiercely against their faces.

'No. I'm not.'

He raised his eyebrows at the fragile stutter in

her speech, frowning pointedly at her slight, trembling frame. A fiery pink blotched her cheeks, her pearl-white skin smacked into colour by the driving wind. He carried spare clothes in his saddlebags, a woollen rug that he could offer her but, judging by her mutinous expression, her stubborn stance, he suspected she would refuse all offers of help. So be it.

'Which way?' he demanded.

'Over there.' Katerina pointed. 'Can you see the turrets of the castle? It belongs to the Earl of Norfolk.'

He nodded, starting to walk again. 'Do you work there?'

'Yes,' she lied. The less he knew about her working situation, the better. She fell into step beside him, not too close, and matched her pace to his. His horse plodded along behind them, docile on the rein.

'And is your husband there? Your family?'

'What?' Unprepared for his question, the toe of her boot snagged on a protruding tussock of grass and she pitched forwards, stumbling into Lussac's left flank. Seeking balance, she snaked her hand out, fingers hooking around his wide leather sword belt. Her knuckles pressed into his back, a flat wall of solid muscle. A wobbling excitement shot up her arm at the contact, bursting, visceral.

She snatched her fingers away, pressing them against her mouth, aghast. 'Forgive me...' she swallowed hurriedly '...I lost my footing.'

'No matter.' His mouth twisted up into a half-smile. 'I was asking you about your family.'

'Er, yes. Yes, they are there.' She chewed anxiously on her bottom lip, reddening the flesh. How different it was to walk alongside this huge bear of a man, compared to the easy companionship of Waleran. All the nerve endings in her body seemed to turn in his direction, like flowers towards the sun, drinking in his vitality, his power, alert to his every move, the low sound of his voice. This man threw her off balance, in more ways than one, befuddling her mind with questions, undermining her hard-won confidence, security. She couldn't think straight. How much longer could she keep this up? How much longer before she said something that would give herself away, reveal her secrets? Throwing a nervous glance forwards, she saw the white flash of the tents come into view and almost wilted with relief. Her salvation.

As the sun reached its zenith, the last remaining wisps of cloud vanishing in the heat of noon, Katerina tramped back into camp. Lifting her eyes to absorb the familiar scenes around her, she breathed out: a long, hard sigh. Her tense muscles eased. She had got rid of him, shaken off his overpowering presence. By the castle gatehouse she had convinced the dark stranger with his pitiless eyes of turquoise that she worked in the Earl of Norfolk's castle, and that, yes, her family were within and she was safe. And he had turned away with a quick nod of instant dismissal. She was glad of it, welcomed it.

Katerina walked towards the circle of patched and stained canvas tents. The troupe, some twenty adults, had set up on a flattish patch of lumpy ground outside the perimeter walls of the castle. The soldiers, patrolling on top of the high wall, would stop and look down on them every so often, watching them practise their acts, or to listen to the music. Huge logs, ashy and blackened, smouldered fitfully within a rough boundary of stones; it was the children's responsibility to collect up enough wood to keep the camp-fire burning day and night, but at the moment most of the children were rushing around, their screams high-pitched and giggling, trying to hide from each other in an extended game of tig.

Over to the right, nearest to the castle moat, the

musicians of the troupe ran through their repertoire, Galen's thin, reedy frame thumping the tight animal skin of his drum, the beat thumping solidly, rhythmically through the air. The other musicians joined in gradually with their pipes, whistles and fiddles. Thomas was on the bagpipes, with old Henry turning the clanking handle of the hurdygurdy. The resulting music was invigorating, overlaid with dramatic intensity, designed to excite the audience with the promise of the exhilarating entertainment to come.

Katerina's heart lifted at the sight of them; within the troupe, she had a place, a valued role. Her act alone had gained the group a certain fame, and, instead of knocking on doors, they were specifically requested to perform for some of the highest-ranking nobles in the land. There was no chance she would be recognised; as long as she maintained a low profile during the day, her elaborate costume and mask would keep her true identity a secret.

And yet, today, she had been exposed, her disguise stripped bare in the most brutal way, beaten by a man and floored completely. A niggle of dissatisfaction lodged firmly in her gut. How had she let herself be caught like that? She never would have believed that he would scramble up the tree after her! A pair of twinkling turquoise eyes, smug, victorious, barged into her mind's eye, and she closed her eyes, a futile attempt to rid herself of the unsettling image.

A tent flap, spotted with black mould, flapped back. The top of a greasy head appeared, followed by huge shoulders, a vast belly straining against the coarse weave of a tunic. It was John: the leader of the troupe, the man who doled out the coin at the end of every performance, the man who decided whether their skills were good enough, whether they stayed or left.

'You took your time,' he growled, spotting Katerina as he straightened up. 'Get out of my way!' he yelled at one of the children who sprinted, shrieking, pursued by another child across his feet. He kicked out, but the children were too fast to feel the imprint of his boot. 'Waleran's been back for ages!' Set in the protruding dirty-white of his eyes, his dark-brown irises seemed very small.

'Is he here? Is he all right?' She glanced around the camp, seeking her friend. Waleran was safe!

'Fine. The soldiers roughed him up a bit, but no harm done,' John growled. 'Where have you been?'

'I went to look for him, became lost in the forest.' She wriggled her shoulders unconsciously, remembering the press of the man's body against her own as he grabbed her, held her. Warmth surged across her belly at the memory, stirred deep; she pressed cool palms to her hot cheeks.

'Well, you'd better start practising,' John said. The bluish-grey skin on his cheeks pulled slack, puffy around his jawbone. 'We're performing to-night.'

'Tonight?' Katerina replied, shocked. 'Surely we all need a day's rest? Our last performance was only a night ago!' She refused to be cowed by John's bullying behaviour. He needed her, and her performance, and that knowledge gave her a semblance of power.

'Aye, tonight, cloth-ears,' John cackled at her. 'For the Earl of Norfolk himself. He has unexpected guests, important ones, so you'd better start practising now. We can't afford any mistakes; it has to be perfect.' He turned away, going over to yell at one of the musicians who continually blew a wrong note.

Katerina wilted with exhaustion. Her whole body ached from the encounter in the forest; the last thing she wanted to do was perform this evening. But she had little choice in the matter; John was her employer, the man who paid out the wages and decided who was in, or out, of the troupe. It wouldn't do to fall on the wrong side of his temper.

She had no wish to be kicked out; the troupe was her livelihood, her life. Without it, she wouldn't survive.

Lussac followed Philippe's rounded shoulders up the spiralling staircase, the soles of his calf-leather boots making little sound on the worn limestone steps. A riot of gold banding against limpid blue, the glowing translucency of the evening sky pushed through the thin arrow slits set at intervals into the curve of the outer wall, shedding a feeble light into the stairwell. The day slunk quickly into twilight, but the hours of daylight would grow shorter still; they had yet to reach mid-winter.

After leaving the maid at the gatehouse, Lussac hadn't had to travel far to catch up with the Queen and her soldiers—she had already arrived at the castle with her entourage, the Earl of Norfolk welcoming her with open arms. As one of her strongest allies, he was as keen as the Queen to see the King deposed, and the King's favourite, Hugh le Despenser, banished for good.

'God's teeth! How much further?' Up ahead, in the gloom, Philippe caught his toe on a shallow step and stumbled. His voice carried the faint whine of irritation; the long day and lack of decent food were beginning to take their toll on Lussac's companion.

'Top floor.' The servant, a boy of about twelve, turned and grinned down at them. 'The chambers up here are the best in the castle.'

'They'd better be,' grumbled Philippe, a sheen of sweat over his florid cheeks. As the servant led the two men into the chamber, set at the top of one of the square towers, Philippe looked around in delight. Two beds, canopied with velvet, stood at opposite sides of the room, piled high with fresh linens and furs. The scent of clean straw from the newly stuffed mattresses filled the space, as did the ashy smell from the glowing charcoal brazier in the corner. The servant busied himself lighting the candles from the brazier, setting them into stone niches and metal candleholders around the walls.

'This is Heaven.' Philippe smiled, his gaze alighting on the wooden bath behind an embroidered screen.

The boy followed his look. 'I'll fetch the hot water for you, my lord.'

'By God, we'll sleep well tonight.' Philippe clapped Lussac on the shoulder, throwing his leather bags down by one of the beds. 'I can't wait to rid myself of this infernal armour.' He grabbed at the heavy buckle of his sword belt, flinging both sword and belt in a jumble at the side of the bed.

'I suggest you take the first bath, you stink to high heaven,' Lussac chuckled, moving over to the window. No arrow slits, but narrow, rectangular windows topped with a shallow arch, one pair set into each of the thick stone walls. Hand-blown glass, undulating, formed an effective barrier against the cold outside. Despite the dimming light, he could still discern several features of the landscape: the frothy white line of the surf out to the east, the forest to the south, the flat marshland, water-filled ditches gleaming in the half-light. Their ships had landed to the south of the vast tract of trees, the reason why, initially, they had no idea of their location. Lussac leaned forwards, palms flat on the damp stone window-ledge, his breath misting the glass. Behind him, the boy had returned, sloshing water liberally into the bathtub.

'Last chance, Lussac?' Philippe said. 'Otherwise I'll go first.'

'Go ahead,' Lussac murmured. He turned away from the window, a restlessness churning his body. His eye swept the room: the charcoal brazier, the fragrant steam rising from behind the embroidered screen, the lavender-scented linens. The domestic niceties burned into his soul, for everywhere he

looked reminded him of the home he had no longer. It had been easier in France; the French king
had constantly needed him to head up the battles
and skirmishes along the borderlands of Aquitaine
and Gascony. The canvas tent had become his refuge: no niceties, no luxury. He longed for it.

'Where did you get to, anyway?' Philippe called
out from behind the screen. 'Mortimer's soldiers
came back long before you did. Did you get lost?'
His chuckle was accompanied by a huge splosh of
water. 'Lussac?'

'Aye, in a manner of speaking.' His mind tacked
back to the girl in the forest. The impact of her soft
curves as they landed together in the pile of leaves.
The touch of her fingers on his back as she stumbled and grabbed his belt. Fire leapt in his belly.
A pulse of burning, outrageous desire.

Annoyed, he sat on the edge of the bed and
pulled at his chainmail coif, yanking it over his
head. What was the matter with him? The girl was
nothing more than a minor distraction—and a puz-
zle. Her skin had been smooth like pouring cream,
velvety. Not the coarse, weather-roughened skin of
a peasant. She dressed as a boy, in rags, yet spoke
with the high, modulated tones of the nobility. A
patched and holed tunic clothed her slight body,
baggy braies folded loosely around her slim legs.

Her boots had been too big for her. He frowned, resting his elbows on his knees, and rubbed his face with his hands. Would he see her again, here in the castle? He couldn't quite believe she was a serving-girl. Her manner had been too arrogant and feisty, a bundle of contradictions, diamond-grey eyes assessing him disparagingly. She had truly believed she could best him. Where had she learnt such a misguided sense of self-reliance?

'Go on in, the water's still hot.' Philippe emerged from behind the screen, his portly frame wrapped in linen towels.

Lussac lifted his face from his hands and began to pull his boots off. Why on earth was that foolish chit intruding on his thoughts at all? He had done his duty and brought her home. The maid had wasted his time by refusing his help, deluding herself by insisting she was safe. She was nothing to him—a mere irritant. He had bigger and more pressing concerns to deal with: a murderer to hunt down, not some will-o'-the-wisp who threatened his iron-clad self-control.

The Earl of Norfolk's castle was constructed in a novel design: a central circular tower of five levels, surrounded by three square towers. The design had been hailed as revolutionary, removing all blind spots and making it difficult for attackers to creep up unnoticed. The double height of the great hall meant that it spanned two floors, allowing for large, wrought-iron chandeliers to be hung from the wooden-planked ceiling. Huge, elaborately embroidered tapestries draped from the pale, limestone walls interspersed with the shields and crossed swords from various members of the Earl of Norfolk's family. The whole effect was one of glittering opulence, of luxury, the rich, glowing colours of red and gold reflected in the light from the candles, from the roaring fire in the grate.

Seated in the centre of the top table, behind an expanse of white-linen tablecloth laid with silver dishes, Queen Isabella laid her small, cool hand on that of her neighbour, Thomas, the Earl of Norfolk. The silk of her rose-pink gown, interwoven with silver thread, sparkled as she leaned a little closer to him. As in the fashion of France, the gown was closely fitted to her slim form, with a low, curving neckline and sleeves tight to her arms, fastened with a long row of tiny horn buttons.

'I don't know how to thank you, Thomas, for your hospitality, for your support.' She raised her voice over the general hubbub of the hall, the usual numbers swelled by the influx of her entourage, her knights. The rest of the mercenaries were camped in the outer bailey, their supper cooked over open fires by the castle servants.

Thomas, his frame big and bulky next to the neat, precise form of the Queen, tipped his grizzled head down to catch her words. His hand squeezed hers. 'You can thank me by ridding this country of your husband's rule; him and that…that infidel Despenser! I fully support your cause, you and Mortimer, and will give you some of my knights, if it will help.'

Isabella tucked a wayward strand of hair back behind her ear; the fine blonde strands had escaped from the confines of her white-satin wimple. The movement was studied, careful. She was fully aware of her effect upon men; indeed, she delighted in seeing Thomas's eyes widen with attraction as the curve of her arm carried upwards. It was only when she caught Mortimer's scowling features behind Thomas that she stopped her flirtatious affectations, letting her hands fall demurely to her lap. To lose Mortimer as a lover would be a mistake; he was instrumental in helping her overthrow the King, as well as being everything that Edward was not: courageous, possessive and ardent in his love for her.

'You are so kind,' she ventured, reaching for her silver goblet, sipping at her wine.

'You and your ladies have suffered much in the journey from Hainault.' Thomas nodded towards the group of whey-faced ladies clustered around a trestle table. 'I will do my best to ensure they have every comfort after such an ordeal.'

'They are exhausted,' Isabella admitted tightly, tilting her head towards him. In the candlelight her skin seemed poreless, smooth perfection, emphasised by the brightness of the escaping wisps of her hair, her white, even teeth. 'None of us slept much on the crossing. The weather was against us all the way, simply foul, unbelievable.'

'Then we must thank the Lord that you are here safe and sound.' Thomas's tone was reassuring. 'And now, you must eat.' His hand swept over the laden table, the gleaming dishes groaning with roasted pheasant and partridge, yeasty bread rolls. 'I have a spectacular show prepared for later in the evening—I hope you will stay to watch?'

Inwardly, Isabella groaned. She had been looking forward to an early night, a night spent in a proper bed that didn't pitch and toss and roll. But one look at Thomas's beaming, avuncular features indicated she couldn't disappoint him. She threw him an encouraging smile, helping herself to a slice of roast chicken.

'Who are your commanders?' Thomas continued conversationally, chewing on a piece of pork crackling.

'Obviously Roger has overall command.' She smiled briefly at her lover; his eyes flicked upwards at the mention of his name, but his face remained neutral. It wouldn't do to display their adultery for all to see; Isabella was still married to the King of England. The public would judge her harshly if she were seen to be embarking upon an adulterous affair. 'Hugh de Fontainbleu, Sir John of Hainault, among others.'

'What about Belbigny?' the Earl of Norfolk asked. 'You do not mention him, yet I see him at the end of the table.' He indicated the tall, dark-haired man.

'No, no. He is here...' the Queen paused, delicately, picking at a loose thread on her linen napkin '...on other business. It's a shame, he's a skilled commander, but unfortunately, at the moment, he has other things on his mind.' She sighed, staring out over the bobbing heads of the crowded hall.

'I heard what happened to his family,' the Earl replied. 'His father was in charge of a garrison on the border, is that right? The whole family was slaughtered in the conflict?'

'It was worse than that. The conflict had supposedly finished and a truce had been established, but someone held a grudge against Lussac's father, returned to the garrison with a group of soldiers and fired the whole place.'

'I had no idea.'

'He will travel with us; he hopes to find someone who can shed light on the identity of whoever killed his family. I don't suppose you have heard anything?'

The Earl of Norfolk shook his head.

'Then let's not speak of it further. I don't want him to hear, not a breath of it.' Beneath Isabella's long white fingers, the gemstones on her rings winked in the candlelight as she crumbled a bread roll to tiny bits, scattering them across her silvered plate.

Thomas studied the man at the end of the table covertly, leaning back in his chair, sipping idly from his goblet. Lussac felt the touch of his gaze and turned, pinning the Earl with his hard, dark stare. Thomas raised his goblet in salute, noting the hollowed-out eyes, the lean, ravaged features. What a waste, he thought to himself, as he switched his attentions to Isabella once more. There's a man who suffers, tortured by what happened to his family. But what man wouldn't suffer after what he had been through?

Chapter Five

Gradually, the evening stretched into full night. The knights, noblemen and their ladies, the peasants in service to the Earl of Norfolk, pushed back from the tables, having eaten their fill of roasted meat, braised vegetables and crusty bread; servants scurried around, scooping up the debris. Trestles were pushed back against the circular walls of the great hall, clearing a large space in the middle of the swept stone floor. Bereft of the safety of their table, Isabella's ladies stood in a miserable huddle, forlorn figures in their silks and satins, gaudy butterflies against the plainer attire of the peasants. Noting their plight, Isabella summoned them up to the high dais, where she ordered more benches to be placed behind her so her women could sit in relative comfort.

Through the curtained doorway, a group of musicians entered, setting themselves up with their instruments to one side, backs against the wall. Most of them looked like they hadn't bathed in a year, a motley collection of scruffy itinerants, with ragged, drooping clothes, missing teeth and lank, greasy hair.

'Christ in Heaven,' Philippe whispered to Lussac, 'where did the Earl find this lot?'

But then they began to play. And the music was beautiful: haunting, lilting, building slowly in rhythmic beats, faster and faster, until the sound reached a dramatic crescendo. A troupe of acrobats ran into the hall, running, cartwheeling, somersaulting, contorting their bodies with amazing flexibility, fast and skilled. Their costumes were fashioned from bold reds and yellows, fitted braies and tunics that allowed them to bend and stretch with ease. The watching crowd gasped in awe at the acrobatic feats, roaring with approval at each daring manoeuvre. Even the Queen, not known for praising any sort of entertainment, was smiling, turning and nodding with approval at the Earl.

The acrobats ran to the middle of the hall, gathering together to form a human pyramid: three men at the bottom, then two climbing up, one man vaulting deftly to the very top. His head was on a level with the wrought-iron chandelier that hung with chains from the ceiling. One by one, he extinguished the candles, pulling the waxy sticks from each holder and tossing them to a companion down below.

As the chamber plunged into dappled shadow, the crowd shifted, a palpable tension running through the room, a ripple of expectation. Isabella looked about her, an expression of curiosity on her face. The triangular formation of six acrobats moved carefully as a group to the other chandelier, dousing the flickering light once more. Now the hall was in darkness, lit only by the flickering firelight and the few candles set into stone niches around the walls.

The crowd began to stamp their feet, chanting; it seemed they had the advantage over the royal guests and knew what to expect. The noise of the chanting rose, swelled, filling the hall.

'What are they saying?' Philippe leaned forward, intrigued.

'They're chanting in Latin,' Lussac narrowed his eyes, trying to decipher the words from the jumble of noise. 'It sounds like silver…silver bird?' He shrugged his shoulders, sprawling back into his oak chair.

A sliver of light appeared in the doorway. A momentary hush fell upon the crowd; they held their breath, collectively. Then the roars and shouts returned, louder this time, insistent. The slip of light moved inwards, transformed into a figure, a girl dressed from head to toe in a white-satin garment, the top half of her face covered by a white, leather mask. Every inch of the satin was covered with tiny beads, faceted so they caught the light, shimmering in the dusky shadows of the hall. Tiny, sparkling beads even decorated the outside edges of her mask. Every movement, every fraction of movement was accompanied by a rippling, twinkling sparkle from the costume.

'I've never seen anything like it before,' Isabella breathed out, stunned, her eyes transfixed upon the pearly figure.

The girl raised her arms and the crowd went wild, the music hitching faster, dominated by a repeated drumbeat. Cut in a bell shape, the sleeves flowed downwards from her outstretched arms, like the spread wings of a bird.

'Silver bird!' Philippe thumped the table triumphantly. 'Now I understand. You were right, Lussac. What a wonder she is, eh?'

Lussac's piercing blue eyes studied the figure, the slender curves, the diminutive stature. His heart kicked up a beat. Despite her masked face, the maid looked remarkably familiar. Was it her, the girl from the forest?

From her demure, gentle entrance, the girl sprang into action, somersaulting in a series of forward flips to the pyramid of acrobats. As her hands hit the floor, her feet lifted upwards in precise, fluid harmony, travelling over to arch her spine in a graceful curve. Placing one small foot on the bent knee of her companion, she climbed the human pyramid to the chandelier. Hooking one leg over the iron loop, she held herself upright, balancing strongly on her hands and arms whilst the acrobats beneath tumbled away in all directions. The audience applauded them heartily as they ran out of the hall, laughing and waving, tumbling and springing.

She waited until the last man had exited, before swinging her body down, sharply, held on to the chandelier by her bent legs. The metal circle swung with her slight weight. In the time it had taken her companions to leave she had attached a short rope around one ankle, tying the other end to the chandelier. Her arms swept out, then one leg came down, forming a right angle with her other leg. She began to spin, slowly at first, then faster, faster, the magnificent cloth of her costume flowing around her like shining phosphorus.

'Good Lord,' Philippe jumped out of his seat,

'she's going to fall, that rope's not going to hold her...'

'I think she will be fine,' Lussac reassured him drily. He was certain now of the girl's identity and hated the way his heart tripped faster with the knowledge. The waif in the forest who had hoped to outsmart him with a jittery combination of bravado, luck and agility. Serving girl, indeed!

Half of Isabella's ladies had covered their faces with their hands; they couldn't watch. The rest of the audience stared upwards, open-mouthed, hearts thumping with anticipation. The girl spun faster and faster until her body became a glittering blur up in the rafters, before she stopped abruptly, shocking them, pulling herself up to release the rope, throwing it joyfully down into the crowd.

Then, dropping her body below the chandelier again, although this time hanging by her hands around opposite sides of the iron loop, she began to swing, the strong chains of the chandelier supporting her. The arc of the swing grew bigger and bigger, until she had sufficient momentum to let go, somersault once in mid-air, which carried her towards the other chandelier. The crowd went mad, an element of hysteria in their approval, a joyfulness that the girl had survived such a daring act. She repeated the swing back again, latching on to the first chandelier. She then swung that, audaciously, over the high dais, jumping down straight on to the top table, in front of the Queen and the Earl of Norfolk. For a moment, the Earl looked apoplectic, disbelieving that a common acrobat had possessed the sheer audacity to land, feet first, before royalty. But Isabella was laughing, exchanging appreciative comments with her ladies, and clapping this unknown acrobat as if her life depended on it. The Earl relaxed.

'You're amazing! Your name! What is your name?' Isabella shouted at the girl above the roar of the audience, half-raising herself from her seat, her face flushed with excitement. But the acrobat sprung away, flipping backwards off the top table in one elegant, bouncing arc to cartwheel across the hall.

As the glittering wing of the acrobat's sleeve vanished through the curtain, Lussac pushed back his chair and stood up.

'Where are you going?' Philippe quirked one eyebrow at his friend.

Lussac threw his linen napkin down on his empty plate. The pewter gleamed in the low candlelight. 'I need some fresh air,' he said. 'I'm going outside for a bit. Coming?'

Phillipe shook his head, indicating the food left

on his plate with a half-hearted smile. 'No, I'll finish this. Besides, I think there's more of the show to come.' He nodded across the hall at the acrobats crowding back into the hall, amidst cheers and clapping from the audience.

'I've had enough.'

As Lussac slipped through a low door at the side of the high dais, Isabella turned ecstatically to the Earl. 'Do you know her name?' she asked, her eyes alight with excitement. 'Where does she come from, who is she with? I have never seen such skill, such flexibility!'

'My bailiff hires the entertainment,' Thomas replied, his hands fluttering forwards in apology. 'I will ask him for you.'

'What a treat!' Isabella smiled over at Roger. 'Wasn't she stunning? She made me quite forget my true purpose here.'

Body prickling with sweat from the exertion of her performance, Katerina's fingers fumbled in the heavy folds of the curtain that separated the great hall from the square entrance area to the castle. Applause roared in her ears, people stamping their feet, clapping their approval at her back. Noticing her struggles to exit, a young knight standing to one side pulled back the thick, double-lined fabric, allowing her to slip into the cooler shadows of the entrance hall.

Once through the curtain, her fellow acrobats clustered around her, congratulations rising into the air. Muscles trembling, the back of her head throbbing from the earlier fall, Katerina smiled at their happy faces, their joy at another success-ful performance, and grabbed their hands as they reached out towards her in gestures of support.

'You were fantastic,' whispered Waleran, at the front of the group. 'The Queen loved you.' His brown eyes darted over her slim figure encased in the shining costume, the white mask obscur-ing her face. Katerina squeezed his hand, grate-ful for his words.

'It's a bit too early to celebrate.' Big shoulders propped up against the wall, John boomed at them, 'Come on, you still have to go out there and per-form the finale.' With an exaggerated groan, he levered his vast bulk forwards and began to shove the acrobats back through the curtain, out again to rapturous applause.

As the acrobats left to perform their finale, Kat-erina moved across the freezing flagstones, her feet in soft, calf-skin slippers making no sound as she stepped towards the huge entrance door.

The circular metal door handle glinted in the meagre light.

'Katerina!' A hand clamped on her shoulder. John!

She spun slowly on one heel, hampered by weighty fingers crushing the fragile bones in her shoulder. 'What is it?' she asked, annoyed. 'Surely you don't have a problem with my performance?' Rolling her shoulder forwards angrily, she tried to dislodge his heavy hold.

'Nay, the crowd loved you.' John replied bluntly. 'But I need you to do something else for me.'

She tilted her head up at him, wishing she could remove the mask so her employer could see the look of defiance on her face. 'You ask too much of me, John. I can do no more.' Her body wilted with fatigue, sinews wrung out by the intricate moves. She needed to push her body through a series of stretches in order to avoid the muscles seizing up.

'Not to perform! Nay, you misunderstand me!' he hissed down at her, a fleck of spittle landing on her sleeve. 'But while most of the castle was riveted by our performance—' he jerked his square-shaped head towards the noise coming from the great hall '—I managed to slip down to the cellar and pilfer.'

'Pilfer?'

'Aye, that's right. Here, take these back to the camp, will you?' He pushed a couple of hessian sacks into her stomach, forcing her to grab hold of them. She staggered back beneath the bulky weight. 'There's enough food in there to feed us all for a couple of days, at least.' Shoving her towards the arched entrance, he thumped his fleshy hand against the vertical planks, pushing the door open. 'Get going, will you! Before someone notices!'

Clutching at the gaping bags, the contents threatening to spill out from the loose, gathered tops, Katerina lurched her way through the gap and out into the cool night air. After the intense heat of the hall, the cold pierced through the gauzy satin of her costume. Perspiration chilled rapidly on her skin and she shivered.

A soldier stood guard outside the main door, pulling himself to attention as she appeared and nodded at her. 'A fine show, miss,' he congratulated her gruffly. 'Do you need any help?'

'Er, no, thank you,' she muttered hurriedly, acutely aware of the lumpy goods shifting inside the sacks: the loaves of bread, the meat and vegetables that John had stuffed firmly down. Flushing beneath her white leather mask, she prayed the soldier wouldn't look inside. The unwieldy bags filled her vision; unable to see her way down the

steps, she inched forwards, her toes in their thin
silk slippers seeking the edge of the top step. Carefully, unable to grasp at the iron hand-rail for support, Katerina edged her way down beneath the
soldier's watchful eye.

She almost made it.

Constructed with a deeper drop than the rest,
the bottom step caught her unawares; she reeled
to one side, her balance thrown out by the heavy
load, her arm banging painfully against the gritty
castle wall. A large glistening ham plopped out
from the one of the bags, landing with a thump
on the cobbles.

'Hey! Stop! What have you got there?' the soldier's voice shouted down at her.

Heart plummeting, she threw both bags down.
The incriminating contents spilled out across the
ground: parsnips, turnips, floury rounds of bread.
Even without them, she would fail to cover the
length of the inner bailey before the soldier caught
up with her; it was a wide open space and he would
gain on her easily. She needed to find a hiding
place and fast.

Plunging down along the castle walls, Katerina
turned a corner, around one of the turrets, seeking the shadows. The beads decorating her white
leather mask, her costume, twinkled in the soften-

ing glow of the September moon as she flew along, her feet barely touching the ground. She gained a second turret, spinning around another corner, and cannoned into a tall, bulky shadow leaning up against the walls.

She had the briefest impression of deep-set, sparkling eyes, of a sculptured jaw, before her hands rose instinctively, frantically, pushing against the soft cloth of a tunic, against a hard, unyielding chest beneath, trying to lever herself away from the impact, to create some distance between herself and this…this stranger.

'Let me pass!' she gasped with a sob. 'Let me go on!'

'In a hurry, Silver Bird?' The sarcastic tone cut through her panic. A familiar tone.

Her mouth opened in a dry scream of shock, and disbelief. The knight from the forest! Katerina recognised him instantly. The bulk of him. The smell of him. She backed away, hands fluttering up to her mask self-consciously, checking her disguise was still in place. Why, oh why, did it have to be him? The full, creamy-coloured orb of the moon washed his face with a pearly gleam, striking the high, rigid slash of his cheekbones, the strong upward curve of his dark brows. He stared down at her, his expression incisive, predatory, silver embroidery sparkling around the collar of his cloak, like clusters of stars.

'I need to go,' she muttered, attempting to slip around his substantial frame, head turned stubbornly away, ignoring him, trying to clamp down on the rivulets of fear that coursed her body, the heightened bump of her heart. She could not allow his presence to deflect her escape and beyond him, around the back of the keep, the shadows were dark, intense. She would hide there, until the soldiers became bored of searching for her.

'Nay.' One lean hand snaked out, whipped around her forearm as she passed him. Her heart squeezed with trepidation; she stared in panic at the muscular fingers wrapped around her beaded sleeve, the cold causing her eyes to blur, shimmer.

'Let go of me!' Katerina hissed, jerking her arm downwards, to break his hold. Her feeble movement had no effect, merely ripping at the muscle in her shoulder.

'That was quite a performance you gave in there.' His voice, low and sensual, curled around her. Beneath the flimsy, slippery material, her soft flesh yielded beneath his strong grip.

'I need to hide!' She jogged her elbow angrily. She had to move out of view! Her costume gleamed out like a beacon of light, an iridescent bird pressed back against the dark towering walls.

'Then you're wearing the wrong clothes,' he said. Before she could stop him, before she even had time to think, steady, decisive fingers pushed at the mask, peeling the leather back to reveal the full delicate beauty of her heart-shaped face, her alabaster skin, silky, exquisite. In the same movement, he plucked back the beaded hood of her tunic, dragging it from her neat, golden-spun hair.

'So,' Lussac breathed out slowly, 'not just a serving girl after all. Is this your other job?'

She brought her hands upwards, slim fingers clutching around his with anguish, hot tears of frustration welling in her eyes. The warm muscle of his hands pressed into the sensitive curve of her palm; she dropped her hands immediately, stung by the intensity of his touch. A lick of heat curled oddly in the pit of her stomach.

'I don't have time for this!' She glanced frantically behind her.

'What are you running from?' His tone was underscored with steel.

She heard the soldiers' clustered shouts from around the corner, gathering momentum. Her heart sank. 'It's too late,' she murmured, chewing nervously on the fullness of her bottom lip. 'There's no point in running now.' Her body wilted, strength leaching from her limbs, but she raised her chin up, tilting her head proudly. 'No matter. I'm sure I'll manage to extricate myself from this situation. I usually do.' Doubt clouded her tone, as if she couldn't quite convince herself of that certainty.

A lock of hair, silvered in moonlight, had escaped from the mound of braids pinned tight against her scalp, falling across her cheek. Without thinking, Lussac smoothed the velvet coil back behind her ear, savouring the fine softness, a silken thread between the rough pads of his fingertips. Desire punched him, deep in his gut—powerful, swift.

'Come here,' he said roughly. He spun her around, swiftly, so her back was against the wall.

'What are you doing?' she squeaked, keenly aware that he had moved much, much closer. The heft of his shoulders blotted out the vast expanse of star-studded sky. The wall pressed into her spine, the lightweight fabric of her outfit rustling against the rough-hewn stone. Her arms dropped, hands flailing by her sides.

'Saving your skin,' Lussac murmured.

'I can look after myself,' Katerina shot back hurriedly, senses scrabbling as his head dipped. 'Nay,' she stuttered out, 'this is not the way…' Her breath emerged in truncated gasps, floundering; her heart fluttered…with fear?

'It is the only way,' Lussac muttered.

He told himself her expression alone had motivated him, for the maid possessed the appearance of someone who was utterly alone in the world, an overwhelming sadness tingeing her exquisite features. He had recognised that fleeting, haunted look, identified with it, the look of someone compelled to rely completely on their own resources, their own resilience. The maid was exhausted; even he could recognise the blue shadows beneath her eyes. Pity, not lust, propelled him to kiss her; in all honesty, she was the last person he would desire: a raging spitfire with a temper to match, scant flesh on her bones. He wanted to help her, he told himself, that was all. But since when had he wanted to help anyone?

At the implacable press of his lips, her hands whirled upwards, shocked, trying to push against his chest, to gain some distance between them. Her body squirmed. His big hands cradled her face, stilling her, thumbs pulsing warmly against her flaming cheeks. Heat surged through her chest, her stomach, her loins. As his lips played against hers, dancing along the delicate seam of her tightly closed mouth, she heard the soldiers call out to him and her cheeks flamed once more at the indecency of their shouts. This was outrageous! He'd reduced her to the level of a common whore!

The soldiers moved away from them, their bawdy teasing drifting on the breeze, but Lussac barely noticed. The faint awareness that he should end the kiss now, that the ruse had worked, tickled at his conscious mind. The thought was an unnecessary irritant; he dismissed it, flicking it away like a fly on the window-pane. The maid tasted of roses, this silver girl who could swing through the air with ease, a sweet powerful nectar that twisted around his senses, winching him in, stronger, closer. Bracing his sturdy frame against her, he curved his big arms around her back, lifting the lithe fragility of her body against him. At the intimate, shuddering impact of his body, Katerina gasped, hands clutching at his bulky shoulders for support. Her feet swung inches from the ground. Against her lips, he smiled, his tongue delving into the warm recesses of her open, unsuspecting mouth. Exhilaration, boiling, spiking, swept through her, a thrill of pleasure as his tongue entwined with hers; and for one single precious moment, she forgot who she was, and where she was, surrendering to the astonishing sensations coursing through her body.

And then it was over.

Wrenching his mouth from hers, Lussac stepped back, his breathing hoarse, ragged. Unsupported, her limbs strangely weak, fluid, Katerina flopped back against the solid stone, bracing herself against the wall with flat palms. Like a piece of linen cloth forced through the mangle, a strange, wrung-out sensation gripped her body. Her lips burned.

'How dare you kiss me like that!' she flung at him, across the tense, icy silence. But her accusation sounded feeble, pathetic, like a mewl of a half-drowned kitten.

'Saved your skin, didn't I?' he growled at her, mouth tense, unsmiling. 'Now make yourself scarce, before those soldiers come back!'

Legs wobbling, shaking from the impact of his kiss, Katerina scuttled away from him, her lips bruised, scorched by the powerful imprint of his mouth. Embarrassment painted her cheeks, flagged red, but her body danced with a spiralling, flickering, new-born flame of desire.

She tucked her head down in shame and ran.

Chapter Six

All night the wind thrashed tirelessly against the loose canvas of Katerina's tent, driving into the sagging cloth to curve it inwards, before sucking backwards quickly to release the fabric with a short, thwacking sound. The women of the troupe, ten or so, slept together in one tent, their rounded bodies rolled into threadbare blankets, rough, scratchy wool tickling their gently perspiring flesh through thin chemises. Old rugs had been thrown down to provide an insulating layer between the cold grass and the sleeping inmates, but in some places were so worn that the thick, grey warp threads were clearly visible.

The relentless noise of the wind kept Katerina awake. She tossed and turned, desperate to find that sweet spot where sleep would claim her and send her into blessed unconsciousness. She longed for it. The cracking of the wind, the fingers of cold creeping up into her aching body from the ground, the muttered snoring of the women around her—all seemed to conspire to keep her awake. Exhaustion clawed at her body, her limbs floppy with tiredness, and yet her mind, her mind seemed alive, dancing with tingling awareness and excitement. The memory of that kiss, the knock of his sturdy frame against hers jolting every nerve-ending in her body to screaming awareness... Nay! She must drive the memory out, extinguish the vivid colour of the image: the lean planes of his face coming down to meet hers, the strong cradle of his forearms against her back...his tongue against hers.

Katerina wrenched at her blanket, twisting it around her body tightly, furiously. Nobody had told her a kiss could be like that. Innocent in the ways of the marriage bed, she had been unprepared, overwhelmed by his devastating nearness. The women in the troupe told her stories, of course, and recounted their various liaisons with the opposite sex; she wasn't completely in the dark. But in all her one-and-twenty winters, she had never been kissed on the mouth like that, never been held hard up against a man's body with all its shocking intensity.

The bristly blanket itched the side of her neck;

extricating one hand, she scratched at her skin, frowning. She would do well to remember the stranger's brutal dismissal, the sudden shadowing of his eyes. To him, the kiss was nothing, meant nothing, a mere diversion at the end of an evening. Maybe he had intended to help her, after all, to save her from a tricky situation. With his sparkling blue eyes, and bold, impassive stare, the man was an enigma, a man she sincerely hoped never to encounter again.

'Katerina! Are you awake?'

Nay, was it morning already? Katerina groaned, turning over on to her back. The air in the tent was hot, heavy, stifling with the smell of female perspiration. A heavy grittiness dragged at her eyes, as if filled with sand. Somehow, at some point, in that long drawn-out, noisy night, she had slept. Yet now, as she opened her eyes blearily, she felt as if she hadn't slept at all. Her mind yawned with tiredness as pinpricks of sunlight pierced the holes in the canvas, sending needles of light shafting down to the mounds of sleeping bodies.

Sitting up, long amber braids falling forwards over her shoulders, Katerina noticed the empty spaces in the tent; some women were already up, busying themselves with the morning chores: lighting the fire, heating up the huge bowl of pottage, a thick soup of oats and vegetables which would feed them all. The blanket fell from her shoulders, revealing the simple T shape of her linen chemise which doubled as a nightgown, billowing out over her slim frame. A vague dissatisfaction niggled at her conscience and she cast her eyes sideways, nose wrinkling with annoyance. Every night, after a performance, she would shake her costume out carefully, checking for any rips or tears, before packing it away in her scuffed leather satchel. Now she stared at the shining bundle thrown carelessly at the edge of the tent, the mask perched on top at a jaunty angle. What was happening to her? What had happened to her to make her throw her costume to one side as if it meant nothing? The costume was her livelihood; it was everything, her whole existence.

'Katerina! Hurry up, or I'm coming in!' Waleran called from outside the tent. 'It's important.'

Stepping over the still-sleeping bodies, Katerina picked her way over to the tent flap and stuck her head out. Waleran stood outside, brown eyes gleaming with interest at her sleep-flushed face, her coiling, coppery braids. Suddenly self-conscious, she hitched her blanket closer around her shoulders. 'What is it?'

'The Queen wants to see you. Queen Isabella. It seems she was quite taken with your performance last night.'

Katerina eyed him in consternation. 'Waleran, nay! Why on earth does she want to see me?'

Waleran shrugged his shoulders, thinking how beautiful Katerina looked in this early morning light. Her skin held a limpid translucency, a shining quality that emphasised the soft grey of her eyes. He wondered when he should make his move; they were such good friends, the transition to becoming lovers would surely be an easy one.

'I'm not going. Go back and say you cannot find me.'

Waleran jerked his head to one side. Following his movement, Katerina saw two of the Queen's soldiers standing on the edge of their encampment.

'Oh, God, have they been sent to fetch me?'

Waleran nodded. 'Katerina, what's the matter? You cannot refuse the Queen's command. All she wants to do is congratulate you. Find something decent to wear…not boy's clothes,' he added, hurriedly, 'and they will take you to her.'

'I don't have any women's clothes, save my costume,' she answered in desperation. 'You know that; I left everything behind.'

'Borrow something.' Waleran smiled at her,

strangely enjoying her discomfort. Normally it was Katerina who bossed him around, confident and self-assured in her own skin.

A look of panic on her face, Katerina's bright head ducked inwards. The tent flap closed with a snap.

In a very short time, all the women in the tent were awake, pulling their finest gowns from their satchels, trying to find something that Katerina could wear to be presented to the English Queen. Most things were either too big, or too stained and patched to be presentable, but, at last, Marta pulled out a dress of silver-grey velvet that was only slightly worn around the hem and everyone decided that this would be the gown that Katerina would wear.

'At last,' Waleran announced, as she finally emerged from the tent.

'How do I look?' Katerina chewed at her bottom lip.

The close-fitting underdress was of light-grey silk, the sleeves tight to her arms and fastened down to her wrists with a row of tiny pearl buttons. The overdress was fashioned from velvet, the colour of pewter, shot through on the diagonal with rows of silver thread. Silver embroidery ran around the hem-line, with only a small section fraying at the back. Marta had parted Katerina's hair in the middle and retied her braids to pin them in a knot at the nape of her neck, while Brunhild, digging deep into her bag, had produced a simple silver circlet that now sat on Katerina's head.

'How do you look?' Waleran was astonished. He had always been aware of Katerina's innate beauty, indeed, he had known her when she was the lord of the manor's daughter, wearing finery like this every day. But he had obviously forgotten how delicious she could look, how utterly desirable.

'Aye, how do I look? Oh, Waleran, I don't feel comfortable wearing this; I'm too like my old self. What if someone recognises me?'

'Nay, it's not possible. We're too far from home.' He touched her arm, a comforting gesture. 'Katerina, you look beautiful. Now, go with the soldiers and accept the Queen's praise. You deserve it.'

Ragged, horizontal bands of gilded sunlight split the grey light of dawn as Katerina followed the tall, broad backs of the Queen's soldiers. Her hem brushed over the dew-soaked grass, the material darkening with moisture. Her feet slopped in borrowed slippers as she walked; curling her toes, she tried to keep the thin leather attached to her feet.

Cold fingers of air sneaked beneath the rounded collar of her dress, touching her exposed collar-bone and the naked hollow of her neck, and she shivered, suddenly wishing she'd thrown her cloak over the whole gleaming outfit. But her cloak was a poor, threadbare affair, not the sort of garment one could wear before the Queen of England. She hoped, nay, prayed, that Isabella would keep the forthcoming interview as short as possible; she had no wish for accolades or praise. Inwardly, she cursed herself for creating a performance that drew too much attention; when she had left home with Waleran, she had had no idea that she would be so naturally gifted. Yet it was her stunning performance that kept her in the troupe—indeed, it was the *only* thing that kept her in the troupe, as John never ceased to remind her. It was her protection, her insurance. She couldn't afford to lose it.

The castle walls rose up before her, towering, huge chunks of dressed stone picked out individually by the slanting light. The soldiers led her across the drawbridge and into the dark shadowed gatehouse, dominated overhead by a heavy portcullis, cruel black spikes pointing downwards. Despite the still, impassive stance of the sentries at this gate, male eyes swivelled appreciatively beneath steel helmets as they tracked the slight figure in the silver gown, the brilliant flare of coiled hair.

The inner bailey, ground shiny with greasy cobbles, was almost empty, apart from a handful of soldiers over by the steps to the main hall, who were washing. A servant worked the handle of a water pump, up and down, sloshing water liberally into the trough so that it overflowed, trickling away along a stone gully towards an open drain.

Katerina flushed, ducked her head. The men were bare-chested, stripped to their braies, their strong muscled bodies exposed, naked. They laughed and joked with each other, their ribald teasing jarring the air as they splashed each other with the freezing water. One soldier noticed Katerina and nudged his companion, whispering something. A fresh peal of raucous laughter broke out and she hunched her shoulders defensively, scuttling quickly after her escort, eyes fixed resolutely to the ground. The sooner she was inside the castle, the better. When she performed, she was in disguise, concentrating hard on each movement, on working her body; she barely noticed the audience's response, oblivious to their close attention as she flew through the air. But here, now, with her hair piled upon her head in elaborate coils, her face and neck revealed, bare down to the collar of her gown, she felt vulnerable, exposed. She hated it, hated this scrutiny, those interested male eyes upon her.

The escort soldiers stopped, flanking the bottom of the steps courteously so she could go up before them. Annoyingly, one of her slippers had come adrift and she wriggled her foot, trying to secure it. An untidy pile of linen shirts near the base of the steps, no doubt thrown down by the soldiers before they washed, caught her eye. She wondered how these soldiers managed to keep the fabric so white, so pristine, while she struggled to keep her meagre bundle of clothes looking anything but smart. Hesitating, with one hand on the iron banister of the steps, she scrunched her eyes up suddenly, a frown gathered between her neat brows. Was she seeing things? A leather cuff, studded with silver ovals, lay on the cobbles beside the shirts. Her cuff.

Her heart gave a quick, treacherous flip. How could she have been so careless? Surely she'd stored it safely away after her performance last night, just like she did every other night, deep at the bottom of her satchel? But, no, there it lay, gleaming quietly, revealing its presence for everyone to see. The cuff that had belonged to her mother, her good-luck charm that she wore for every performance. The last, single link to her old life, her previous existence.

Heart racing, she bent down, seized the cuff between her slender fingers. Yes, it was hers. Swiftly she traced the silver ovals and felt, rather than saw, the etched outline of a single dogrose on each one, before curling it tightly, hiding it in the curve of her palm. She must have dropped it last night, in her haste to flee the castle, the bags of stolen goods held treacherously against her chest, before… Her thought process stuttered to a halt. No, she had no wish to recall what had happened after that. Spinning on her toes, she smiled up at the escort soldiers, who waited patiently for her to climb the steps.

'What do you think you are doing?'

The low, guttural voice emerged from nowhere, striking the back of her head like a physical blow. She stumbled under the weight of it, her hand reaching, scrabbling once more for the iron railing on the steps; her fingers tightened around the cold metal. It was him. She knew it was him, before she even turned around. The knight from the forest, the man who had kissed her…and left her wanting more. She sensed his hard, piercing stare drilling into her stiff, unyielding spine, his gimlet blue eyes resting on the nape of her neck, her bound and circleted hair.

'I said, "What do you think you are doing?"'. His voice rapped again at her, insistent, demanding.

Katerina pivoted, adjusting her chin upwards to meet the eyes of the man who seemed to dog her every move, to thwart her at every turn. He towered above her diminutive figure: restless, threatening, like a prowling animal hunting quarry. What would he do now? Denounce her to the Earl of Norfolk for her thievery last night? A flicker of panic coursed through her, but she stamped it down, snuffed it quickly. Surely she had dealt with bigger problems than this?

Lussac glared down at her, expression fierce in the tough hewn angles of his face. Droplets fell from his wet hair, falling to the bare, polished skin of his shoulders. Like the other soldiers, he was stripped to the waist, the bulky musculature of his chest and shoulders gleaming in the rosy morning light. He had seen the maid the moment she had come through the gatehouse, spotting her slim, delicate profile long before his boisterous companions at the pump. She had emerged from the shadows like an ethereal light, shining out from between the two hefty soldiers. The sight of her sweet face stilled his movements, the cold water trickling down his face, as he tracked her grace-ful progress across the cobbles, unexpected feminine curves revealed by the silver-grey gown. Shot through with iridescent thread, the pewter velvet of her overdress deepened the stormy grey of her eyes, emphasising the pinkish bloom upon her cheeks. Heart squeezing, he had remembered his hands on that lithe body, the soft touch of her mouth against his own in that fleeting, passionate kiss.

'I…er…' Katerina began, stuttering inanely. The solid nakedness of his chest seemed to drive all conscious thought, all logic from her brain. For some insane reason, she seemed unable to concentrate, to find any words, let alone the right ones. She dragged her gaze upwards, forcing herself to look at his face, but that was worse! The generous curve of his bottom lip mocked her, reminding her; she stared at it in dismay. Her palms warmed, pearling with the slick of perspiration, the silver discs of the leather cuff cool against her skin. 'I… the Queen wanted to see me.'

Her mouth dropped open as he grabbed her hand, twisting it roughly to pull her fingers open, revealing the leather cuff. 'I meant "this",' he said thickly. 'What are you doing with this?'

He must have seen her pick it up. 'I haven't stolen it, if that's what you're insinuating!' she flared back at him, annoyed at the powerful clutch of his fingers around her own. His big, calloused thumb dug into the base of her palm.

He ignored her protest. 'Does it belong to you?' His eyes searched her face, flinty, challenging. Katerina drew a deep unsteady breath. He was closer now, surely, so close that she could see the bump of his heart beneath the solid plates of his chest. Water flicked from his hair on to her pale, exposed wrist, a glistening trail sliding across the net of blue veins beneath the pallid skin. His threatening manner made the hairs on the back of her neck stand on end; fear threaded like ice along her veins. Was she in danger? The cuff formed the only link back to her family, her identity: she must be careful about revealing any connections.

'No...no,' she breathed out. 'It belongs to a friend of mine. They thought they had lost it; they asked to me to keep an eye out.'

His fingers tightened, crushing the cuff into the centre of her palm. 'You're a little liar, Silver Bird, or whatever your name is,' he ground out. 'It belongs to you, doesn't it?'

'I told you,' Katerina replied, wide grey eyes burning with hostility, 'it belongs to a friend.' She tried to jerk her hand downwards, out of his punishing grip, but his hand, his arm failed to move. 'Let go of me!' she cried out in frustration. Twisting her head around frantically, she glanced at the Queen's soldiers, standing impassively by the steps. 'Help me!' she shouted to them. 'Do something!' Beneath their helmets, their eyes went immediately to the man who held her, awaiting his order.

'Leave us,' Lussac bit out the command. 'Tell the Queen I will bring Silver Bird to her later on.' In a trice, he dropped his grip, whisking up his shirt from the messy pile on the ground. Pulling it haphazardly over his head, followed by a dark-blue tunic, he strapped a thick belt around his waist, then thrust his sword with its jewelled hilt into the leather scabbard. Katerina began to edge away from him, slipping her small feet across the cobbles in the direction of the gatehouse, heart knocking frantically against her chest wall.

'Oh, no, you don't!' He snared her wrist once more. 'No, you stay with me, until I have some answers!'

His strident tone drove straight into her, needled her. Her breath punched from her lungs in a burst of anger. Cheeks flaming, she drew herself upright, holding her ground. 'How dare you treat me like this! You have no right! No right at all!

I've told you, the cuff belongs to someone in the troupe; it's nothing to do with me.'

'Then tell me who it belongs to,' he said, more softly, now. 'It's important; I need to know.'

Katerina stared up at the grim line of his mouth, the turquoise chips of his eyes. 'Why? Why does it mean so much to you?' she asked suddenly.

'Because this cuff is mine,' he spoke tersely, in a voice held under tension. 'I took it from my wrist and threw it down next to my shirt before I washed. Odd that you should recognise it.'

Fear lumped, wedged like a great slab of rock in her chest. She swayed, her body sagging under his intense perusal, the striking turquoise velvet of his eyes. The cuff burned like a brand into her hand, scorching her skin as her mind skittered for answers, thinking of a way to throw him off, for some way out of this mess. How, in Heaven's name, could the cuff be his? He was no part of her family—the man was a stranger to her! She didn't even know his name.

'Have it back then,' Katerina replied shortly. Pretence was her only way out of this predicament. 'Let go of my hand and take it back. I saw the gleam of silver...' she tilted her head sideways at him, attempting a wry smile '...and I thought it was my lucky day. Those discs alone would fetch a good price at market.'

He should have believed her. From all he had witnessed so far, the maid was a proven thief, light-fingered, adept at pilfering and doubtless escaping all blame for such crimes. With her milk-white skin, and those wide dove-grey eyes, few would suspect her. But Lussac didn't believe her. He knew she was lying. He could smell her deceit a mile off, could see terror lurking in her beautiful eyes. The maid knew something and he intended to discover what it was.

'Who are your people, Silver Bird? Where do you come from?'

A strengthening breeze tugged at the hem of her skirts, pressing the fabric against her slim legs. The lump of fear in her chest grew bigger. Katerina shook her head, lips pressed into a mutinous line. 'It's none of your business.' One arm moved defensively across her flat stomach.

She was too thin, he thought suddenly. The bodice of her dress was too big for her, gapping dangerously at the neckline, hinting at the shadowed bosom beneath. Her collar-bone stood out from the fine, white skin of her neck; he noted the shadows of exhaustion beneath her eyes. He released her wrist suddenly, shamefully aware that his grip was too forceful, too punishing against her fragile bones.

'I'm not going to hurt you,' he said, his voice lowering. 'But you're wrong. The moment your fingers touched that cuff, it became my business.' Although he had released her hand, the big frame of his body curled around her, a cage of solid flesh and muscle, trapping her against the stone steps. She wanted to scream and shout at him, to beat her fists against his chest, to be angry, but all she really wanted to do was cry. To sob. All her hard work, all her efforts to hide the traces of her family, the clues to her past, all had turned to ash. All because of one stupid, foolish mistake. She should have left that leather cuff alone and walked straight past it, her head held high.

'Lussac!' Mortimer's dark head appeared in the doorway. 'What in Heaven's name are you doing? Bring the maid up here now! Isabella is demanding to see her.'

Lussac hooked his arm around Katerina's, effectively pinning her to his side. His forearm lay along her forearm, the rounded muscle of his upper arm nudged against her shoulder. Through the flimsy linen of his shirt, the heat of his skin burned through her sleeve. Her body leapt in recognition at his closeness, while her mind unravelled with

terror. 'This is what we're going to do,' he said quietly, his voice measured, controlling. 'We will visit
the Queen, together, and then afterwards you will
tell me the things I need to know. I need answers
and I will get them, one way or another.'

Chapter Seven

Isabella took a delicate sip from her pewter goblet, grimacing as the watery mead slipped down her throat—would she ever become accustomed to this insipid English drink? In France they drank red wine from the moment the cock crowed till eventide. How she wished for its full-bodied fortification today, the day when she began the pursuit of her husband, the useless King of England. She tapped her fingers on the table, restless. Where was everybody? She looked up as the heavy curtain over the arched doorway of the great hall twitched, then drew back. Mortimer strode in, the slanting sun from the high windows polishing his straight black hair to the sheen of a raven's wing. 'Ah! Roger, at last! Did you find her?'

Mortimer nodded. 'She was with Lussac, at the bottom of the steps.'

'Bring her in here quickly,' Isabella snapped. 'We haven't much time; we must move on today.'

'I'm well aware of that fact,' replied Mortimer, drily. He sprang up the steps to the high dais and threw himself into a carved oak chair next to the Queen. 'The Earl has suggested lodgings for tonight, and then we can head for Bury the day after that. The sooner we catch up with Edward, the better.' A terse smile crossed his face. 'I have heard that London has turned against him. And—' he grinned wolfishly, showing a perfect set of white teeth in his tanned face '—I have learned he has put a price of £1,000 on my head.'

Across the pristine white tablecloth, Isabella pressed her forearm, a tiny, discreet movement, against Mortimer's. 'You are worth far more than that,' she teased gently. She allowed herself this small liberty in their relationship, for although they had to keep their affair secret for the sake of the support of the English people, at this hour the great hall was deserted; there was no one to see this gesture of affection. September was a busy month; the peasants had broken their fast before the sun rose and were already out in the fields, harvesting the crops before the winter.

Isabella frowned slightly as Lussac strode into the room, his face stern, impassive. On his arm was a young woman, supposedly the incredible acrobat from the performance the night before. Was this slight, diminutive figure really the person who had swung from chandelier to chandelier, astonishing them all with her daring acts of bravado?

The Queen cleared her throat. 'How kind of you to bring the maid to me, Lussac.' She inclined her head towards the tall knight. 'I wasn't aware Mortimer had sent you to fetch her?'

'He didn't.'

The Queen waited, but one look at Lussac's impenetrable expression told her she wouldn't receive any more information on the subject. She sighed. As a friend of her brother's, she had known Lussac since childhood, but the man had become a stranger to her now. Still formidable in battle, an expert strategist and skilled at commanding an army, he would plunge into skirmishes like a man possessed, even more so since the tragedy that had befallen his family. Charles relied heavily on him in France and trusted him with his life, but she knew, on this campaign, Lussac's motivations lay elsewhere. Charles had expressly told her that she could not call on Lussac to help her: Mortimer would lead her army and Mortimer alone. Still, she couldn't help hoping that Lussac would find what he was looking for sooner rather than later, and come back to serve her in the campaign. It had been too long.

She switched her attention to the maid, speaking with the gentle, cajoling tone she reserved for the peasant class. 'Come, come closer, my dear, do not be afraid.' Half-rising from her chair, she indicated the exact spot on which Katerina should stand. The jewels on top of the Queen's head twinkled crazily in the streaming sun, needles of light piercing outwards into the crepuscular gloom of the great hall.

Lussac. So that was the name of her tormentor, Katerina thought. It didn't seem to fit him, somehow. The name implied light and joy, an enthusiasm for life, but one look at the darkly scowling face at her side made her think of anything but that. As if in a trance, Katerina stumbled forwards, Lussac's arm providing a support she yearned to throw off. She curtsied clumsily before the Queen, velvet skirts brushing the grey expanse of flagstones as Lussac bowed. He was not going to let her go. She stared down at his arm wound snugly around her own, the tanned fingers covering hers, strong, capable, warming her icy skin. A scratch crossed one of his knuckles, she noticed, a thin red line of dried blood. Panic rose in her gullet and she bashed it down; fear would not help her now.

All she had to do, all she must do, Katerina told herself sternly, was to get through this audience with the Queen, and then…

'I said, "What is your name?"' the Queen repeated testily. Really, was she to be surrounded by dunces in this country?

'I am Silver Bird, my lady.'

Isabella smiled benevolently. 'I mean, your real name. Where are you from?'

'Yes, tell us, Silver Bird,' Lussac muttered under his breath.

Katerina tried desperately to ignore the man at her side, the warmth of his hip bumping intimately against her left flank. She shrugged her shoulders diffidently. 'People know me as "Katerina". I have been with the troupe for a long time.'

'You were born into it?'

'Something like that,' Katerina replied, attempting to keep her answers as vague as possible, without telling an outright lie.

Isabella's fine eyebrows shot upwards at the obvious dissembling. Her lips tightened imperceptibly. 'Your act, last night, was truly wonderful. Where did you learn such skills?'

'I was taught by a member of the troupe, my lady.' This, at least, was true. Waleran had taught her everything she knew.

'And your parents? Are they with the troupe?' Beneath a jewelled net, Isabella's blonde hair shone in two precise rolls. Intricately cut diamonds studded the simple gold band that circled her head.

'Er…no, no, they passed away,' Katerina managed to stutter out.

'Utter rubbish!' Mortimer said suddenly, shoving his pewter goblet down upon the table. A drop of wine shuddered out, splashing on to the cloth at the firmness of the movement.

'I beg your pardon?' Isabella glared at him.

'Oh, for goodness' sake, Isabella!' Mortimer smacked the table with the flat of his palm, his manner triumphant. 'It's obvious who she is! Where have you seen that colour of hair before? It's not exactly common!'

A churning feeling welled up in Katerina's stomach—a gathering, roiling nausea. Blood roared in her ears and, for one horrible moment, she wondered if she were going to faint. This was it. Mortimer knew who she was. He had recognised her from the colour of her hair. Her damned hair! She watched in horror as his mouth opened wide, focusing wildly on the dark, cavernous interior of his gullet.

'She's Katerina of Dauntsey. You know, the Dauntseys, who live out at Longthorpe. Thomas's daughter. He has an older brother, remember. They've all got that hair. I'd recognise it anywhere.' He pinned his narrowed eyes upon Katerina. 'I'm right, aren't I?' His booming voice echoed around the great hall, across the trestle tables swept clean, up across the colourful embroidered tapestries that adorned the high stone walls.

Lussac acknowledged the soft sag of Katerina's body against his right flank as Mortimer spoke the name and watched as the neat head, pinned with delicately braided amber coils, nodded in proud defeat. Maintaining his hold on her, he wondered if she were about to collapse. Her face was grey, ashen with shock. Why was she so afraid of people knowing who she was, her identity? Mortimer's revelation had supplied the answer to Lussac's earlier question. If the cuff belonged to Katerina, and, despite her fervid protests, he was in no doubt that it did, then that simple leather band was connected to the Dauntsey family. Knowing that, it wouldn't take him long to track down his murderer. He should have been as triumphant as Mortimer up there on the top table, beaming away at his Queen. But somehow, as he watched the defiance, the stamina drain out of the woman at his side, it didn't feel like a victory at all.

* * *

In the rising sunlight, horses thronged the inner bailey: huge, muscled destriers, warhorses, tramping and colliding with each other as the stable-boys darted between them, throwing the heavy saddles on to their backs. The animals jerked their heads up, eyes wide and rolling, snorting hot plumes of air from widened nostrils, scraping at the cobbles with restless hooves. And above this seething, heaving chaos, the wide bowl of sky was blue, carrying the promise of heat later in the day.

'So, Katerina…' Lussac spoke her name for the very first time, dipping his head to her ear as they stepped out together from the great hall. 'Katerina of Dauntsey.'

'Please, please do not speak that name,' she whispered. Her toes were frozen within the insubstantial shoes as she balanced precariously above the churning chaos of men and horses.

He barely heard her voice. 'I don't understand. Why do you deny who you are, when you have such talent? Why do you hide behind the trappings of your performance, disguise yourself as a boy?' His searching gaze swept the length of her, across the pale-grey silk hugging the neat indent of her waist before it flared out over the gentle curve of her hips. 'It's almost as if someone is searching for you, as if you don't want to be found.'

She stared at him, aghast. Her world was in pieces, saliva turned to dust in her mouth.

'You don't want to be found.'

A small sob tore at her chest. 'I have to go! I have to leave…now!' She plunged away from him, her broad-shouldered tormenter in his surcoat of dark blue, down, down the steps and into the swarming mass of animal flesh. Injustice shook at her, seizing her breath in a fierce, shuddering clasp. Her whole existence, her livelihood, was in jeopardy. Her identity had been revealed, but if she vanished now, hid for a while, she might be able to salvage some small fragment of her current existence.

Reckless now, desperate to escape from Lussac, she shoved at a rounded, glossy rump that blocked her way towards the gatehouse, glaring at the wall of chestnut horseflesh when it refused to budge. Stalled, she nibbled at her bottom lip in worry, now fully aware that she drew many interested glances. All she wanted to do was to reach the gatehouse and disappear out to the tents, to pack her bags and flee—was that too much to ask?

'Excuse me, my lady, but maybe I could be of some assistance?' A knight appeared at her side, a well-padded, portly knight, only a few inches taller than herself. Laid over his chainmail, his dark blue surcoat, decorated with embroidered fleur-de-lys, stretched tightly across his protruding stomach. His rounded face, fleshy cheekbones, held a kind, considerate expression as he addressed her in a beautiful, modulated tone. 'Philippe, Count of Garsan, at your service, *mademoiselle.* Please, allow me to escort you from this…this…' He struggled to find the appropriate word to describe the mayhem happening around them, and, failing to find it, simply waved his hand over the inner bailey, before extending one gauntleted hand towards her. Despite the iron band of panic winching around her chest, Katerina smiled at the knight's generosity. She refused to glance behind—was Lussac following her?

'Aye, thank you,' she blurted out in relief. The tight bundle of her breath released suddenly. She clutched at the knight's glove, the hard leather of the rigid, creased fingers catching at the soft skin of her palm.

'She's with me, Philippe,' the stern voice spoke behind her. The knight's hand dropped away beneath hers, a look of surprise crossing his face; in consternation, she realised the leather cuff was still gripped within her palm. Lussac stood at her side. 'Let's go somewhere quieter,' he said, his voice cutting low and powerful across the noise of the bailey.

'I don't want to go anywhere with you!' she squeaked. 'Please, please, leave me alone!' Her protests fell on deaf ears, his bare fingers curling around her own. He forged through the horses, shoving the gigantic animals aside as if they were nothing more than common dogs or sheep. She skipped to keep up with his extended pace, cheeks flaming with the cold, with embarrassment, as they crossed the drawbridge and moved in the fields of pasture outside. She lost one shoe in the process, now probably stamped to shreds by those massive horses; the wetness from the thick grass soaked through her stocking.

Lussac stopped abruptly, facing her in the patch of grass between the high castle walls and the huddle of white canvas tents. He pushed one hand through his dark-brown hair, silky strands falling back over his forehead, like ruffled feathers.

'I think you can help me, Katerina.'

'No, I can't.'

'Listen to me.' He reached down, disentangled the cuff from her trembling fingers. The silver ovals winked in the light. 'I don't care about who you are, or what you are hiding from. It means nothing to me.' He held up the cuff, inches from her face, blue eyes glittering. 'But this does. This means everything to me. I need to find out who this belongs to.'

'I thought you said it belonged to you,' she said crossly. Did he not realise her whole existence teetered on the brink of destruction, the fragile glass walls of her life about to topple, to lie in broken shards around her?

'I found it,' he said shortly. 'And you recognise it... No—' he held up his hand to silence her speech '—no protests, please. And as we now know you are Katerina of Dauntsey, courtesy of loose-lipped Mortimer back there—' he jerked his head in the direction of the castle '—I suspect that the owner of this cuff is a member of your family.'

Katerina crossed her arms over her stomach, hugging her sides. Freezing liquid ran in her veins. Overhead, a pack of gulls wheeled and circled, their eerie cries piercing the sun-soaked air.

'Take me to your home, Katerina. Take me to Longthorpe. Go into your tent, now, and pack your things.'

'Never, I refuse to do it. You cannot make me.' But even as the words spilled from her mouth, she realised the stupidity of them. How could she hope to best him? Physically, never—he towered above her—but maybe, just maybe, she could outwit him.

'I can make you do anything I want,' he replied bluntly. 'It's your choice: either I drag you from this place, kicking and screaming and making a spectacle of yourself, or you'll come quietly. It's your choice.'

'Please, I can't, I can't go home.' The sudden fear, the pleading in her voice, shocked him. Guilt scoured his tongue, a thick, bitter liquid.

He scowled down at her, trying to ignore the rigid set of her jawline, the devastated expression in her pewter eyes. Why was she making this so difficult? 'Yes, you can, Katerina. Like it or not, you are coming with me.'

Chapter Eight

Frustration clouding her eyes, Katerina plunged into the relative safety of her tent, thankfully empty, hearing the heavy canvas flap shut behind her. Her fingers shook as she ripped off the borrowed veil, the elaborate gown, wrenching brutally at the fine fabric to pull it over her head. One of the small buttons snagged in the coils of her hair and she ripped at the material, dislodging several strands that drifted around her head, a spun net of amber.

She dropped to her knees, the dress spilling into a forlorn puddle at her side, and rummaged in her bag for more comfortable boy's clothes: dun-coloured braies, fawn hooded tunic. She tipped up the bag, shook it, dislodging all the contents.

And there it lay, on the faded stripe of the rug. The leather cuff. Her leather cuff, falling from her bag like a curse. The cuff she had unfastened from her mother's wrist on the day she died. The man prowling outside her tent, the man who waited for her, had not lied. The cuff she had found in the bailey belonged to him. How, she had no idea. The tears that had threatened all morning began to pour down her cheeks; Katerina sobbed as she secured the cuff high around her forearm, pulling the tunic's bristly wool over her head, the long, wide-cut sleeves covering the shining discs. She sobbed for her life, her identity. Staggering to her feet, she hauled on the braies, fastening them securely around her waist, stuffing her costume back into her scuffed bag. It was all she had in the world, apart from a few measly coins in a pouch that hung from her belt.

Slinging the long strap crosswise across her body, she stood up, scrubbing brutally at the tears on her skin, reddening her cheeks. It would do no good feeling sorry for herself. Self-pity would not help her now. She relied on her wits, nay, prided herself on them; she would extricate herself from this mess, no doubt about it. But she needed time to think. Time, which that horrible, arrogant man, pacing about outside, would not allow her to have.

The tent flap punched back. She jumped.

'Who's that man out there?' Waleran said, as he came in. The outer corners of his nut-brown eyes crinkled as he smiled. The sounds of the camp being dismantled followed him: the flap and snap of sagging canvas as taut guy ropes were released on the tents, the indignant snorts of the mules and horses as stuffed panniers and saddle-bags were loaded on to their backs.

Katerina stared at Waleran, trying to push back the sense of desperation, of hopelessness that threatened to overwhelm her. Against the white canvas background of the tent, he appeared smaller, more wiry, an expectant, encouraging smile fixed on his narrow features as he waited for her to speak. 'Who is he, Katerina? What's happened?'

Katerina shook her head. 'Oh, Waleran,' she said softly, 'the worst has happened.' She fastened one of the loose straps on her bag, her hands drifting forlornly to her sides. 'Roger Mortimer, the Queen's commander, recognised me and all because of this! My stupid wretched hair!' She touched her head in anguish, knuckles against her skull. 'He knew my name, Waleran. He spoke it out loud.' She pulled the hood of her tunic firmly over her head, obscuring the glistening colour.

'Are they going to make you go back to your father?' Waleran spoke slowly.

'It's worse than that. I was so stupid, Waleran, so

stupid! You know the leather cuff I wear? Around my wrist?'

'Your mother's?' he confirmed, frowning.

'Aye. Well, for some obscure reason, the knight who waits for me, Lussac de Belbigny, has an identical cuff. And when I saw it in the bailey, I thought it was mine!'

'And you picked it up.'

'And I picked it up. Oh, Waleran, I wish to God I hadn't done so. He wants me to take him back to my home!' Her voice rose, tremulous, shrill. 'And you know what will happen if I go back there!' In the gloom of the tent, dirty-white, her eyes widened, alert, serious. Memories crowded into her head. The bitterness between her father and his older brother, the constant fights and petty bickering, all so worthless, so useless. And her own hand, promised in a marriage so inconceivable that she had no wish to partake. Lifting her head, she forced a wan smile towards Waleran.

'I had better go,' she said. 'Otherwise, he'll come barging in here to drag me out.'

Stunned, Waleran eyed her in disbelief. 'You can't leave, Katerina, John will go completely mad! The troupe is nothing without your act. You cannot go with that man.'

Katerina shook her head. 'I have no choice.'

'No, Katerina. You need someone to take care of you, to look after you. That man out there wouldn't dare take you away if you had a protector.' Waleran's voice adopted a curious lilt. He traced one silky wing of hair spilling forwards from the voluminous hem of her hood, a swag of undulating satin in the dimness of the tent.

Katerina arched one eyebrow, catching his odd tone. 'What do you mean?' she answered slowly, suspiciously. 'I don't need anyone, I can look after myself, you know that.'

'Aye, I know,' Waleran replied. 'And up to now, it's been fine. But you're so vulnerable, being a woman. You're the only maid in this camp with no protection. All the other women have husbands, or fathers in the troupe.'

Katerina shifted uncomfortably. She never liked to dwell for too long on the precariousness of her situation.

'I can help you, Katerina,' Waleran continued. 'If you were married, or even betrothed, that French knight out there would think twice about carting you away.'

'What are you saying?' she whispered.

'I realise this might come as a shock, Katerina. We've been friends for a long time, and, well, I've come to think of you as more than a friend.

I didn't intend for all this to be such a rush, but your current situation demands it—I think we should marry.' There, he'd said the words, finally, the words that had swirled around in his head for nigh on a year now.

Nay, nay, nay! Why did he have to go and say such things?

'You don't have to do this,' she muttered.

'I want to do it.' Waleran beamed back at her. 'I've wanted to say those words for a long, long time. I love you, Katerina.'

Face flushing, she dropped her gaze to the neck of his tunic, the embroidered eyelets that carried each loop of leather lacing. How could she tell him the truth? That she had no wish to marry for anything other than love.

'Waleran, I had not...I...you're like a brother to me,' she stumbled over the words, her tongue big and clumsy in her mouth. She folded her arms across her chest, bracing herself away from him, defensive.

Waleran's mouth tightened at the gesture. 'Let me be more than a brother to you,' he suggested gamely, although a note of doubt crept into his voice, wavering, unsure. He tipped forwards, unexpectedly, grabbing clumsily at her shoulders, pressing his lips against hers.

'Nay!' Katerina wrenched her mouth away, appalled at his behaviour. 'Waleran, stop this. It isn't right, it doesn't feel right!' She scrabbled to her feet, away from him, dragging her sleeve across her face, wiping away the feeling of his mouth against hers. Her lips felt numb, assaulted. 'Why are you doing this? It will make no difference to that man out there; I suspect he'll insist on dragging me off whether I'm betrothed or not.'

'I'll stop him,' boasted Waleran. 'He'll listen to me, listen to reason.'

'That man will listen to no one,' Katerina replied. 'Have you seen him?' She recalled his breathtaking speed, his agility in the forest as he pursued her. 'I know what that man is capable of, Waleran; we have no hope of besting him, at least physically. It is best if I pretend to go along with his plans, then try to outmanoeuvre him in other ways, outwit him.'

'It's because you're unmarried, on your own, that he thinks he has authority over you.'

'I suspect he hasn't even thought of that.' Katerina placed a hand on Waleran's arm. 'Look, I understand what you're trying to do for me, and I thank you for it, but—'

'Sorry to break up the fond farewells...' Lussac stuck his head through the tent opening, observing the pair of them with a bleak, wry smile '…but we need to make headway, Katerina.' The diamond glitter of his eyes struck hard, to the very centre of her. Her stomach flipped with a roiling emptiness. Lussac's knowing look took in the closeness of the couple: the hectic colour washing Katerina's pale, high cheekbones, Waleran clutching possessively on to her arm.

'You can't do this, you know!' Waleran pushed in front of Katerina, facing the broad-shouldered knight. Against Lussac's towering frame, Waleran looked like a child.

'Are you the husband?' Lussac glowered at him.

'No, I…er, yes, yes, I am.' Waleran flushed with the lie, a dull red colour washing over his neck and jawline.

Katerina stepped up to Waleran's side. 'I am unmarried,' she pronounced simply. 'Waleran is trying to protect me.' Her clear, melodic tone cut through the thick, uneasy atmosphere. She turned to her friend. 'Let me go, Waleran. And remember, I will be all right. I can look after myself.'

Queen Isabella and her entourage finally left the Earl of Norfolk's estate around mid-morning, clattering out on horseback from the gatehouse, heading towards Bury St Edmunds. Even at this hour, a somnolence lay across the land, the warm air carrying a relaxed, ambling feel. It was as if the countryside had retained the high heat from early summer, storing it deep in the earth, and now released it shivering into the mist that hung over the river valley to the south. The breeze, drifting across the coloured wagons, the glossy horseflesh, the proud, snapping banner of the Queen, touched faces with warmth.

Sheep dotted the patchwork fields, white woolly spots against a backdrop of green, breaking away in anxious knots as the horses approached. A golden light bathed the shallow, undulating hills as the peasants busied themselves in the fields, cutting the wheat, bundling the cut grass into stooks to make hay. The shadow of the great famine hung over everyone; people had seen many friends, relatives, die of starvation. In that bleak summer a few years ago, when the rain never stopped and the air was cold, the crops had failed, rotting away to black mush in the fields where they had been planted; livestock had drowned. No one wished a repeat of what had happened and now the importance of preserving the crops through the winter took on added significance.

From the vantage point of Norfolk's castle, Lussac observed the Queen's party moving away, before sticking one booted foot into his stirrup and swinging up into the saddle of his destrier. The gold fleur-de-lys embroidery on his dark-blue tunic glinted in the sunlight, the side-seams deliberately split in order to ease riding. Beneath his woollen braies, his thigh muscles formed bulky indentations, flexing strongly as he controlled the excited skittering of the animal beneath him.

He half-twisted in the saddle, flicking a wayward strand of dark hair out of his eyes. 'Have you everything that you need?' Doubtfully, he eyed the small bag slung over Katerina's shoulder, resting on her hip.

'Yes.'

He frowned. Surely the chit must have more possessions than those that would fit into a leather satchel? His own effects had been neatly packed by a helpful servant and secured to the back of his horse in two large saddle-bags.

'Shall we go then?' he asked.

Katerina, perched on top of a sweet grey palfrey, merely scowled at him. She had already refused to ride side-saddle, insisted on sitting astride in her ridiculous boy's outfit. The flaming gold of her hair was hidden by her customary sack-like hood. Already he missed the pearl-grey dress that caressed her curves, revealing her slim, lithe form. 'I suppose so,' she replied grudgingly, seizing the white leather reins between her small hands.

'I'm glad you decided to come.'

She rounded on him hotly. 'Did I have a choice?'

'No.' His eyes were blank, unreadable. Every muscle in his body itched to drive his heels into his horse's flanks and ride, ride like the devil until he found the man for whom he was searching. The murderer. He sighed. 'I promise this will not take long. I'll deliver you back to the troupe before they even notice that you've gone.'

'If you say so.' Her manner was churlish. 'Although I'm sure John will not be happy when he finds out about my disappearance.'

'I spoke to John while you were packing your things. He seemed most amenable to the whole idea.'

'What!' Katerina frowned, pinned her large grey eyes upon him. 'I don't believe you! How dare you meddle in my affairs?'

'You won't lose your position. I offered him some money to cover any lost performances.' His gaze swept over her, blank, unconcerned.

Her blood boiled at his interference and she screwed up her eyes at him, trying to stare him down. She hated to be beholden to anyone, let alone this man, with his extraordinary turquoise eyes and carved, handsome features, but in his implacable presence, she became powerless, intensely vulnerable, a fragile leaf knocked about by the violent winds of his determination. She hated it.

'Which way?' Lussac said, bunching up his reins in one tanned, gloveless hand. 'North?'

'South,' she said firmly, driving her knees into the rounded sides of the palfrey to lead the way down, across the marshes. She twitched her head sharply around so he wouldn't see the lie in her face. It wouldn't hurt at all to lead this arrogant knight on a wild goose chase, to stall him a little so she had time to regain some of her lost control, time to find a way to escape. She had no intention of returning home. Ever.

Tiny, loose stones spitting out from beneath her palfrey's hooves, Katerina led the way across the dusty causeway bisecting the still, glistening marshland, deliberately curbing her horse's gait to a slow trot. The causeway was too narrow for both her and Lussac to ride side by side, and she took great delight in weaving her horse from left to right, so that he had no hope of passing. A heat haze shimmered over to the east, blurring the line between ground and sky, and in the distance she could see the shine of the wide river estuary, the gleaming line of the sea. Metallic ribbons criss-crossed the plateau, ditches dug by legions of Flemish immigrants to drain the impossible, sponge-like land.

'How far is it from here?' Lussac said, his gruff voice falling on her from behind. He kicked his horse so that the animal moved alongside her, forcing her horse to move closer to the hedge on the right-hand side.

'Oh…er…' she stared studiously ahead, as if marking the route '…at least another half-day's ride.' She squinted at the southern horizon, wondering how long she could keep up this pretence, wondering how long it would be before Lussac became suspicious. She had scant knowledge of this area and prayed that this causeway led to somewhere significant, like a town, as opposed to the middle of the marshes. In a town, there were people, crowds, crowds in which she could lose herself, quickly.

'I hope you're not lying to me,' he said slowly, his turquoise gaze pinning her uncomfortably to the saddle. A jolting weakness entered her knees at his words, her hands tightening imperceptibly on the reins. Her heart lurched with guilty conscience. Was he about to accuse her of leading him astray? What would he do to her? 'But it would make no sense if you were,' he continued, musing aloud, 'no sense at all.'

It made every sense, Katerina thought wretchedly, if he knew what was to be her fate if she returned home. Which was worse? she wondered. Risking Lussac's wrath if he found out she was leading him in the wrong direction, or going back to a father whose mind seemed warped by loss, torn to pieces by her mother's sudden death? She hoped to extricate herself from the situation before she had to do either.

Reaching down, she plucked some glossy blackberries from the sprawling hedgerow that lined the raised causeway, popping them into her mouth. The sweetness burst on to her tongue and she savoured the delicate, flowery taste within her mouth, the taste of autumn. Her stomach growled; she had eaten nothing since before her performance last night. Hopefully she could find enough of these delicious berries to stave of the worst of the hunger pangs.

'What are you doing?'

'I'm eating blackberries,' she replied. Her horse had slowed even more, the bridle tinkling merrily as the animal settled into a barely perceptible walk.

'We need to be moving faster than this.' He pushed one exasperated hand through his hair.

Silky fronds fell back over his forehead, tousled. Katerina's heart seized in her chest; how beautiful he was, she thought, the shadowed planes of his tanned face, the square-cut, powerful jaw-line. Her eyes drifted to the firm line of his mouth, the full generous curve of his bottom lip.

She shuddered, ashamed by her blatant perusal, tearing her eyes away from the carved beauty of his face, away from the mouth that had kissed her. Leaning over, she stuck her hand into the brambles, risking scratches as she wrapped her fingers around another bunch of blackberries.

Strong fingers curved around her upper arm, hauling her slight figure upwards, hoisting her from the saddle. 'I swear you are doing this deliberately,' he growled, searching her flushed face, her lips stained with purple juice. 'I've a good mind to throw you up in front of me and lead your horse. It would certainly be faster.'

'No, absolutely not!' she declared, outraged, squirming beneath his close scrutiny. The thought of riding so close to him, her body knocking against his…that rigid, iron-clad chest, those hefty thighs! Hot colour washed over her pale skin in shame. 'I'm hungry, that's all.'

'Then let's ride on to the next town and buy a decent meal,' he said, irritation threading his tone.

'I'd rather do that than nibble away at hedgerows. You'll never fill up that way.'

But this is how I eat every day, she thought. A few scraps here and there—sometimes days without anything but a thin watery gruel. Occasionally they would manage to poach or steal something more substantial. This was her existence and it had become nothing unusual to her.

'Besides, you look like you could use a decent meal. There's nothing of you.'

Stung by the accusation in his voice, the sheer arrogance, she hauled her tunic hem down over her slim legs, a wild, self-conscious movement, and stuck her chin out stubbornly. 'I don't deliberately starve myself, if that's what you think!' she flashed back. 'How do you think I live every day? Dining on roasted swan off silver platters? Supping on fresh yeasty bread washed down with rich French wines? Think again, Lord High-and-Mighty.'

'No, you misunderstand me.' A ruddy colour flooded his cheekbones as he struggled to find an answer to placate her. 'I only meant to say...' He trailed off. What had he meant to say? That her body was lithe, and slim and exquisite; that it was exactly the right size, but too delicate, too fragile to be living this harsh life on the road? She would slap him for that, no doubt. The maid obviously prided herself on some misguided idea that she was invincible, could protect herself. But her cutting words made his own existence feel indulgent, coddled—an existence in which he gave no thought to the source of his food, or heat, or water. He was spoiled, a spoiled member of the nobility, and her simple speech left a sour taste on his tongue.

On the other side of the hedge, the sad, mournful cry of a redshank filled the air. Katerina glared at him, spine stretched ramrod straight, rosebud mouth set in a stern line, her whole frame brimming with hostility. Her expression was so raw and so outraged that for one insane moment all he wanted to do was hug her, to fold her in his big arms and feel her tight against him. Like last night.

He shook his head, dismissing the tempting image. 'Let's keep moving,' he said, snatching up her bridle so that her horse was forced to match its pace to his.

Chapter Nine

Ducking his sleek head beneath a dilapidated inn sign swinging from the stone archway, Lussac steered his destrier on to the flattened earth of the inn's courtyard, pulling Katerina's horse in alongside him. It seemed like the pair of them had ridden for hours across impenetrable countryside, a landscape of boggy, unstable ground and huge brilliant skies that made his eyes ache with the solid intensity of light. Often, they were forced to double back, retrace their steps in order to find ways to cross deep muddy ditches, or skirt around thickly planted forests. He wasn't convinced that Katerina was certain of her direction; her eyes adopted a vague, hazy look when he questioned her. At least now, in this bustling market town, he would hopefully gain a clearer idea of the way to go.

Two-storey, timber-framed buildings rose up on either side of the yard, crumbling white plaster criss-crossed with dark wood struts: the inn's ac-commodation. A stable-boy ran out to grab the horses, flicking an admiring glance at the tall knight. Lussac's blue tunic was cut from a fine woollen cloth and shone with a lustrous sheen; he had pushed back the scalloped edge of his hood so that the material gathered in close folds at the base of his neck. The stable-boy's gaze slipped across the young lad who rode alongside the knight, barely grazing his attention.

'What is the name of this place?' Lussac flipped the lad a silver coin. It spun through the air, oscil-lating, and the boy's grimy face split with a huge grin as he reached up and caught the twisting sil-ver in one dirty fist.

'Why, Framilode, my lord.'

'And how far is Longthorpe from here? The Dauntseys' place?' Lussac dismounted in a creak of leather, moving around to the front of his horse, patting the animal's nose.

Katerina froze, breath snaring in her throat. Her fingers, suddenly icy, curled woodenly around the reins, clutching on to the narrow leather straps as if her life depended on it. Could she twist her horse around now, in this narrow space, and make a run for it, a desperate dash for freedom? But Lussac would catch her in no time; she had to be cleverer than that.

'Longthorpe?' the lad was saying, 'I'm not certain. Let me think...' He trailed off, peering up at the inn's sagging, wooden shutters as if they would provide an answer.

Lussac pinned Katerina with a withering glance. 'Come on, Katerina, surely you must know the way from here? How far is Framilode from Longthorpe?'

'Oh, I...' She stared down at her hands, her short pink nails digging into the white leather reins. 'I—'

'No, I remember now,' the lad chirruped, interrupting. 'You're heading in the wrong direction. Longthorpe is north from here. You need to follow the old Roman road that heads to Ipswich, and then on to Bury.'

Lussac's features hardened. In two long strides he was beside Katerina's horse. 'Come here,' he said, menacingly, all but yanking her from the top of the horse. His strong fingers burned into her waist through the thin stuff of her tunic, leaving an imprint.

'What are you going to do?' she squeaked, confidence deserting her at the fury in his face.

'You lied to me, Katerina,' he ground out, his tone unstable, volatile. When her sturdy boots touched the ground, he kept one hand on her shoulder, pressing her down, holding her to the spot. His eyes blazed over her, threatening. 'And I bet you've had a great laugh at my expense, leading me a merry dance all morning.'

'Can you blame me?' she threw back at him, voice wobbling beneath his anger. Fear clutched at her windpipe as his fingers clenched at her shoulder. 'I told you I couldn't go home, yet you kept on pushing, demanding that I come with you! You've dragged me away from my life and my work, insisting that I go somewhere that I have no wish to go! What was I supposed to do? Sit back and allow myself to be led home, like a willing dog on a lead?'

'Yes!' he roared at her. 'That's exactly what I expected you to do. That's what most women would have done; they would have done as they were told!' But even as the words burst from his mouth, he realised how misguided they were. From the first moment he had encountered this luminous slip of a girl, he had always suspected that she would do exactly the opposite of what anyone asked her to do. Why had he not heeded his own instincts? He was a fool, an idiot, drawn in by her sweet, innocent face, entranced by a lithe, graceful figure in the saddle, allowing her to lead him astray like some dumb animal.

She folded her arms defensively across her chest, mutinous, bunching the rough, threadbare fabric of her tunic. 'Well, I am not "most women".'

Catching her chin between thumb and forefinger, he tipped her face up, causing her hood to slip from her head. Sunlight struck the intricate coils of her flame-coloured hair. 'You have no idea what this means to me, do you? How important this is to me?' His speech was raw, bereft of emotion.

She jerked her head to one side; his fingers dropped away. 'I have no idea how important this is to you, Lussac, because you have told me nothing. I have no idea why you want to go to Longthorpe, no idea how you came by a cuff that has been in my family for generations...' His eyes widened at her revelation. 'Yes, I admit it. Every member of my family wears a cuff like the one you wear on your wrist. My father, my uncle, my mother...God rest her soul. So how, how did you come into possession of such a thing?'

The smell of charred wood pierced his nostrils; the memory of sickening, suspended quiet as he climbed the fire-blackened stone steps cloaked him. His sister's small feet peeking out from beneath her silken hem, the leather cuff clutched within her lifeless fingers, her other arm stretching out across the floorboards, fingers trying to reach her fallen mother. Were they trying to link their fingers together before they finally succumbed to the smoke? His heart gripped with blackening sadness, breaking, splintering. How could he speak of such atrocities, or put into words what had happened to his family, explain? And how could he tell the maid at his side that he believed one of her family members as being guilty of such a crime?

'Lussac?' Katerina tilted her head to one side, her dark-fringed eyes quietly assessing. He gave the tiniest shake of his head, as if trying to negate something, his eyelashes shuttering fractionally to hide the diamond glitter of his eyes. But not before she saw it. Saw the bleak desolation cross those turquoise depths, acknowledged the raw, bitter intensity of his ravaged expression.

'My God,' Katerina whispered abruptly, 'what happened to you?' Instinctively, she reached out, catching up his loose fingers that hung by his side, snaring her hand with his, a fleeting touch of recognition, of support. Of connection. Heat burned from his roughened knuckles into the soft cup of her palm.

Warmth, desire, he knew not what, swirled in his chest as he savoured the polished silk of her fingers, before he turned, pulling his hand from hers. 'It's a long story,' he replied. A story he was unwilling, or unable to tell. 'Come, we will have some food and then we will start again. The right way, this time.'

She followed his broad back on shaky legs, into the inn. He had found her out, discovered her ruse and she had survived. But his determination, his need to reach Longthorpe, was plain for all to see. She had read the desperation in his eyes. He was not going to let her go. She needed to find a way out and fast.

Inside, the inn was almost deserted. A couple of men sat at one end of the long trestle talking quietly whilst another man, thick-set and burly, swept the floor. The delicate nature of the twiggy broom looked incongruous against the man's fat, stubby fingers. The two men broke off their conversation as Lussac and Katerina entered, staring blatantly at Lussac's expensive tunic, the jewelled hilt of his sword, the powerful muscular presence of the newcomer with his servant trailing behind him.

'Pull your hood up,' Lussac muttered quickly. He ran one finger in the gap between his neck and his hood; sweat slicked across his fingertips.

Warmth flooded her belly at his request—surely he felt no responsibility for her? Obscured in the

shadows behind Lussac, Katerina obeyed his command, blinking in the dim, smoky light of the interior. Despite the unseasonable heat outside, a slow
fire sputtered in the centre of the room, the smoke
trailing up and out of a ragged hole in the roof.

Lussac gestured to a bench alongside a trestle,
indicating that Katerina should sit. He slung himself on to the bench on the other side of the un-
evenly-planked table, nodding at the landlord to
bring him some ale.

'What do you want to drink?' he asked Katerina.

'Just water, please,' she replied, wrinkling her
nose at the reek of horse-dung, the rank smell of
tallow fat from the guttering candles.

He noted her grimace, threw her a quick smile.
The unexpected gesture lit up his face, made him
seem younger, more boyish, somehow. 'Surely
you've been in places worse than this?'

'Hardly.' She raised her eyebrows at him,
haughty. 'We sleep in the open air, remember. No
inns for us. Too many undesirable people.' She
stared at him, the heated curve of her cheek half-
obscured by the lip of her hood.

Lussac shifted uncomfortably. It was almost as
if she levelled the accusation at him. No doubt he
deserved it. In these past few years of battling, he
had forgotten how to treat women, preferring to

bark orders at unwilling soldiers or retreat into the solitary silence of his own brooding company. He had forgotten their softness, their sweetness.

'Look…' He cleared his throat. 'I'm sorry if I've been rough with you—'

Katerina's eyes flicked over him. 'Are you?' she interrupted. 'I don't think you care one jot about anyone else. All you care about is achieving your own ends, whatever they might be, running roughshod over anyone who gets in your way.' She dropped her gaze, picking with her fingernail at a loose splinter on the table.

'I'm not as bad as you think.'

'No?' She arched one fine eyebrow in his direction. 'Then why do you glare at me as if I've crawled out from beneath the nearest stone? As if I'm the last person on earth you want to be with? I thought you wanted me to help you?'

Was he really such an ogre? 'I did. I do.' He smiled with devastating suddenness, turquoise eyes sparkling in the dim light. 'There, is that better?'

The smile lit up his chiselled features, softening the hard lines of his face. Her heart squeezed dangerously, driving the breath from her lungs. 'I suppose so,' she responded shakily, unable to control, to pacify, the accelerating beat of her blood.

Why had she said anything to him at all? Her own resources simply couldn't cope; it was far easier to deal with his cold, detached authority than this, this look of…understanding?

Lussac nodded in thanks as the landlord dumped a tankard in front of him, slopping the ale on to the coarse-grained wood. The man plonked another tankard in front of Katerina, then held his tight-skinned fingers out for payment. Lussac placed a few coins in the outstretched palm and the man shuffled off, resuming his sweeping.

'Ugh!' Katerina peered down into the murky depths of her tankard. Flecks of dirt floated across the surface.

'You can't drink that, you'll be ill,' Lussac said. 'Here, have some of mine. The brewing takes away the nastiest bugs.' She watched as he slid the tankard across the table towards her, spine tingling with awareness. To share this man's drink seemed unexpectedly intimate, to touch her lips to the same vessel that his lips had touched. But she needed it, needed the fluid and the energy it would give her. Winding her hands around the chill pewter, she lifted the tankard to her mouth. The cool liquid slipped down her throat, reviving her, and she licked gratefully at the last drops, a plan forming slowly in her mind.

'Thank you, that was lovely,' Katerina murmured softly. 'But now, I think I need to...er... pay a visit?'

Lussac, mesmerised by a single errant drop on Katerina's bottom lip, frowned. 'What do you mean?'

'I mean I need to go to the garderobe,' she hissed. 'Women's business.' There, that should keep him away for a bit. Men normally couldn't stand such things.

He raised his eyebrows. 'And I'm supposed to believe that?' It was as if he had read her mind, she thought with dismay.

'Lussac, I need to go!' she hissed at him. She extricated herself from the narrow gap between trestle and table. 'It will be at the back somewhere. I'll go and look.'

Lussac stood up, the links of his chainmail hauberk glittering in the gloom. Behind him a tallow candle guttered and danced in a wall niche.

'What are you doing?' She clutched onto her bag in consternation, fiddling with the long strap.

'Coming with you. You don't think I'd let you go there on your own, do you? After your performance this morning? Think again, Katerina.'

Katerina fumed and fretted as Lussac followed her towards the back of the inn, directed by the innkeeper. The garderobes were positioned for convenience over the wide, swirling river, with narrow windows cut high into the stone walls for ventilation. Lussac stuck his head inside, making sure there was no way Katerina could escape, retreating quickly at the foul smell.

'Are you coming in there with me?' she taunted, setting her head on one side in question. 'Or am I allowed a modicum of privacy?'

'I'll wait out here,' he announced companionably. 'You don't want to spend too long in there.' Leaning his broad shoulders against the stone wall, he folded his arms high over his chest.

'Well, I might be some time,' Katerina warned. He shrugged his shoulders, unperturbed.

She shut the makeshift door, gulping nauseously at the hideous smell pervading the cramped, confined space. Looking up, she could have cried with relief. The window was small, a narrow slit cut in the stone. Lussac had obviously noticed it and thought it presented no problem. But Katerina knew she could climb through, and she was quick about it.

By noon, she had reached Ipswich, the market place alive with people thronging in the small cobbled square. Teetering, narrow buildings surrounded the space, built cheaply and quickly with cob walls and thatched roofs. Leading off from the market place, the streets were muddy, rutted and uneven; a central gulley ran with stinking water. Rubbish lay everywhere, randomly strewn about; broken crates and empty barrels towered up in high, precarious piles. Merchants shouted from their stalls, each vendor trying to outdo his neighbour in selling his wares and make himself heard above the general hubbub. The space filled with noise, colour and people. But not Lussac.

He had not come after her—of that she was certain. He wouldn't waste his time in pursuit now anyway—he had been told the direction to Longthorpe by the stable-lad; he had no need of her. She made her way along the row of trestles, keeping her head low, her eyes averted, until she came upon an old woman selling floury rounds of bread. Her mouth watered. Handing over her pennies into the wizened fingers, she clutched the warm loaf in one hand, resolving to find a quieter place in which to eat it.

Behind her, a horse screeched in alarm; instinctively, she turned towards the sound, as did the other people who jostled around her. On the other side of the square, the same animal reared up, forelegs pawing the air as the crowd scattered sideways, outwards, anything to avoid the powerful, thrashing hooves, the rider leaning forwards and clinging to the mane to stay in the saddle, to avoid falling.

The rider.

The warm, yeasty roll dropped from Katerina's fingers, spinning along the filthy cobbles to lodge beneath a nearby trestle, snapped up moments later by a hungry dog. The horse dropped back to the ground, eyes rolling white and wild, whilst the dog that had nipped at the horse's legs in the first place slunk away to a dark corner of the market, ribs moving visibly under mangy fur. Garth Trevallyan. Katerina stared and stared at the man, her face pale, distraught. She should move, fade away now, but her limbs were frozen, rooted to the spot, her feet like vast lead weights, pinning her to the cobbles. Garth Trevallyan was a hired soldier, hired by her father and her uncle to search for her, to bring her back home. Home to a marriage that made the bile rise in her throat at the very thought of it. A marriage to which her own father had agreed, had actively supported! She recognised the square, florid features, the cheeks stained permanently red from too much drink and the fat, protruding stomach straining at the fastenings of his surcoat. The surcoat embroidered with her family crest.

She passed a hand across her face, scrubbing roughly at her eyes. Maybe her sight played tricks upon her? But, nay, the silver dogrose on the red background gleamed across the market square, unmistakable, the same emblem that adorned the tapestries, the shields, even some of the pewter-ware in her home. And the cuff clasped high around her forearm. Her mind cast back to the many ferocious arguments witnessed between her father and her uncle, the petty jealousies, the wrangling. There had only been one day, she recalled, when they had been in the same room without arguing. The day she had inadvertently overheard their muted conversation, her uncle's proposition and her father's agreement; the same day she had packed her bags and fled with Waleran.

And now.

Now, Garth Trevallyan was here. Was it by chance, or had someone seen her, given him the knowledge that she was in the area? She had no intention of staying around to find out. Pivoting on her toes, she turned abruptly in the direction of the north-west route out of town, towards Bury. That was where the troupe was headed; she would rejoin them, and be safe.

'My lady?'

A young man stood before her, a rough-coated dog on a chain at his side. A tall, burly young man who blocked the way, who wore an identical surcoat to Trevallyan, embroidered with the silver-rose emblem of her home.

In a trice, she ducked her head, allowing her hood to drop further over her face, shadowing her features. Panic rose in her gullet, a lightning streak of pure, unadulterated fear that weakened her knees, dragged at her shoulders. For one single, insane moment, she thought of Lussac, wanted that tall, powerful knight at her side, protecting her. What a fool she was! She was on her own, now, just like she always was. And she had to make the best of it.

Katerina ignored the young man's words, hoping to give the impression that he addressed someone else in the crowd, despite the fact that he stared directly at her with bland, hazel eyes. She made to pass by him, on the side without the dog, but a gauntleted hand on her forearm rippled her tunic sleeve, prevented her moving forwards.

'My lady Katerina?' he said politely. 'You are to stay with me.' As if to emphasise his point, the dog let out a low, rumbling growl.

'Nay, you are mistaken,' she replied, as gruffly as she could.

In reply, he knocked the hood back from her hair with one bunched fist, revealing the glorious auburn shine of her tightly bound hair, her delicately wrought features, the sprinkle of tiny fawn freckles across her nose and cheeks.

He smiled, an unpleasant twist to his mouth. 'I don't think so.' His teeth sat in a crooked row, stained and yellowing. Beneath his knee-length surcoat, made of red wool, he wore a chainmail hauberk, the links rusty and inflexible. 'Over here!' he shouted above her head towards Trevallyan, who had managed to calm his horse and was edging his way through the crowds towards them.

'My, my, my,' announced Trevallyan, a triumphant note in his voice as he dismounted clumsily, with a great deal of puffing and panting. He eyed Katerina up and down, absorbing the masculine details of her attire. 'And dressed as a lad, who'd have thought it?' One grimy thumb grabbed at her chin, painfully, forcing her to look into the bloodshot whites of his eyes. 'You've been lucky, my lady, that you've been able to evade us for so long. But now it looks like your good fortune has run out.' Katerina knocked his hand away, hating the greasy touch of Trevallyan's fingers. Why couldn't it have only been him who had found her? She could have outrun him easily. But it was the other, younger soldier, and the huge hound at his side; the pair made her wary, afraid. The dog followed her with his big brown eyes, strings of saliva falling from his lolling mouth. He would have her between his teeth in an instant if she tried to flee. 'You can't make me go with you,' she protested furiously, 'I am a free woman, I have rights!'

'Correction,' Trevallyan viewed her slim figure nastily, a smug smile plastered across his pudgy face. 'You are a woman, which means you have no freedom, and no rights to speak of within the law of this country. You have to do as your father says until you marry, at which point you have to do what your husband says. You're going home, Katerina of Dauntsey.'

Sitting on the damp ground, staring out across the mirrored surface of a wide, slow-moving river, Katerina looped her tied wrists over her bent knees, hugging them close. They had spent all afternoon following the muddy, rutted tracks north from Ipswich, until the point when the sun began to slip towards the horizon. As the light faded from the sky, her captors had decided to set up camp for the night.

'Here.' Trevallyan threw a blanket in her direction, narrowly missing the dog's nose.

'You cannot expect me to sleep like this.' Katerina lifted her wrists with derision.

'You will sleep like that,' Trevallyan stated, yawning widely. De Courtney laughed, a rough, sycophantic sound, pandering to the older man's authority. 'You've evaded us for long enough; I'll take no chances with you.' He levered himself down on to the rug beside the spluttering fire, his expression as eager as de Courtney, who, already sitting, unwrapped a package of what she suspected was food. Obviously, they were not going to share it with her.

Despite her bound hands and feet, Katerina managed to pull the blanket around and over her, curling over to lie on her side, turning her back to the soldiers, and the dog, pretending to sleep. But in truth, her mind worked furiously, plotting and planning an escape; she had no desire to wake up in this spot tomorrow morning.

Time elapsed slowly; she had no idea of how long she had lain on the cold, knobbly ground. The tempting sludginess of sleep crept along her eyelids, pulling them down, desperate to carry her off into the depths of unconsciousness. But she fought against the seductive feeling, determined, working steadily at her wrists with her teeth to undo the rope. As she persevered consistently, quietly, so as not to alert the soldiers to her actions, the sun's warmth slipped from the air, a veil of mist rising above the river's silky flow. The light disappeared to the west and, against the dark velvet nap of sky, the moon rose, mottled-cream, three-quarter's full, edged with a milky-blue haze. Katerina tugged once more with her teeth; the length of rope slithered from her wrists like a white snake, coiling on the ground. Rubbing her wrists beneath the cover of the blanket, she drew up her knees carefully to release the rope around her ankles. The bump of her heart picked up a notch with the anticipation of what she was about to do. Very, very slowly, within the confines of the coarse, prickly rug, she rolled over to face her captors and their fearful hound, her eyes sweeping the darkness to pinpoint their location.

The dog lay a few feet away, large bristly head resting on outstretched front paws, body slumped sideways in what she hoped was sleep. But the dog opened his eyes immediately, alerted by the small noise she had made in rolling over. He lifted his head, the chain attached to his collar rattling faintly. Fear skittered through her veins. Beyond the hound, tucked up in blankets around the glowing embers of the fire, lay the two men, both snoring heavily, both confident that the dog would alert them instantly if she tried to escape.

Tentatively, she stretched one hand out towards the dog; in his relaxed form, the animal appeared much less threatening. If she could stroke his head, or scratch behind his ears, maybe he wouldn't make any sound when she left the camp. A low growl, accompanied by a dangerous curl of his upper lip, made her snatch her hand back, heart thumping. Lifting her head, she judged the distance to the river. Not far—she could probably make it in four long strides. Both soldiers still wore their chainmail; if she reached the water before them, the heavy mail would prevent them swimming after her and drag them down before their feet even lifted from the river bottom. But this dog? She had no idea how far, or for how long, this hound would pursue her once the soldiers released him from the chain. It was a chance she was willing to take.

Vaulting up, casting the blanket to one side, Katerina sprang towards the river, throwing herself full length into the gleaming, slick liquid. The water was cold, much, much colder than she'd anticipated, and she gasped, her lungs contracting in shock, before striking out with a strong, confident stroke. Adrenalin fuelled her movements, driving her on; she refused to turn, to look behind. As the water swirled around her, she heard the frantic barking, the shouts and bellows of the men from the shore. The movement of her limbs became jerky with the cold, but she swam with the current, cutting a diagonal path across the centre of the river, where the water ran far deeper, exerting a powerful pull on her legs.

Without warning, the dog was upon her, at her back, huge teeth catching at her clothes, her tunic, nipping savagely. Hot tears of frustration sluiced down her cheeks; she battled to twist away, spiralling in the water, thrashing the glittering surface to push herself free. But the dog advanced, incisors clamping down heavily on her left shoulder, teeth driving like spikes into her soft flesh. She screamed in pain, kicking out furiously, blindly at the rough, wiry coat. To her surprise, the dog released its jaw, tiring, starting to sink with the effort of keeping afloat and keeping a grip on her. Katerina seized the moment to disappear, taking a deep breath to drop below the surface, scissoring her legs to push herself towards the other bank. The wound in her shoulder burned; she ignored it, realising the cold water had a numbing effect on the pain. Although satisfied that the dog's energies had slackened, that he would give up, she knew she had to climb out as soon as possible. Trevallyan would simply follow the river until he found her again.

Her lungs seared with the effort of holding her breath; she rose to the surface, carefully, treading water, moving her arms either side to keep herself afloat. The fresh air, sweet and vital, surged into her lungs, filling her chest. She blinked the water droplets out of her eyes. The opposite bank rose before her, a steep muddy incline on a sharp curve of river; further down, the flow became more gentle, widening out into a patch of reeds. The wind sidled through the stiff stalks, tawny pale in the moonlight, rippling the surface of the water into a series of ridges. Turning her gaze upstream, she searched the darkness, for the dog, for her captors. Nothing. Everything was quiet, unnervingly quiet, except for the rapid jerk of her breath and the fear bumping wildly against the wall of her chest.

She headed for the reeds, clambering through the sharp stalks, crawling through on all fours, head down, the grass scratching at her face, her clothes. The temptation to lie down in the reed bed, to sleep, was overwhelming. As her clothes dripped forlornly from her slight frame, all the energy that had powered her escape drained from her, vanished. Gritting her teeth, she fought the sensation, continuing doggedly to place one hand in front of the other, to lift one knee to complete the movement forwards until she reached the place where river mud gave way to solid ground. Cautiously, Katerina lifted her head, knowing the tall bleached grass, topped with fluffy plumes of seed, would screen her. She prayed that the men were still on the other side of the river, that there was no bridge, no ford, by which they could cross. Across the flat plain of grass, she spotted the dark, undulating outline of a forest. She would hide there for the rest of the night.

Chapter Ten

Jabbing the arches of his feet against the hard metal stirrups, Lussac raised himself in the saddle, stretching out his leg muscles. The sheer temerity of the maid, her bravado, was astounding! Women's issue, indeed! He had waited and waited outside that garderobe, like an idiot, thinking he would give her a little bit more time, when all the while she was inching herself through that tiny window and haring off through the countryside! How on earth she had scrabbled through that narrow space was beyond him. A slight smile turned up the corners of his mouth, a grudging admiration at her tenacity, her determination. Surprise jolted him. In truth, he missed her feisty companionship, her truculent ways, her breathtaking beauty. He had only met her yesterday, yet already Katerina filled his thoughts, pushing away the darker images to the edges of his mind.

Donning his chainmail, his chausses and hauberk at the inn, he had ridden off in pursuit of her, thinking to find her easily. She wouldn't get far on foot. He had galloped over countless fields, along countless hedgerows, occasionally stopping and searching the horizon for that slim, elusive figure with her bright, red-gold hair. Nothing. At least, by heading north, he was heading in the right direction for Longthorpe, but still, he needed her. She knew what her family members looked like; she could identify them. With her help he would be able to work out who had been in Gascony four years ago, the man who had given the command to torch Lussac's home.

He was on the point of giving up for the day, until he came to Ispwich. A group of market traders, eyeing the royal emblem on Lussac's surcoat with wary admiration, recalled an altercation between a young red-haired lad and two soldiers. The lad had left the town with them, but not by choice, they told him eagerly, left the town on the road heading north-west.

An odd sense of trepidation gripped his innards as he galloped in that direction. He rode towards the evening sun, the golden orb setting in a dramatic riot of gold and blue-grey clouds, finding it difficult to explain his sense of unease. If the 'boy' in the market-place was really Katerina, then who were the two men she was with? He frowned.

Soon, he would have to stop for the night; the light leached quickly from the day. Having followed a wide, curving river for most of the afternoon, he finally crossed it at a ford: a narrow point, the shallow water rippling over the stones. The horse's hooves splashed through, droplets of water flying up, clinging to his leather boots, his chausses, the velvet nap of the horse's coat. Up ahead, the dark billowing shadow of a large forest loomed; he would find shelter beneath the trees.

Lussac heard the frantic barking first, far away, in the distance—a dog going berserk. He pulled on the reins, listening carefully. Sounds travelled further over water, especially in this still, pellucid air of evening. And then a scream. A chilling scream of pure fear, piercing the air, rising clearly above the smooth rush of water. It was her; he knew, instinctively, that it was her. Heart-rate picking up, he turned his horse towards the sound, scouring the dimming landscape: the silvery flat of the water, the bulk of forest and the fringes of the river, clagged with straight, bone-coloured reeds. Urging his horse on, he rode along the river, skirting the edge, searching. His keen eyes soon noticed something within the rustling reeds: a tiny move-ment, a shifting.

Heart lightening, he rode towards it.

Fighting a sickening lassitude, Katerina rocked back on her heels in the rigid grass, knees sink-ing into the soft mud, as she stared up at the man on horseback. Did her befuddled mind play tricks on her? In the twilight, the man was tall, broad-shouldered, chestnut hair falling thickly across his forehead, the golden fleur-de-lys stretching taut across his chest. He wore no helmet, the hood of his hauberk falling back on his shoulders in thick, metallic folds, the glinting steel mesh emphasising his tanned, powerful neck, the square, inflexible cut of his jaw-line.

'No…o…o!' she gasped out on a wavering note, disbelieving, gaze dropping to study the bluish hue of her fingertips, resting feebly in her lap. The tight coils of her wet hair pulled cruelly at her scalp. Had the cold water possessed her common sense? 'No, it can't be you!' Despite the heaviness of her head, the drooping weariness, she lifted her eyes once more, regarding the figure before her, dazed. The dwindling light struck the man's fea-tures, highlighting the bleak, hard contours, the dramatic, forceful sweep of his dark brows.

A wry smile curled his lips. 'Aye, it's me,' he acknowledged gruffly, one eyebrow quirking upwards at the horrified expression on her face. He threw himself down from the horse, strode over to her hiding place in the reeds.

'W-what are you d-d-doing here?' Her head lolled back as she looked up at his towering figure. Lussac opened his mouth, about to bawl her out like one of his foot soldiers, to haul her roughly from the reeds and remonstrate with her about running away, but the words died on his lips. Anger sapped from him; her face was ashen. Her faint words stuttered out as she shook with cold, swaying, her clothes claggy and wet, plastered to her neat shoulders, the curve of her chest. Water dripped from her hair, the tips of her ears. Droplets clung to the pearly column of her throat, tinged with pink from the setting sun.

He crouched down in front of her, balancing easily on his heels. Close up, his breath gripped. 'My God, Katerina, what has happened to you?' His voice punched the air, guttural, concerned. Her skin was pale, so pale, her lips tinged with the blue of cold. Instinctively he caught at her hands in her lap, clasping his rough, warm fingers around her frozen wrists. Suddenly the whole reason for him pursuing her, the help he sought, mattered not, vanished. Katerina needed help. His help.

'What happened?' he asked again. Her fingers were like icicles.

'I…I was in the river,' she stammered back. 'The…those….' Katerina swayed, her exhausted brain clawing for the right words, to explain. In the distance, a dog barked, a wild, ferocious sound. To Lussac's surprise, she recoiled in fear at the noise, lurching forwards so the top of her head almost touched the front of his tunic. 'They set their dog on me,' she mumbled. 'The river was the only way I could escape.' She glanced around, fearfully, searching for something upstream.

His blood ran cold at her explanation. What sort of men were these, who would set a dog on a woman? Following her gaze, Lussac saw nothing, only the flowing sweep of the water, a flock of birds skimming low, picking up the flies hovering about the surface. He frowned. 'But who? Why would someone do that to you?'

Fringed with wet, spiky lashes, the sparkling grey crystal of her eyes met his. Shivers racked her frame. He was certain only sheer will forced her to hold her spine ramrod straight before him; her whole demeanour told him she was ready to collapse. Patches of blue smudged beneath her eyes, dusted the high curve of her cheekbones. Now was not the time for revelations; she would tell him soon enough.

Forcing herself to concentrate, to gather up any scant vestiges of energy she had left in her body, she lifted her chin purposefully. 'I...I need to get out of here,' she whispered, trying, and failing, to disentangle her hands from his. 'Can I borrow your horse? I'll give him back...later.' A long wisp of hair stuck haphazardly across her cheek. Lussac felt a sudden urge to gather that bundle of fragility into his arms, to protect her.

He laughed softly. 'Katerina, you're in no fit state to ride anywhere.' Besides, he was not about to let her slip through his fingers again.

'I need to get out of here!' she repeated, glancing round once more. He caught the edge of panic in her voice.

'I agree.' He bent down, placing two big hands beneath her armpits, intending to lift her. She wiggled her shoulders violently at the contact; he caught her sharp intake of breath.

'I can do it!' she hissed.

He ignored her protests, in no mood to wrangle, sweeping her up easily from the shelter of the reeds. Within the powerful circle of his arms, her body was light, fragile, muscles tensing beneath her shoulders.

'Can you walk?' he asked, setting her on her feet at the edge of the reeds.

'Of course I can walk!' She levered her shoulders angrily from his supporting grip. A raft of dizziness swept through her, making her sway. The wet wool of her braies, her tunic, dragged heavily against her skin, itching uncomfortably.

Lussac stood away from her, huge arms folded across his chest, waiting.

Screwing up her eyes, scratchy from river water, she stared across to the spot where his horse cropped the wispy vegetation. The distance seemed huge, humiliating. She wanted to weep with disgust at her own ineptitude. All morning she had plotted to escape Lussac and had been successful, only to be caught by the very men who would take her home anyway. Out of the frying pan and into the fire, her mother would have said.

She took one huge step forwards, trying to overcome the debilitating weakness in her legs, then another, before her knees creased with lack of energy and she stumbled, sinking into the bleached grass. She'd had enough; let him laugh at her, mock her. If she had any hope of escaping from those men at all, then Lussac de Belbigny was her only hope.

'You win,' she murmured dully as he scooped her up from the ground, throwing her easily against his chest.

'It's not a competition,' he replied. 'You are in no position to fight.'

Flushed with shame, knowing he was right, Katerina held herself rigidly away from him as he carried her towards his horse. She hated this weakness, this inability to fight for herself. He made her feel vulnerable, exposed, out of control. Lussac's hand clutched strongly at her thigh, the weight of his forearm heavy against her hips. She struggled to maintain the furthest possible distance between their two bodies, ignoring the inexplicable flutter in her belly.

'For God's sake, lean against me,' he growled in her ear. 'I'm going to drop you at this rate.'

She gritted her teeth, refusing to give in, to relax against him, every nerve-ending in her body fighting him, refusing to acknowledge the tantalising closeness of his touch. The muscles along her spine strained with the effort. She sighed with relief as he threw her up on to his horse, her lungs releasing, breath flooding out, then tensed once more as he jumped up behind her, bulky chest pressing heavily against her back. In response to the contact, she leaned forwards dramatically, bending over the horse's mane, desperate to keep the space between them.

Lussac chuckled. 'Fighting me will merely slow us down,' he pointed out slowly, regarding her odd unbalanced position with a smile. 'Do you really want those…whoever they are…to catch up with you?'

Who did she prefer? she wondered. The soldiers, hired by her father and uncle at great expense to bring her back home, or this knight at her back, handsome and dangerous, whose very nearness spiked her body into every increasing spirals of desire. With Lussac behind her, solid thighs cradling the soft roundness of her hips, his arms pressed heavily against her shoulders, Katerina questioned whether she was in even greater danger than she had been before.

Digging his knees into the muscled flanks of his horse, Lussac pulled on the reins, directing the animal towards the darkening wedge of trees that fringed the flood plain. 'It will be dark soon,' he announced. 'We need to find a place to shelter.' He stared down at Katerina's wet hair, her damp, sopping garments. 'And you need to change.'

The jerky movement of the horse forced her back

into the broad solidity of his chest. Her limbs felt weak. Finally deserted by the strength to pull herself forwards, she sank into the warm, comforting brace against her spine. Her rigid, self-imposed restraint crawled away, dissipated into the limpid twilight; her eyelids drooped with fatigue. All she wanted to do was curl up and sleep.

As she sagged against him, shoulders nudging his chest, her pliable body resting against his, Lussac gritted his teeth, unwilling to acknowledge the flick of desire through his veins. What, in Heaven's name, was the matter with him? He told himself the physical response was completely normal; it had been a long time since he had held a maid in such a way. The faintest smell of rose petals lifted from her soaked, straggling hair. She seemed so small, so light within the cradle of his arms, it was difficult to equate the woman before him with the fighting, spitting termagent he had first encountered in the Earl of Norfolk's forest, the same girl who had twisted and spun through the air before the Queen. She seemed to possess more courage, more daring than many of the soldiers he had encountered. He understood how much it had cost her to accept his help, to acknowledge her own vulnerability. As he negotiated his horse around the outlying trees of the forest, he wondered who or what she was running from.

'Katerina?'

Lussac's voice seemed to come from a great distance, the low husky tone piercing the layers of blissful sleep. Lifting her head, she struggled to open her eyes. Her clothes stuck in uncomfortable layers against her damp flesh, the coarse wool of her braies itching the delicate skin on her thighs. Her eyes widened as Lussac lifted her down, her legs slithering off over the horse's neck, jolting awkwardly.

As he set her on the ground, his hands lifted immediately from her waist but, her feet were numb; she couldn't feel her toes! Teetering stiffly, her cheeks reddened with embarrassment, she clutched at Lussac's forearm; she hated herself for using him as a support. 'Ouch! My feet!' she gasped, as the blood began to rush back into them, prickling painfully.

'Take your time,' he murmured. In this translucent half-light, her skin was like smooth marble, the huge sparkling gemstones of her eyes viewing him warily. She looked ethereal, other-worldly, as if she had taken one step sideways out of the magic of the forest. Stung, astonished by his fanciful thoughts, he stepped back smartly as soon as she found her balance.

'Where are we?'

She followed his gaze to what appeared to be a tumbledown cottage, roof sagging crazily, set in a glade of silver birch. The setting sun caught on the silvery leaves, the breeze stretching each papery shape to reveal a white underside, some loosening, spinning down to settle on the moss-covered thatch of the cottage, like snowflakes. Some distance off, an owl hooted, answered in return by his mate, the call echoing through the trees.

Bending his head beneath the tilting lintel, Lussac disappeared. Moments later, he stuck his head back out again. 'Are you coming? I realise it's not the Earl of Norfolk's castle, but it will do well for tonight. There's no one here…and hasn't been for a long time.'

Her brain fully awake, she felt the first trickle of unease, coupled with an unusual giddy sensation. Was he really expecting her to spend the night with him, in there? Her legs, stiff and cold, remained fixed to the spot, the bite wound in her shoulder beginning to smart, fiercely. 'Er…well, I could sleep outside; it might make things easier.' Her voice sounded feeble in the cooling evening air.

Emerging on to the uneven, cobbled courtyard,

he covered the distance between the doorway and her frozen, statue-like figure in three longs strides. 'Easier? In what way?' he rapped out. 'It's September, it's cold outside at night. Why would you not want to sleep inside, where it's warmer?'

Because you would be there. With me. The vivid thought knocked into her brain.

'Um…it's not right, Lussac.' Her teeth were chattering now as she fought to explain her doubts. 'And we're not married…' She trailed off, miserably.

'It's a bit late to worry about maidenly modesty, Katerina.' Up close, Lussac loomed over her, his diamond eyes intense, missing nothing. 'You seem to have spent a great deal of time rewriting the rule book in that respect, leaping about the place dressed as a boy.'

She shuffled uncomfortably, placing one hand against the horse's neck to balance herself. The wound in her shoulder stretched painfully.

'Here…' He thrust the blanket into her arms, his voice gruff, edged with jolting formality. 'Go into the cottage and take off those wet things. I'll collect some firewood.' He extracted a length of fabric from the saddle-bag, crumpling it on top of the blanket. 'Wear this; it's probably too big, but at least it will keep you warm whilst your clothes dry.'

Through her utter exhaustion, she frowned at him, her expression guarded.

He laughed, a short, toneless bark. 'Don't fret, you're not my type. I will call out to make sure you're safely garbed before I come back in. Your only concern should be to get warm and dry.' Heat flooded her cheeks at his words and she turned away, embarrassed by his bluntness. As she stumbled awkwardly towards the cottage entrance, the heated intensity of his gaze pierced her spine.

The interior of the cottage smelled damp, musty. At first she couldn't see anything, only an impenetrable blackness. Gradually, her eyes adjusting to the dim light, she began to discern the interior in more detail: the firepit in the centre, with an open hole lined with slate tiles in the roof above, the mud-packed floor, the cob walls bowing gently inwards, straw sticking out from the dried mud in random fashion. There was no glass at the windows; one window sat open to the elements, the other still retained one of its two shutters, hanging forlornly from a broken hinge.

She clutched on to the blanket, the tunic, almost too frozen to move. But she had to move. Lussac would not be long collecting wood; she had to change before he returned. Her befuddled mind wondered if he would punish her for her earlier disappearance, but strangely, he didn't appear to be angry at all. She couldn't make sense of it, of him. But right now, common sense prevailed; she would accept the help that he offered, simply because she had no other choice. Survival was her *modus operandi,* survival by any means possible.

Katerina struggled with her sodden tunic, heaving the heavy folds up across her body, over her head. The wet material resisted, sticking unpleasantly against her injured shoulder, before suddenly releasing; she screwed her eyes up at the searing pain. Stepping out of her loose leather boots, her woollen braies, she managed to wrestle with the thin fabric of her chemise, allowing it to fall to the floor in a heap. Naked, she closed her eyes, teeth chattering uncontrollably, limbs drooping with fatigue; it all seemed like so much effort.

She sank to the earth-packed floor, black waves swirling in her head. She wanted to sleep. Shaking her head fiercely, she tried to dispel the horrible feeling of lassitude, telling herself she had to go on, to look after herself, to take care. No one else would. On her knees beside the cold circle of fire stones, she clutched at the blanket and scrubbed herself dry, her fine pale skin turning red-raw with the brisk activity. Rippling shivers possessed her body as she pulled Lussac's tunic over her head, the luxurious wool kissing her skin, warming her.

Her drying braids dragged at her scalp, and she pulled out the hairpins, scattering them to the floor. Two long braids looped down, falling to her waist. She ran her fingers deftly through her loosened hair, separating out the damp strands. Wrapping the blanket around her tightly, bundled like a cocoon, Katerina swayed, then sank gracefully to one side, curled up on the ground, allowing sleep to claim her. Let Lussac de Balbigny do what he liked; she simply didn't care any more.

'Katerina?' Lussac knocked and called. Then knocked again. Something was wrong. Arms full of wood, he shoved one shoulder against the rotten planks, crashing the wide oak door inwards. Dropping the collected branches into a rattling pile, he picked out her hunched-up form in the gloom of the interior, hunkered down swiftly by her side. Was she breathing? His decisive fingers sought the pulse in her neck, found the regular beat of blood. His heart steadied. He snatched his hand away, conscious of the silken touch of her skin against his fingertips, of another feeling building slowly, inexorably, in his chest.

Katerina lay on her side, spine curved around knees drawn up to her chest, hands bunched into little fists against her neck. Her hair, her magnificent hair, lay loose and beautiful over her shoulders, spilling in a glorious amber puddle on to the floor. Drying tendrils curling softly around her face, resting against her cheek. Her skin gleamed. Why did his fingers itch to touch, to test that velvet softness of her face, against the better judgement of his conscious mind, the cavernous hollow that formed his soul? He should know better than to be tempted, to be entranced by such beauty. Normally, the utter blackness of his spirit, the void that consumed him, overpowered such desires, but with Katerina? In her presence, despite her wilfulness, her misguided self-reliance, all seemed different. With this maid, the bad feelings seemed to vanish, to be replaced by a lightness of heart that he had not known since his youth.

His gaze switched to the wet clothes strung across the floor. She had managed to change into his tunic at least. The fabric that had covered his own body now clung lovingly to her curves, the rounded press of her breasts, the raised flank of her hip. A smile tugged at the corners of his mouth; she obviously had no idea his tunics were split to the waist along the side seams to ease riding and now, the front panel of fabric had fallen forwards to reveal her pale, shapely thigh, a lean calf and narrow ankle. He suspected she hadn't planned to fall asleep before he returned; her whole demeanour was that of a woman constantly on her guard, ready to fight her corner at every opportunity. But this time, the experience, whatever that experience had been, had obviously been too much, even for her. The blanket wound chaotically around her neck and shoulders; she had failed even to pull it down over her body for warmth. Carefully, so as not to wake her, Lussac teased out the blanket folds, one knuckle brushing against her hot, silky cheek, and pulled the woollen fabric down over her, tucking it in around her toes.

Chapter Eleven

Katerina had no idea of how long she slept, but she had a very strong idea of what had woken her. Shifting on to her back in her sleep, the wound in her shoulder bumped against the solid ground and she cried out with the searing pain, forgetting where she was; who she was with.

'Katerina?' In the glimmering darkness, Lussac called out to her, his voice low, hushed.

Lussac?

Her eyes popped open, brain struggling to comprehend, fighting back the layers of drowsy sleep. For a moment she savoured the warmth suffusing her body before her current situation rushed back, details vivid, uncompromising. Her capture, the dog attacking as they thrashed in the water; her own belittling humiliation as Lussac caught up with her, saw her beaten and wasted, cast up on the river bank like a wrung-out length of cloth.

And now she lay, wrapped in his tunic smelling of sweet, lavender washing-soap, a tunic that belonged to a man with dangerous eyes, who slept a few scant feet away from her.

Except that he wasn't asleep.

She struggled to a sitting position, head fuzzy. Stubby flames danced in the fire-pit, a thin trail of bluish smoke rising lazily to the chimney-hole in the roof. Several layers of slates had been set round the hole to prevent sparks alighting on the thatch. Lussac sat opposite her, hair like polished chestnut, bulky shoulders propped up against a dishevelled pile of straw. One leg stretched out before him, his booted foot almost touching the white-grey stones of the fire-pit, the other leg was bent, one arm resting loosely across his knee. His fingers were long, tapered, she noticed, the ridged sinews in his hand prominent in the flickering light. Alongside him, her wet clothes were draped across a broken chair, the fabric steaming gently in the heat from the fire. A kernel of odd delight skipped within her at the thought of his strong hands upon her clothes, busy in the menial domestic duty that she should have performed herself. Or would have performed, if she hadn't fallen asleep.

'How long have I been…?' Her voice croaked,

throat dry and parched, and she swallowed rapidly, trying to force the words out.

'Asleep?' he supplied. His eyes, charcoal-dark and sparkling, moved over her, touched the gold-spun magnificence of her hair cascading over her shoulders. The glowing light from the fire made his lean features appear chiselled, as if from stone. 'Not long. Were you dreaming? You cried out.'

She swallowed once more, attempting to dispel the dusty coating within her mouth. 'Dreaming? Er, no, I'm not sure.' She was reluctant to draw any attention to the real reason for her waking: the flaring pain in her shoulder. 'Have you anything to drink?'

'Here.' He rummaged in the saddle-bags beside him, then leaned forwards with his leather water-bottle.

'Thank you.' As she shifted to take the bottle, making sure she used her right as opposed to her left hand, the blanket slithered from her shoulders, pooling down around her hips.

'Is anything the matter?' he said sharply, noticing her awkward movement.

Flinching under the diamond-intensity of his eyes, she pulled the stopper on the flagon, tipping the vessel to her lips. The fresh cool spring water slipped down her throat. Slowly, she replaced the stopper, keeping her eyes lowered, studying the dirt-ridged floor with exaggerated concentration. 'No,' she replied carefully.

In one rapid, easy movement, he stood beside her, towering over her. The toe of his boot nudged at her hip. 'There's blood on the back of my tunic.' His voice was blunt, matter of fact.

'I'll make sure I wash it before I give it back,' she replied hastily. 'What are you doing?' Cool fingers moved the silken bundle of her hair to one side and slid down the back of her neck, proprietorially, lifting the garment's decorative collar. Her heart stalled at the blatant over-familiarity, the graze of knuckle against her skin. A blade rasped through the material, slicing down with expertise, then air rushed over her injuries, exposed.

'Christ alive!' Lussac stared, shocked at the pulpy mess of her shoulder, the deep puncture marks in the white skin, the torn edges of each bite mark already purpling. 'You little fool! Why didn't you tell me what happened?' His acerbic tone attacked and dismissed her in one go, chewing relentlessly at some fragile, vulnerable part of her. He jammed the knife back into his belt, crouching down beside her, folding back the fabric even further to view the extent of the damage.

'Leave me alone!' she flared back at him, wiggling her shoulders violently to deflect his fingers. Snatching at the blanket, she struggled to cover her bare skin, the offending shoulder, but it seemed inextricably lodged beneath her hips. Tears prickled at the corners of her eyes.

'Leave you alone? And let your wound fester, so it becomes infected?' Anger jolted through him, anger at those people who wished to harm her, who threatened her safety. 'Even you, foolish as you are, should know better than that.'

Katerina hung her head. Tears slid down her cheeks, dropping freely; her spirit sapped. 'I do. I know. I would have sorted it out,' she mumbled, watching the hot tears splatter into her lap, trickling across her slim wrists.

'Are you crying?'

Stung by his acid tone, her head whipped around; she fixed him with a wild, furious stare. 'Aye, I am, and there's not a thing you can do about it! If you don't like it you can go—I'm not asking you to stay. I never asked you to help me.'

Her tear-stricken voice nipped at him, burrowing deep within some inner core; shame flooded his body. He had been too harsh. Since their first meeting, she had sparred with him at every turn, stood up to him, condemned him, matching him in verbal, if not physical, strength. Her initial feistiness had led him astray. He had misjudged how helpless, how broken she was at this moment; she spat at him like a wounded vixen, cornered. She was not some soldier he could bawl out on the battlefield; by attacking her at her lowest ebb, he had cracked through her seemingly impenetrable shell of spiky self-confidence. Dropping down beside her, he reached for her hands. The rough pads of his fingers rubbed the soft skin.

Lussac took a deep breath. 'I'm sorry,' he said.

She glanced around at him, wary, blinking away the wetness from her smoke-grey eyes, her lashes soot-black, stippled with teardrops. A deep shudder coursed through her. 'I bet that's the first time you've ever said that.' Her voice wobbled dangerously, then steadied.

He smiled slowly at her, curiously relieved. 'Will you let me treat that wound? I have some salve in my bag which should help.'

Katerina nodded doubtfully, nibbling on her bottom lip, unsure. She told herself her own health was at stake, nothing more, but a whisper of caution scratched at the inner recesses of her brain. Through lowered lashes, surreptitiously, she tracked Lussac's powerful strides as he made his way over to his bags, observed the way his close-fitting tunic clung to his strong haunches, his thighs, before falling to his knees. Despite all that had happened, a lightness danced around her heart, flickered new-born in the pit of her stomach; a lightness she couldn't explain. As Lussac turned, holding the earthenware pot of salve, she averted her eyes, wrapping her arms securely around her raised knees in an attempt to keep the damaged tunic from falling down.

She tensed as he hunkered down behind her, pouring water from his drinking bottle on to a pad of cloth. 'This may hurt a little,' he warned. He began to dab gently at the wounds on her back, his touch light, considerate, then threw the cloth down, dipping his fingers into the salve.

Without the separation of the damp cloth, the first touch of his fingers was a shock. Katerina closed her eyes, sucking in her breath abruptly. As he smoothed the thick honey-smelling ointment across her skin, she willed herself to control her breath, the wild pitch of her heart, forced herself to remain upright, rigid. Her skin tingled, grew warm.

Her reaction was not to the pain, but to the man kneeling inches behind her, energy radiating from his big body, encompassing her—the searing brush of his fingers, the *smell* of him: an intoxicating tangle of leather, woodsmoke and horse. Heat kindled within her, growing and blossoming, sparking suddenly to…what? What was it? A strange looping, coiling excitement, that drove her heart to beat faster, harder against her ribs, and snatched at her breath. In a desperate slide of realisation, she longed for his hands to stop their ministrations and smooth downwards, around, to slip beneath the flapping sides of the tunic, to draw her back, into him.

Her heart-beat skipped, then accelerated; she fought to draw in more oxygen to keep up with the rush of blood around her body. This will be over soon, she repeated to herself, a mantra, a prayer. This will be over soon. But, in truth, she wanted the feeling to last for ever. It was as if she were on the edge of an unknown precipice, with her own body becoming a total stranger, an unknown entity. She had never known such an addictive, intoxicating feeling, such a fierce, unbounded reaction…ever.

Katerina lurched upwards, legs weak, rickety as a puppet, finding some hidden strength to tear away from his irresistible touch, staggering over to the door. 'I can't breathe!' she gasped out. She crossed her arms fiercely across her chest, anchoring the slipping tunic to her breasts. The air emerged from her lungs in short, panicky gulps.

* * *

Kneeling on the floor, one dark eyebrow quirked upwards, Lussac studied her closely. What was the matter with the maid? Her face was flushed, as if she were running a fever. Her expression was one of haunted panic. He tried to ignore the creamy flash of her naked shoulder, bathed in the glow from the fire, for the warm velvet of her skin beneath his fingers had begun to gouge serious inroads into his own self-control. Against the muscle-bound wall of his chest, his heart thudded dangerously, an uneven strike.

'Come back,' he said, gently. 'Let me finish.'

Katerina backed up against the door, the thick oak planks supporting her trembling limbs, cheeks hot. 'I'm not sure…' she hedged. Her eyes were reflected pools of light, silver-grey. She cleared her throat, trying to gather some tattered shreds of her dignity together. 'It's just that…well, you should know I'm not in the habit of doing things like this.' Although her voice trembled, she managed to inject a triteness, a formality into her tone. 'It's not usual behaviour for me.'

Lussac chuckled, resting back on his heels, placing the pot of salve down by his side. Lit by the flames, his huge shadow bounced on the crumbling wall behind him. 'I would love to know what "usual behaviour" is for someone like you,' he replied. 'Everything I have seen so far has been distinctly unusual: poaching rabbits, climbing trees, not to mention swinging on chandeliers.'

'No, I didn't mean that…' She paused. 'I meant, this, being with you, a stranger, a man…' she shuffled uncomfortably '…alone.' She closed her eyes, mortified, hunting for the right words to explain. 'With you…like this.'

'It's nothing to be embarrassed about,' he replied. 'It's nothing I haven't seen before. I said I would help you.' He deliberately kept his tone brisk, practical, refusing to acknowledge that the gapping edge of the tunic had slipped even further, the taut flesh below her collar-bone shining like a pearl. His loins clenched deceitfully.

'Yes, but I don't think…' She turned worried eyes upon the sculptured angles of his face. *I don't think I can control myself.* She gasped out loud, balling one hand into a fist against her chest. Had he heard? Had she said those words out loud— those words that clamoured treacherously in her head? *I don't think I can control myself around him.* In what way? She couldn't even begin to imagine.

'I've said I would help you, and help you I will. And if you come back here, I can carry on.'

'I cannot.'

'I've told you, I'm not going to hurt you. I promise. I need to put the salve on and then we're done.'

How could she tell him it wasn't the pain, it was him, the confident press of his fingers, the draught of his breath sifting across her naked shoulders, stirring her hair? It was these things that made her hesitate and resist moving back. How could she announce something so outrageous? The lean, wiry maid who dressed like a boy—why, he would laugh in her face! He had made no secret of the fact that he had no desire for her. No secret at all. She had to prove to herself she was equally immune to him, immune to his presence, his touch upon her. She was strong, she could do it; she would make herself do it. Forcing her unwilling legs to move, she settled back down in front of him, sinking to her knees, her arms clamped severely to each side, holding the tunic in place, keeping her eyes focused on the flickering embers before her.

Faced once more with the sweet, bare curve of her shoulder, Lussac knew he had lied. And that he had to be quick and finish the job. He gritted his teeth as he massaged the salve in firm, deft circles across her skin. His body reacted to the maid's nearness in a way he did not like, in a way he seemed unable to control. Her loosened hair tumbled forwards over her shoulders in a riot of rapidly drying curls, the colour of amber. He longed to plunge his hands into that mass of glorious abandon, to lose himself within the silken tresses; longed to trace the mesmerising curve from ear to shoulder, to run his fingers down the notched rope of her spine, pale and vulnerable, inches from his ministering fingers. He was supposed to be helping her, for Christ's sake, not imagining her beneath him! As that clear, evocative image drove into his brain, his loins gripped with inexplicable desire, stabbed through him, brought him sharply back on his heels. His hand dropped.

'All done,' he croaked.

She turned her head, looked back at him over her shoulder. It was then that he saw it. Saw the desire burn in her eyes, those wide pools of light devouring him.

A lump of charred wood fell sideways in the firepit; sparks shot upwards.

'You feel it too,' he whispered.

Her mouth was mere inches from his, the delicious rosy curve half-open, expectant. In that breathless hush of stalled time, he sensed the tension within her, read it in her rigid stance. What did she want from him? He had nothing to give. If she had any wit at all she would back away now, retreat to a shadowy corner of the cottage, away. But her huge, luminous eyes held on to his, diamond-bright, drawing him in; he shuddered with desire. He rounded his palms on her shoulders, meaning to steady her, to reason with her, to speak some nonsense about settling down for the night, to drink, to eat, anything that would take his mind off that mouth of hers, the enticing brilliance of her eyes.

At his touch, the smallest sound escaped from her lips: a sigh.

Logic fled, deserting him, ripping away the last fragile remnants of his self-control. He tipped his head forwards, down, lips scuffing the corner of her mouth. Flames leapt within him, tore at the very core of him, the brief flutter of her mouth against his. He wanted more, much more. Hands that had intended to set her away now pulled her close, hard, chest to chest, stomach to stomach, roping tight around the flexible curve of her back. Beneath the tunic's voluminous folds, her figure was lean, but soft and pliable, cleaving to him, matching him. His mouth sealed down over hers, harder, questing, tongue roaming over the sensitive seam of her lips.

Katerina could hardly breathe; she was lost, sunk in a ferocious tumult of emotion: new, untried, feelings so exquisite that she wanted to shout aloud, to sing her joy to the skies above. Her limbs burned, liquefied under the relentless onslaught of Lussac's mouth, heart thudding recklessly, unevenly against the iron-clad wall of his chest. Powerless to resist, the touch of his mouth was inevitable and she had welcomed it. She craved the taste of him, the feel of his strong body against hers; she wanted this piece of time, this boundless spell of delicious intensity, to last for ever.

Lussac tore his mouth away, breathing heavily. Sitting back, he stuck one hand roughly through his hair, sending the silky dark locks spiking upwards. 'My God.' He stared at her, eyes bleak, fathomless, as if he were trying to work out what had just occurred between them, decipher the logic of the attraction, the kiss. 'That was unforgivable of me.'

I forgive you. But the strength to voice the words deserted her; his kiss had sapped the toughness from her speech. Katerina shook her head weakly at him, negating his words with the gesture. Nay, it was not unforgivable. It was the most beautiful thing that had ever happened to her.

'Cover yourself up.' He rose to his feet, snatching up the blanket where it lay strung out in gathered folds across the floor. He threw it at her.

Passion shrivelled, died within her. It was if he had taken a bucket of icy water and doused her with it. How could he change so quickly? How could he be kissing her one moment, pulling her towards him as if the moment would never end, then shove her away, hostility in his eyes? He couldn't even look at her. *He had tried and found her wanting.* The simple explanation sprang into her head: she was not woman enough for him, for one as experienced as him. The kiss had revealed her innocence, her lack of knowledge when it came to men. What a fool she was, for having even one iota of hope, of expectation. Despite the stony expression on his face, he was no doubt laughing at her inside.

Alongside the feelings of loss, of hopeless rejection, caused by the blunt finale of his kiss, temper erupted within her, fiery and haphazard, unstable. 'How dare you treat me so!' she blazed. 'Don't even think to take your pathetic frustrations out on me!'

'What on earth are you talking about?' Lussac frowned.

She hunched her shoulders. 'I'm so sorry if I failed to live up to expectations!'

So that's it, Lussac thought, walking over to his saddle-bags on the other side of the room. *She thinks I've used her, found her wanting and have now discarded her.* How wrong could one woman be? Her eyes burned into him, hating him, hot, fiery coals of wrath; even with his back to her, he could feel her disdain, her anger. Maybe it was better this way; maybe it was better if she hated him. He sank down against the bale of straw once more, watching Katerina as she yanked the blanket over her shoulders, curling herself into a tight, miserable ball with her back to the fire and to him. Aye, it would be easier if she hated him; that way, she would never be hurt. He wouldn't wish that on anyone, but especially not on her.

He sighed, tilting his head back, closing his eyes. It was going to be a long night.

Chapter Twelve

It was early morning when Katerina woke again. Somewhere near the open chimney-hole, a blackbird trilled frantically, a continual bombardment up and down the musical scale, warbling and squawking. The air in the cottage was chill; lying on her back, Katerina saw her breath form a white cloud above her face as she exhaled. Lifting her hand, she brushed one finger across her lips, remembering. The sensitive flesh tingled, stung slightly, as if bruised. Something wilted inside her, twisted her gut. She switched her head abruptly to the left, eyes travelling over the fire's ashy remains, seeking out the space where Lussac had slept. Empty. Loose strands of straw poked out from the bales, drifting listlessly in the slender draught from the open window. She wondered where he was, but doubted he had gone far, after her exploits yesterday.

A long slow breath escaped her lungs. Last night, she had been lucky. Fortune had been on her side; *he* had been on her side, scooping her up on the river bank last night when she was down, at rock bottom, and tending to her wounds. Any decent man would have done it. Of course, not any man would have kissed her, but from the way he had ended it, he had no intention of ever trying that again. She stared at the ground miserably, recalling the hot, white-light intensity of his touch, his eager, skilled mouth against hers. How could she have known what such closeness, such connection could feel like? She was naïve to the ways of men, an innocent.

She raised one arm in the air, stretching her muscles, testing, then raised the other arm with her damaged shoulder, assessing the strength of the movement. The healing, overly taut skin across her shoulder strained cruelly, ached. She couldn't afford to be injured, couldn't afford to be unfit to perform. Did those men her father had hired know she was with the troupe? Or had they been lucky in Ipswich, catching sight of her across the market?

Reaching for her clothes, dried stiffly over the chair, she lifted Lussac's tunic up and over her head, the movement awkward with her damaged shoulder. She folded the fine material carefully, smoothing her hand across the creases. Her naked skin puckered in the cool air and she shivered. The folds of her own tunic had clumped together and she held the garment across her bare thighs, tugging irritably at the unwieldy fabric.

The door sprang open. Lussac filled the opening.

Instinctively, Katerina hunched over, clasping the tunic across her naked bosom, dragging it down so it covered the tops of her bare thighs. 'Lord in Heaven, you might have knocked!' she blurted out, horrified.

'I thought you would still be sleeping,' Lussac replied, breath snaring in his throat. One gleaming swell of naked breast peeked out from the inadequate covering, framed by the delicate cage of her collar-bone above. Her legs were slender, feet pink-tipped with tiny, shell-like toenails. He couldn't remember the last time he'd seen such small feet. His fingers gripped around the edge of the door, fighting to steady himself, fighting for equilibrium. 'I'll be outside,' he announced jerkily, dragging the heavy, unwieldy door back into its frame with unnecessary force.

Desire thrummed through his broad frame as he staggered back from the door, away, away from the lustrous perfection of those limbs, the tempting slope of bare bosom, her sweet, enchanting face. Christ, she acted upon him like a siren of old, calling to him, luring him in with those staggering grey eyes, that magnificent hair. Seeing her there, with that flimsy piece of fabric barely covering her nudity, he had truly believed he would lose control and take her there and then, rolling around in the hard, corrugated ground.

It was imperative he remained focused on his purpose in this country and the reason he had searched for her. Katerina's family held the key to everything, the key to his life, his salvation. He needed to reach Longthorpe and he needed Katerina to take him there, willing or not. He had to avenge the death of his family, nothing more, nothing less; his own physical desires should never have come into it. And that was all this was. Physical desire. It was a long time since he'd been with a woman; the cold hollowness of his spirit had made sure of that and now this delectable morsel was thrown before him. His body, devoid of physical contact for so long, was responding in the only way it knew how. He frowned. But why now? After all these years? He simply couldn't explain it.

Fully dressed, Katerina tugged at the door, then slid out into the fresh morning air. Her braies were damp around the ankles as she tucked the loose ends into her leather boots, but everything else, her chemise, her hooded tunic, was dry. Wrenching her hair back, she had plaited it roughly, allowing it to swing down her back, securing the braid with a leather lace. The sunlight picked up the golden flecks in the bronze strands, flaming her hair with a lustrous beauty.

In front of the cottage, the grass in the clearing grew thick, with vigour, soaked with a heavy, clinging dew. Tiny spiders' webs clung to single blades, stretched into uneven octagons, like tented lace. Viewed from above, the grass appeared coated in a diaphanous veil of white. Katerina hesitated on the threshold, reluctant to move into the clearing, to find Lussac. She had no wish to face him. His humiliating rejection of her, after their kiss, preyed on her brain, and the embarrassment of him barging in on her naked made her want to hide, to slink away without seeing him.

But there he was, crouched down at the side of the clearing over a small fire, adjusting some kind of trivet from which hung a small iron pot. He poked at the ashes with a long stick, one chainmail sleeve pushed back, revealing a lean forearm roped with muscle. Strong, skilful arms that had held her, pulled her in tighter, harder. Her heart flipped in shame, the urge to run away almost overwhelming. She must have made a sound, a small movement that gave her presence away. His head lifted, features unsmiling, chestnut hair falling in silky spikes over his forehead.

He said nothing, not a word of greeting, no acknowledgement. Above his head the drooping branches of a beech tree bobbed in the breeze, scattering the shadows that fell across his face.

The silence stretched between them, grew ominous, laden.

'I...I'm all dressed,' Katerina blurted out—anything to fill the silence!—and tried to ignore the quiet fire of his observation. It was as if he saw beneath her skin, pierced her soul; she wriggled uncomfortably, her words constricting her throat. The dew darkened the toes of her boots as she moved across to him, every step beset with awkwardness, her limbs without grace like those of a new-born colt. The rising steam from the cooking pot bathed her face in warmth. Katerina tucked a wayward strand of shining hair behind her ear.

'Lussac, I must return to the troupe,' she announced firmly, fiddling with the frayed rope around her waist, a makeshift belt for her tunic. Maybe he would let her go. It was worth a chance.

'Here.' He produced a floury bread roll from the

bag at his side, a hunk of cheese balanced on top. Had he failed to hear her words?

'Thank you.' She accepted the food gratefully, sat down cross-legged in the grass opposite him. She cleared her throat. The curve of his top lip was firm, well defined, a sensuous tilt at the corners of his mouth. Concentrating hazily on the nobbled bark of the tree trunk behind his head, she chewed unconsciously at the corner of her mouth, reddening the flesh. 'I need to find the troupe again, Lussac—' she shoved the words out in a rush '—otherwise John will never have me back.'

'No, Katerina. I'm sorry, but there it is. You have to come with me.' His eyes observed her calmly. 'And this time, I'll keep a closer eye on you.'

She ignored his veiled reference to her earlier escape. 'But you know the way to Longthorpe now,' she squeaked, baulking at his authoritative tone. 'What could you possibly need me for?'

Because you bring a joy and warmth and vitality to my life. My heart feels lighter when I'm with you. The unexpected thought barged into his mind, unbidden.

Frowning, he scratched at one ebony eyebrow, rubbing his eye in the process. 'You know what your family look like, Katerina. Your father, your uncle. I want you to point them out to me. I want you to identify them for me.'

'Other people could do that for you,' she replied grumpily.

'I want to be sure, Katerina. I want to be sure I have the right person.'

'Why? What do you want with my family?' she breathed. Something in his tone snared at her subconscious, something wild, dangerous. 'This is all linked to the cuff, isn't it? What is it about that cuff?'

He shoved the stick violently into the fire, let it burn. A black trail of smoke rose in front of his face. 'It's best that you don't know.' His voice was clipped, formal, devoid of emotion.

Tension hung between them, suspended in the air like dense fog.

Katerina took a bite of the bread roll, chewing hungrily. He was not going to tell her, however much she poked and prodded him for a reason. She swallowed a piece of the fragrant bread, savouring the taste. It felt good to have something substantial in her belly.

'What did those men want with you, Katerina?' Lussac swung the iron pot towards him, carefully pouring the contents into a pewter mug. 'Here, have this.' He handed her the mug and she clutched it, gratefully, between two hands.

'Where's yours?' She placed her lips on the edge of the cup, but the liquid, warmed mead from the smell of it, was too hot; she would wait.

'I only have one cup. Ladies first.' He propped his broad shoulders against the trunk at his back. 'Tell me, Katerina.'

She studied him over the rising steam. This was it. This was the moment where she should tell him, confide in him. Could she trust him? Or would he turn against her like all the rest, like her own family had done? But if she confided in him, surely he would see how impossible it was for her to return home. Maybe he would understand.

'Over a year ago now, I left home. I disguised myself as a boy, because, as I'm sure you are aware, single women, travelling alone, are fair game.' She took a sip of mead, wincing as the hot liquid stung the tip of her tongue.

Lussac kicked irritably at a log that had rolled out from the fire, nudging the smoking wood back into the hot ashes; he would prefer not to think of her out there on the road, defenceless and vulnerable.

'I wasn't completely alone. I had a friend, a good

friend, who helped me, taught me some skills, skills that meant I could work as a performer.'

Waleran, he thought. Obviously more than a good friend to her. A lover? He recalled the pair of them in the tent at Norfolk's castle, the way the pair of them had sprung guiltily away from each other when he barged into the tent. An unpleasant churning sensation crawled within him. He stared at the luminous, perfect oval of her face, her wide, storm-grey eyes, the fall of her glorious hair, and wanted so much for it not to be true.

'But my father wants me back home; those men were mercenaries, soldiers hired by him to find me. There's....there's a price on my head, good money.' She took a deep, shuddery breath. 'I've managed to evade them up to now.'

'And then I came along and spoiled it all.'

Katerina ignored his quiet, level response, voice rising with emotion. 'I should have walked straight past that leather cuff! And Lord Mortimer, recognising my hair!' Disgruntled, she yanked at her plait dangling over her left shoulder and down across her front. The curling end, bound in leather strips, lay in her lap. 'The colour gives me away. I'll have to cut it off and dye it. It's too unusual, too obvious.'

'No,' he breathed. His gaze brushed the bound

glittering rope, aghast at the idea of her doing such a thing. 'You mustn't do that.'

Katerina glared at him. 'How else am I going to keep myself hidden?' Draining the contents of the mug, she plonked the empty vessel down between them. Lussac refilled it from the pot. Above his head, the breeze sifted through the beech tree, sending a volley of amber leaves across the clearing.

Lussac took a sip of mead. 'Maybe you should ask yourself how long you can keep going like this? he replied finally. 'I suspect your father will not give up until he finds you. Do you really want to keep running, to keep hiding for the rest of your life?'

Her shoulders sagged; no, she didn't. But what choice did she have? Mentally, she pulled herself upright. 'I've been quite good at it so far,' she replied briskly.

'Aye, I'm sure of it.' His eyes twinkled. 'Your methods of self-protection are admirable.' A brief smile tugged at his lips as he recalled the stolen horse and her mad, haphazard scramble up the tree, away from him. Her impossible escape through the narrow garderobe window, giving him the slip in the inn. 'But those mercenaries caught you yesterday, Katerina, and they will catch you again—'

'And I told you, I was unlucky,' she interrupted, springing to her feet. 'I would have got away with it if you hadn't come along.'

'If you hadn't died of exposure first,' he muttered grimly, remembered the blue shadows around her lips from the night before. Did she not realise how vulnerable she was? Lussac watched her pace across the clearing, the cut of her braies emphasising the slenderness of her legs, strong emotions playing across her face.

'Is the prospect of returning home really so dreadful?' he ventured.

She stopped, whipping around to face him. 'I told you it was, didn't I? That's why I had to escape from you!'

'Yes, you told me, but you didn't tell me *why.*'

A sharp blade of fear sliced her gut; her cheeks washed chalky-white. 'You're right' she whispered, falling to her knees beside him. 'I didn't tell you why.'

She was so close, he could have touched the downy lobe of her ear, trailed his fingers down the smooth column of her throat. Instead he drove his clenched fists into the spongy ground at his sides. 'It can't be that bad,' he responded, keeping his voice level to hide the tremulous desire that snared his larynx. 'What's your father trying to do? Marry you off to some poor, unsuspecting halfwit?'

His teasing words scoured into her, goaded her. He made light of a situation that was hateful. 'You have no idea!' Her voice rose, shrill.

'Am I right? Is it marriage?' he pushed, astonishing turquoise eyes focusing on her distraught face, intimidating.

'Aye,' she exclaimed in a rush. 'Aye, it's marriage! Marriage to a man twice my age, a man who is my father's brother! Now do you see? I could never go back to that!' She stuffed a fist against her mouth, stifling a half-sob that threatened to break free. She would not, could not dissolve into tears.

His fingers grazed her cheek.

'Don't touch me!' She snatched her head back; if he showed her the slightest sympathy she would crumble, collapse against him. And after the mortification of last night's kiss and his subsequent rejection of her, that would never do.

'My God,' he breathed.

'I would rather die than go home,' she declared, her voice rising. 'Now can you see why I had to get away from you? You were taking me back to the one place that I never want to return to!'

Lussac arched one eyebrow at her dramatic statement. 'I do see, Katerina. I understand. But a marriage like that would never happen, would never be allowed. Surely you know that. Such marriages within families are against the law of the land. The blood tie is too close.'

'Not if my father consents…'

'Not even if your father gives his consent. It will never happen.'

'How can you be so sure?'

Because I will never let it happen. I would protect you from such an ordeal. The words popped into his head.

'Because…' He searched for a viable answer, one that would never let her guess his true feelings. 'Because Queen Isabella would never allow such a marriage; it goes against everything she stands for. The law of this land will protect you.'

Katerina was already shaking her head. 'I fear my family believe themselves to be above the law. My uncle does, at least.'

Lussac scowled. Of course they would. Those sort of men always did. It made perfect sense. They were murderers who considered themselves to be above the normal rules that governed the land. Propelling himself to his feet, he poured the dregs of mead on to the fire, stamping the remaining flames out with the sole of his boot.

'What father would agree to such a thing for his

child?' he asked roughly, sticking his hand out towards her. Katerina grasped it; he pulled her lightly to her feet.

'After my mother died, he became extremely over-protective; it was almost unbearable. My freedom was curbed, stifled. I knew he would arrange my marriage, but to someone more suitable, but not him, never him!' Her voice rose in a trembling panic and she reached out, clinging to Lussac's sleeves. 'Please, Lussac, I beg of you, please don't make me go back there!'

He read the utter desperation in her eyes, her fear. Her shoulders hunched over as she dropped her hands from his upper arms, wrapping them defensively across her chest. A pallid greyness covered her face; she was exhausted from the previous day. His stomach churned; the maid had been running for her life, her future, living on her wits and skills in a world weighted in favour of men. The odds were stacked against her.

'You have to stop running.'

Her eyes flashed at him, smoke-grey, indignant. 'How, Lussac? How am I supposed to do that! Surely you can see the impossible situation I'm in?' Her question ended in an indignant screech.

'I might be able to help you, Katerina,' he said

slowly. He raised his eyes heavenwards. What on earth did he think he was doing?

She tilted her head to one side, arms still clamped across her middle, mouth tight.

'Queen Isabella has travelled on to Bury today; she will be there tonight. Bury is on the way to Longthorpe—am I right?' He could scarce believe what he was saying.

Katerina nodded, breath trapped in her throat, silently hoping.

'We will go there tonight. I will ask the Queen to draw up a writ, forbidding the marriage to your uncle, and you can sleep in a decent bed. I think you need to rest, Katerina.'

She drew herself more upright. 'No, I'm fine,' she protested. Her hair, amber threads, glinted in the sunlight.

He smiled, shook his head. 'No, Katerina, you are not fine. Any idiot can see that. You need to rest before you take me to Longthorpe. You will be in no danger, as the Queen's writ will protect you.' *And I will protect you, too,* he thought.

Her rigid stance wilted, drooped a little, before him. She allowed herself to lean on the solid calmness of his suggestion, her body cleaving slightly towards him. How wonderful it would be to collapse in his arms right now and for him to take

care of her, to make everything all right. She had
been fighting her own battles for so long, she had
forgotten what it was like to rely on someone, to
trust someone.

'Do you think it will? Do you think a piece of
paper has the power to stop this?' she asked, a
doubtful note in her voice.

'Yes, I do,' he said. 'We can help each other. I
will secure a writ from the Queen, and you will
take me to Longthorpe. Call it a simple business
transaction. We will both achieve what we want.'

A business transaction, she thought, a chill sliding through her. Of course, that is how he would
see it. Why would he view it any other way? It
wasn't as if he cared one jot for her, for what had
happened in her past, or what was to happen in the
future; she was simply the means to an end. But if
it meant her hateful marriage could be called off,
then she would do anything at all.

Steep banks rose up either side of the muddy
track, inclines of dark, crumbly earth smothered
in dark green trails of ivy, punctuated by the vertical columns of ribbed ferns. Above their heads, the
high branches of the tree met overhead forming a
green canopy, a shadowed tunnel. Lussac walked
up front, one hand grasping the reins beneath his

horse's head, leading. His tunic hood was thrown back, chestnut hair feathering upwards in the slight breeze. Katerina sat astride the horse, legs dangling free of the too-long stirrups, adjusted for Lussac's superior height. He had offered to alter the length for her, to make the riding easier, but she had told him she had no need of stirrups to help her balance on a horse.

Tipping her head back, enjoying the kiss of sunlight against her face, she watched the lacy green net of leaves file before her vision. It was a strange experience for her, being led on a horse; she felt lazy sitting there, static. She rolled her damaged shoulder experimentally. Already it seemed much better; the pain had eased, and the stiffening stretch between the wounds had lessened.

The soft nap of the horse's nose bumped against Lussac's cheek, as he strode along. His horse was strong enough to carry both of them and the journey would have been accomplished more quickly, but this way, it was safer. The further he could keep the sweet touch of Katerina's delectable body away from his own, the better. It would give him more of a chance to regain the scattered remnants of his self-control. His mind reeled with the circumstances that had led Katerina to leave home; trapped and frightened by the prospect of a horrible marriage, she had taken the brave, risky option. She had run. Not many women would have made that decision; they would have accepted the hand that Fate had dealt them, accept the situation imposed on them by a superior male authority. But not Katerina, no. A smile tugged at his lips. Frightened she might have been, but lacking in courage, in bravery, she was not. She had challenged her father's authority, refused to go along with his plans, using her wits, her physical skill, to extricate herself from a distasteful situation. He couldn't imagine her doing anything else.

A small sound at his back made him turn his head, squinting in the strong sunlight that pierced the trees. An extraordinary sight met his eyes: Katerina, balanced upside-down on her hands, toes pointing skywards, her tunic falling back to her neat waist in loose gathers. The intense light faded her hair to the colour of sand, a pale gold; her braid snaked across the saddle and down his horse's flank.

'Katerina?'

'What…? Oh!' Her voice was muffled, obscured by her tunic falling over her mouth. Scissoring her legs down smartly, her toes touching the horse's rump, she knelt in the saddle, lifting her head up. 'Sorry…what did you say?' She grinned at him, her face flushed, sparkling with a radiant energy, a luminescence.

Something tugged at his heart.

'What are you doing?'

Her tunic remained bundled up somewhere around her chest; he caught the flash of white chemise peeking out from beneath the dun-coloured fabric. She yanked the material down abruptly. 'I have to practise…' she shrugged her shoulders '…for when I get back to the troupe. I wasn't sure if my shoulder…might affect my performance.'

'On the back of my horse.' He was incredulous, more than anything. 'Couldn't you have waited until we stopped?'

A sheepish look crossed her face. 'I'm not used to sitting idle on horseback, I usually walk.'

Lussac raised one eyebrow. 'Are you telling me that you're *bored?*' He wanted to laugh out loud; most women would do their utmost not to walk anywhere and now this maid was practically begging to be allowed not to ride! 'Too slow for you, is it?' he murmured.

Katerina bounced down from the saddle, coming round to meet him at the horse's head. Her grey eyes sparkled, the colour of pewter, shot through with streaks of silver. 'Why don't you ride for a bit and I'll lead? Let's swap.'

This time, he did laugh out loud, teeth white and even in his tanned face. 'Katerina, where have you been for the last few years? Have you any idea of the notion of chivalry? Men are supposed to take care of women, not the other way around. How would it look if I rode into Bury on horseback, with you leading me?'

She shrugged her shoulders, enjoying the sound of his laughter; it made him seem more boyish, more approachable somehow.

'A noble lady is like a delicate flower, not supposed to do too much, to become too tired, or too dirty,' he explained, amusement threading his voice. 'Surely you experienced a life like that at home?' They walked together now, each either side of the horse's head.

'My mother was always telling me to stop rushing about, to stop going outside, stop behaving like a hoyden.' Katerina sighed. 'She was always telling me to act more like a lady. It's been so long, I suppose I have forgotten. I'm so used to fending for myself now.'

He wanted to tell her that he would take care of her. But how could he take care of someone, when he couldn't even take care of himself?

She stopped suddenly, placing one hand on top of the horse's nose. Her pale fingers were fine, tapered, he realised, her skin so delicate against the coarse woven fabric of her sleeve. How could he ever have mistaken her for a common wench? Her hands were those of a noble lady. 'Even if the situation is sorted out with my father, I'm not sure I could go back to that kind of life—I've had a taste of freedom and, for all the hardships, the cold, wet nights, the lack of food, I think I prefer it. It makes me feel alive. Instead of the prospect of days and days inside, working away at some dull tapestry, I get to throw my body through the air, to perform, to entertain. Do you understand?

Lussac nodded slowly. He did understand. She was like a wood-sprite, a nymph of the forest, dancing lightly through the green-soaked glades, ethereal, magical. How could anyone curb that energy, her passion for movement? He would hate to see anyone try to do such a thing to her.

Chapter Thirteen

The high, towering frontispiece of the abbey at Bury St Edmunds was built in a white dressed stone, huge blocks forming two towers either side of a wide, central doorway. Niches had been carved into the front, curved columns like clusters of pipes on each side, topped with a sharp, triangular arch above. Intricately carved statues of saints had been set within each of the niches, a head bowed here, an arm outstretched there, giving the whole abbey front an impressive level of detail, and no doubt delighting the steady succession of pilgrims who made their way towards the shrine of St Edmund, situated behind the high altar.

As Lussac and Katerina walked across the busy cobbled courtyard, Lussac's horse trailing behind them, a large rotund figure squeezed out from a small door at the side of the abbey.

'Philippe,' Lussac murmured. 'Brace yourself.'

His friend hoisted one arm in the air, a dramatic gesture of welcome as he bustled towards them, his glance darting curiously back and forth between Lussac and Katerina. 'Lussac, what are you doing here? Have you…?' He struggled to find the correct words. 'How are things?'

'We encountered a few problems,' Lussac replied calmly. His deep, rich voice cut straight through Philippe's incessant burbling, the lurching hand gestures. 'One of which I hope Isabella will be able to help with.' His bright gaze touched the burnished top of Katerina's head.

'She's settled herself in the great hall, with her ladies,' Philippe said. 'We've only just arrived here ourselves.' He raised his eyebrows conspiratorially. 'I warn you, Lussac, she's not in the best of moods.'

'Katerina!' Three sets of eyes turned in unison towards the masculine voice.

'Waleran!' Katerina cried out, recognising the lithe, sinewy figure of her friend coming around the corner of the chapter-house. She lifted her eyes towards Lussac, her face radiant and happy. 'It's Waleran!' she said, by way of explanation.

'I can see that,' Lussac responded drily, through gritted teeth. A grinding irritation clamped around his chest; he had an insane desire to curve his arm around Katerina, a definitive gesture of possession, of proprietorship. His hands bunched into fists at his sides, nails digging into the hard skin of his palms. Katerina belonged to no one; he would do well to keep his hands to himself.

'What are you doing here?' Katerina exclaimed as Waleran approached, almost skipping across the cobbles towards her. A smile wrinkled his narrow face. He grasped her hands, then pulled her close, hugging her in his lean, sinewy arms. She tensed slightly as his arm moved across her painful shoulder, before drawing back.

'Sorry,' Waleran said suddenly, a dull ruddy colour seeping across his jaw-line as he recalled their last, awkward conversation, his offer of marriage. 'I was so pleased to see you, that's all.' He threw a shifty glance up at Lussac, scowling darkly at him over Katerina's neat head.

'But what are you doing here?' she repeated, shaking her head in disbelief. 'I don't understand.'

'John's over the moon. The Queen enjoyed the performance at the Earl of Norfolk's castle so much, she asked the troupe to accompany her to Bury. Will you come around to the camp or...?' Waleran glanced past her to Lussac, as if asking for permission.

'It's probably the last time I will see everyone,'

Katerina said quietly, her fine eyes searching the chiselled lines of Lussac's face. 'And in this last year, the troupe have become like a family to me. I need to say goodbye before I return home.'

Lussac handed the reins to a stable-boy, who had finally emerged from the low buildings to the left of the main abbey. Every bone in his body told him not to let her go. He wanted her by his side, where he could see her, especially with her so-called friend, Waleran, hanging around.

'We've set up on a piece of rough pasture, behind the abbey hospital,' Waleran added, as if that would help his decision.

'Are you planning on running away again?' Lussac muttered softly.

She shook her head. A gold-spun tendril of hair fell across her cheek. 'No, Lussac. You are right. I have to stop running, stop looking over my shoulder, worrying every day that my father's henchmen will catch up with me. I must face my future.'

His hand cupped her shoulder. 'I will go and see Isabella about the writ. If you go back to your camp and say your farewells, I will come and find you later. Stay close, Katerina.'

He followed her graceful progress across the courtyard, arm in arm with Waleran. Was he a fool for allowing her to do this? 'Philippe, go after them and keep an eye out,' he said suddenly. 'Don't let her go anywhere.'

The afternoon was hot; layers of shimmering heat lay across the land, pressing down on the earth, muting birdsong. Bees swung lazily amongst the flowers in the abbey gardens. Harvesting took place; scything wheat, the peasants in the fields stopped periodically to mop the sweat from their faces with their sleeves. The monks, dressed in their serviceable brown habits, silver crosses dangling on beaded threads from their waists, engaged in less physically demanding activities: gentle weeding in the vast vegetable gardens, or picking apples from the heavily laden trees in the orchards.

'It felt so sad, saying goodbye to everyone,' Katerina said quietly.

'You'll see us again, I'm sure.' Squatting down on the shallow, curving bank of loose stones, Waleran attempted to keep his voice jovial. He reached out and dipped the wooden pail into the deeper part of lazy flowing river.

'Maybe, when everything is sorted out, I will come back,' she mused.

'John would welcome you with open arms, Katerina. It's your act that draws the crowds.'

'I'm going to miss everyone, so much.'

Trees hung low over Waleran's head, casting his features in an eerie green light. 'You'll see me again, Katerina. I plan to come back to Long-thorpe, to visit my family. I just hope that Belbigny is right, that the Queen's word will change your father's mind. You're giving up so much.'

'I have to take that risk, Waleran. Lussac is right; the time has come to stop living like a fugitive.' Katerina sat on the bank, legs outstretched on the loose shingle. Two full buckets of water balanced on the stones either side of her.

Lussac. The way she spoke that man's name, in a delicate lilt, made him fume. She'd not even known him above a handful of days! He glanced down at the water, a sickening jealousy swirling in his gut. Beneath the clear surface, a shoal of tiny fish darted, jerking in unison, first one way, then the other.

'Well, he doesn't trust you,' Waleran bit out resentfully. 'Look at the way his man regards us.' He nodded in the direction of the tents, where Philippe's solid build in dark-blue surcoat could plainly be seen.

'I can understand it,' Katerina replied. 'I've already given him the slip once—why should he trust me again?' She fiddled with the little stones at her sides, rolling them around between her fingers. Warmth flooded her body at the thought of him, of his big frame against hers, his mouth across her lips. She blamed the heat; even beneath the trees, it was oppressive, pressing down on her like a thick blanket. Whereas before she had been the right temperature, now she felt uncomfortable, out of sorts. Perspiration prickled along her spine; she scratched at the back of her neck, feeling the slick of sweat.

Waleran staggered up the bank, dumped the bucket beside the others, water slopping. Beneath the green tunnel of trees that curved over the river, Katerina's face shone out with a pearly luminescence. There was so much he didn't know, so much she hadn't told him; she, Katerina, who normally confided every last detail. So much he couldn't ask. Where had she spent the night? Had she been alone, or with him? His fingernails gouged into the calloused flesh of his palms.

He grasped a bucket in each hand, feeling the muscles pull across his shoulders as he lifted. 'Are you coming?' Waleran tilted his head to one side, studying her seated figure, her sweet face, sprinkled with freckles.

'You go on,' she replied. 'I'll come back a bit later.'

Waleran stared down at her, frowning, as if trying to decipher information from her closed, beautiful face. He wondered at her reluctance to accompany him, felt the surge of regret.

'Don't look so stern, Waleran.' She laughed at him. 'I'll be along, soon enough. '

'You'd better not be too long, or that one will be after you.' He nodded in Philippe's direction.

Katerina sat quietly for a while, chin balanced on her knees, listening to the sound of Waleran's retreating footsteps, the trill of birdsong in the trees high about her head. The continual flow of the water exuded a hypnotic, melodic quality and she watched the slick of water as it curved over the bigger lumps of stone, deepening the colours of the rock; seams of bronze, blue and ochre sung out from beneath the surface. Her tunic sleeves clung stickily to her arms, the fabric cloying. She knew what she wanted to do, now, right at this moment—did she dare? She glanced about, checking her surroundings, making certain she would not be observed; Waleran would nearly be back at the camp now. In a trice, she tugged her tunic over her head, stepped out of her boots and braies. Falling to mid-thigh, her gauzy chemise stuck to her skin, but modesty made her keep it on as she walked barefoot into the cool water.

* * *

Beads of sweat gathered at the back of Lussac's neck as he strode out from the abbey, a renewed sense of purpose fuelling his stride. Isabella, horrified at the prospect of such a marriage, had readily agreed to scrawling her signature at the bottom of a writ drawn up by her scribe. Lussac had paced that dark, gloomy hall, listening to the scratch of the clerk's nib against the nubbled paper. It had seemed like an eternity before it was finished, but now he had it, stored safely in his saddle-bag—the paper that would secure Katerina's freedom.

The grass grew up in thin dry wisps, parched and crisp, scratching at the cloth of Lussac's braies as he walked across the field. Where was she? Where was Philippe, for that matter? The camp seemed deserted, apart from one wizened old man sitting cross-legged on a threadbare rug in front of one of the tents. He plucked idly at a lute, the pale, polished wood reflecting like a mirror in the sunshine, the single notes rising sweetly into the thick, heavy air. Across the horizon, grey, bulbous clouds gathered strength. The old man's fingers paused on the lute strings.

'Where is everybody?' Lussac asked. His huge shadow fell across the man, casting him into darkness.

The man hunched his narrow shoulders, placed his instrument tentatively down on the lumpy rug. Some of the woven threads had come apart, fraying at the edge. 'Your man's over there.'

Lussac followed the jerk of his head, spotting a pair of dusty boots crossed at the ankles poking out from behind one of the tents. The boots belonged to Philippe, his portly frame stretched out in the long, hot grass behind one of the tents, his head propped up on a canvas bag, snoring gently.

'Oh, for God's sake, Philippe, can't I trust you to do anything?' Lussac shoved his toe savagely into his friend's rounded side. 'Where's Katerina? I told you to keep an eye on her.'

Philippe held his hands up before him, a placatory gesture. 'It's all under control, Lussac.'

'It looks like it.'

'Katerina is down by the river, with that friend of hers. They went to fetch some water.'

'Really? And you let them go?'

'Stop fretting Lussac, look, I can see her from here.'

Squinting across the shimmering heat haze of the afternoon, Lussac spotted two figures, moving under the trees. 'I thought she was supposed to be saying goodbye to all of them, not just him,' he muttered. 'Why did you not go with them?'

'I thought I would give them a little privacy,' Philippe cleared his throat delicately.

'What? They're not together, if that's what you mean,' Lussac shouted back, beginning to stride across the field. Jealousy flared in his gut, spurring his steps. He should not have let her out of his sight.

Chapter Fourteen

What was it about this maid and water? Lussac thought. Was she compelled to move towards it, against her will, like iron filings aligning towards a lodestone? He strode through a waving sea of grass, the feathery plumed tops tickling his hands, brushing against his boots, scratching the leather. The air was heavy with the scent of warm grass seed, kernels of oil heated in the hot sun.

In front of him, a curving line of deciduous trees marked the line of the river. The countryside was deserted, save for a single figure heading towards him, features shaded by a wide-brimmed hat, struggling along the hedgerow between two heavy pails. Waleran. Katerina's friend. Katerina's lover?

He didn't want to think about that.

'She's down by the river,' Waleran puffed out under the weight of the slopping buckets, before

Lussac even had time to open his mouth. There was a note of resignation in the young man's voice, a hint of sadness in his eyes.

Lussac nodded, moving past him. Encroaching from the west, the clouds piled up in ominous pleated folds, darkening. Once at the tree-line, he stopped beneath the spreading branches of an oak, breathing in the dank air of shade. The neck of his tunic stuck to his skin; he tugged at it in annoyance, feeling the damp sheen of sweat on his throat. Had Katerina moved along from the spot at which Philippe had pointed? He couldn't be sure. Against the river's constant burble, he listened for any clue to Katerina's whereabouts. In the grass, out in the scorched pasture, insects whirred and hummed.

He moved upstream, working his way around thickets of brambles, the tree-roots and trunks that crowded the river-bank. Boots scuffing against the dry, hard-packed earth, he took a side step out into the field again to avoid a cluster of tightly packed trunks.

A flash of white caught his eye, glimmering out from the dark shade. His heart eased with relief. He paced towards the gleam, intending to call out, to shout her name, to remonstrate with her for leaving the camp.

His speech fled.

Half-turned away from him, Katerina stood in the middle of the river, the thin white stuff of her chemise floating softly on the water's surface, like the satiny petals of a flower. Her hair hung loose, rippling tresses of deep amber, coiling down her back in a shining fall of copper. Eyes closed, she scooped the water up in joyful handfuls, flinging the cool liquid over her neck and face. Crystal droplets tracked down the slim column of her neck, pooling in the shadowy hollow at the base. Then suddenly, she sank, bending her knees so that the water swirled over her shoulders. The chemise billowed upwards, revealing the rounded, naked curves of hip and thigh, gleaming with a pearly luminescence, white marble beneath the smooth slick flow.

Lussac braced himself against a tree, fingers digging into the ridged bark. His breath stuck to his ribs. Passion rushed through him. He had to remain immune to her, for all their sakes! A voice clamoured in his brain—the voice of sanity, of self-restraint?—telling him to go now, to leave, but his feet seemed welded to the spot, limbs leaden, unresponsive. She would catch him spying on her and he would never hear the end of it, caught like a naughty child pilfering cakes steaming hot from

the oven. He closed his eyes, shutting out the mesmerising sight, but her image remained, forged into
his brain. His body shook with desire, blood rattling through his veins with relentless fury, building.

'Who's there?' The trill of her voice threaded
sharply across the water. Now he was trapped;
if he tried to move, to disappear, she would see
him and accuse him of watching her secretly. He
would have to brazen things out, pretend he had
just arrived.

'It's me.' Lussac cleared his throat, moving out
into the dappled shade so she could see him, trying
to inject a note of irritation, of disapproval into his
voice. 'I've been looking for you everywhere! Why
did you leave the camp, when I told you not to?'
He shoved his hand against his hot scalp, tetchy,
leaving silky strands of chestnut hair awry.

'I offered to fetch the water with Waleran,' Katerina said. 'Philippe knew where I was.'

She drank in the glorious details of him as if she
had forgotten what he looked like, drank them in
anew. His tall, unyielding figure, long sturdy legs
planted solidly on the bank, his lean jagged features, watching her. The generous curve of his bottom mouth, surprising in the hard set of his face.
Her pulse knocked heavily against her heart. His

cheekbones were flushed; a light sheen of sweat coated his skin. He had dispensed with his chain-mail, a green-hooded tunic clinging instead to his broad shoulders, the leather laces coming adrift at the throat to expose the corded muscles in his neck. Fawn-coloured braies encased his legs, stuck into familiar calf-length leather boots. His eyes shone over her, bore into her, the irises widening, dark-ening.

'Did you get it?' she said, hurriedly, voice thick-ening in her throat.

'What…?' Lussac frowned. He couldn't concen-trate. What was she talking about?

'The writ? Did you get the writ?' Rising out of the water, Katerina hunched her shoulders, wrap-ping bare, slender arms across her body, conscious of his penetrating gaze.

'Yes, yes,' he assured her. 'I have it safe.'

'That's good news.' She smiled doubtfully. 'Isn't it?' A shaft of sunlight pierced the shifting green canopy of leaves above, struck down on her fig-ure, illuminating the whiteness of her shift, the peerless quality of her complexion. One side of her chemise had drifted down revealing the delectable globe of one shoulder, the pale, flawless skin. Her hair blazed like golden fire.

'It was the water,' Katerina carried on, trying to

explain across his continuing silence, 'the water, in this heat—' her face lit up '—it was too tempting. I couldn't resist.'

'I know what you mean.' He scarce knew what he said, the words cleaving like soggy wool to the roof of his mouth. The wet gauzy fabric stuck to her like a second skin, moulding lovingly to her curves. Beneath her crossed arms, he could see the push of her breast against the fabric. A warning voice shrilled loudly in his brain, but he thumped it down, smashed it to smithereens with the fist of his desire. His breath emerged in short, ragged gasps.

Katerina flinched under the intensity of his gaze. Something was not quite right. Despite the stillness of his stance, she sensed a dangerous tension running through him, a wildness. Her heart trembled. The air thickened, stretched tight; even the birds fell silent, as if anticipating the approaching storm.

'I thought I had a bit more time,' she continued shyly, shivering a little as the water swept around her waist, tugged at her chemise. Her voice seemed overly loud, booming out over the rippling chuckle of the river. 'Could you throw my tunic over to me?' She pointed at the small heap on the shingle, hoping to deflect the potency of his gaze. 'I'll come out now.' Nudging her feet over the sharp little stones, she took a tentative step forwards, arms wedged firmly across her bosom. Rivulets of water coursed down her body as she rose from the river, leaving the soaking cloth clinging to her narrow ribs, her flat belly, the flaring curve of her hips.

'For God's sake, stay where you are!' Lussac growled, jerking his eyes away roughly. Snatching up her tunic, he waded into the shallows to shove the cloth over her, as if warding her away, covering the distasteful sight of her body. As if he couldn't bear to look at her, she thought sadly.

'Why are you so angry with me?' She clutched the bulky fabric to her chest, like a shield. 'I'm sorry, Lussac, I thought you wouldn't mind me coming this far.' Tipping her neat chin up towards him, she frowned, trying to comprehend the thoughts behind his stern expression. Her eyes were pale grey, the colour of a dove's wing. A single droplet of water ran down her cheek, resting on the pink lush fullness of her upper lip.

Lussac shook his head at her words, the shallow water running over his boots, darkening the leather. Only a few inches separated them; he could smell the freshness of her skin, the faintest scent of rose petals rising from her wet cascading tresses. A thousand reasons teemed within his brain, reasons to stop, reasons to carry on. He stopped reasoning. 'I'm not angry, Katerina,' His voice swung over her, a velvety caress, rough with desire.

'What then? What is it?' She reached across, fingers curling around his arm.

Beneath her touch his body loosened, ruptured. 'This.'

His big hands seized her shoulders, closing the small distance between them, pulled her tight up against him, hard. In the distance, thunder rumbled.

She gasped out loud; the rugged muscles of his chest crushed against her. Sensations tumbled over her: the smell of leather, of smoke; the overwhelming closeness of him. Her blood began to race, pick up speed. His fingers clamped around her upper arms, supporting her. She knew now, she knew what was about to happen; she sensed it in the tough, rigid stance of his body, in the fathomless depths of his eyes, the rawness of his expression.

His mouth brushed against her hair, his voice hoarse, unsteady. She heard his sigh. 'Push me away, Katerina, stop me, before it's too late.'

She should. She should shove at his chest, beat at his shoulders and fight for her freedom, break out from the strong prison of his arms. But as her brain rapidly erected barriers, her body cleaved towards him, traitorously. Ligaments sagged like wet rope, weak, the immediacy, the nearness of him fuelling flickers of desire, new-born, untried, deep in her belly. He had kissed her before and found her lacking; she was under no illusions.

'I cannot push you away,' she breathed, tilting her face up to his. 'I will not.' She wanted this, she wanted *him*.

He groaned, the sound of raw need echoing around this magical, shade-dappled place. His muscular frame shuddered against her. As he gathered her close, fixed in the circle of his arms, his mouth descended, warm and pliable, fastening over hers. Desire seared through her; her fingers clawed at the fabric of his tunic, snagging, before winding around his neck, pulling him closer, instinctively.

Lussac felt her cool fingers at the back of his neck, drawing him down, nearer to her, and thought his heart would explode with the sweet sensation. Her skin was cool, fragrant and dewy; he arched back, so her slight weight fell against him, deepening the kiss. His lips moved along hers deliberately, inexorably, playing along the closed line of her mouth, inquisitive, demanding. His hands spanned the neat curve of her waist, before moving higher, one thumb grazing the soft underside of her breast.

Breath catapulted from her lungs; she tore her lips away, rocking back violently from his intimate touch, in shock, in delight?—she knew not what. How to explain the incredible feelings that coursed through her, feelings that severed conscious thought from need? 'What...' she clutched at Lussac's shoulders '...what is happening to me?'

In response, he moved one hand beneath her knees, swung her above the lilting water. The thin, threadbare linen of her shift formed the only barrier between her hip and his hand splayed out possessively. The clear taste of his breath fanned over her face. 'It hasn't happened yet,' he murmured, striding up the shallow bank with her, shouldering her easily.

Excitement ripped through her at the unspoken promise of his words, her innards liquefying. Lussac laid her down in the tall, long grass, in a place where the sun met shade, where the hot drifting grass encountered the low, overhanging branches at the side of the river. The crushed grass beneath her back tickled, releasing the delicious scent of summer, warm, languorous. She closed her eyes, trying to steady her rapid heartbeat, the breakneck rush of her blood, sensing Lussac settle alongside her.

Her eyes popped open. A rippling musculature

of chest met her stunned expression, dark whorls of hair matting the polished, unyielding surface. 'You're naked!' she squeaked. Her limbs dissolved beneath the brilliant heat of his gaze, diamond blue.

His hand shook as he placed his palm flat in the middle of her belly. Flames of desire shot out from the spot, greedy, demanding, a tumultuous whirl-pool of sensation that made her gasp with delight. Melting beneath his touch, her whole body lost grip on reality, the ropes tying her to the shores of reason, of logic, fraying rapidly, unravelling. She was adrift. The river, the fields, her life—all were consumed, devoured by that simple touch.

He moved over her then, folding her into him, his hands in the glorious tumble of her hair, his mouth kissing the smooth skin of her forehead, her cheeks. Her diaphragm contracted, squeezed tight with delicious awareness, exhilaration leaping through her veins, pulsing through her heart. She wanted to scream out loud at the glorious sensation of his body, his hard, sinewy length against hers, chest against chest, hip against hip. His questing fingers worked their way down the slim column of her neck, nudging her delicate collar-bone, scorch-ing along her body, down, down until she thought she would explode beneath his touch, the pulsating storm of need building forcefully within her.

His hand caressed her hip, lifting the damp hem of her chemise. Warm air fluttered against her bare satiny skin, as his mouth captured hers once more, tongue plunging, exploring deep as he eased into her, slowly. Her body went taut, rigid, all sense of reason deserting her; she clung to his face, latching on to the feral glitter of eyes; her breath, her heart strung out with passion, vanquished. She made a small sound, a gasp of longing, of desire, moving her hands to his shoulders, then around to the muscular rope of his spine, clasping him closer.

He heard that faint sound, the sound that broke down the last fragile barrier of his self-restraint, the promise to move slowly with her, to go easy. He surged into her, overtaken by a passion so exquisite that he lost all control. The brief resistance of her innocence checked him momentarily, before he buried himself in her, wholly, utterly. He moved within her, measured and slow at first and she began to move with him, the pale, slender column of her legs wrapped around his thighs, his calves, thick ropes of muscle. Katerina shuddered beneath him, marvelling at the swelling, eddying fullness within her, her fingers digging into the solid flesh of his back, his skin slicked with sweat. She closed her eyes, matching the increasing pace of his rhythm with a delighted eagerness of her own, feeling no pain at the loss of her virginity, but only pleasure, sweet, undiluted pleasure, building slowly, layer upon ecstatic layer to a point where she thought her heart would burst. Her flesh burned, hummed beneath his powerful thrusts, spiralling higher and higher, stretching taut. Ripples of desire began to roll through her body, gathering, threatening to consume her— nay, to overcome her! The man above her drove the very breath from her body as she clung to him, helpless, blinding flashes of light sparkling through her, cascading down in a shower of stars.

She cried out then, as Lussac surged into her one final time, and the delicate, straining bubble that had held them together in thrall, swelled suddenly, then burst, ripping through them both with blistering violence, flooding glorious waves of desire through their exhausted, wrung-out bodies, spent. Lussac collapsed across her, breath in tatters, his body heavy, sated and alive.

Stunned, they lay there, bodies tangled across the scorched, flattened circle of grass. Hidden by tall, waving seed-heads, the beat of their blood slackened. Above their heads, a buzzard wheeled and circled, calling, a strange hollow cry across the sun-soaked land. Yet grey billowing clouds, great frothy lumps began to veil the sun, slowly eating into the patch of bright blue; a storm was imminent.

Katerina had no wish to move, no wish to disturb the delicious heaviness of the man sprawled across her, his sturdy frame pinning her to the earth; she relished it. If only this moment could last for ever, the powerful muscle of his legs entwined with her own, the reassuring thump of his heart against the roundness of her breast. Her body quivered, thrummed from their love-making; how could she have known, predicted even, that a man and a woman, together, could find such ecstasy? Katerina smiled, hugging the blissful memory close, tucking it near to her heart. She would never forget.

Slumped across Katerina like some uncouth lout, fingers embedded in the silken coils of her hair, Lussac knew he should move. But to move would be to admit what he had done and he wasn't sure he wanted to face up to his own failings, not yet. Opening his eyes, he stared grimly at the squashed grass stalks a few inches from his face, flecks of floating seed brushing his lashes. Katerina's cheek pressed against his, peachy skin rasped by his rough, prickly bristles; the pliable curve of her bosom nudged his chest.

Could he admit to himself what had actually happened? He couldn't quite believe it himself. In the past he had slept with countless beautiful women—why had this encounter been so very different? Because this time, he had lost control. For one single, glorious, unstoppable moment, he had forgotten who he was. The man he had been, a man stricken by trauma, beset by haunting, brutal memories—that man had vanished. And this maid, this beautiful, unconventional maid had done that for him. She had given herself to him freely, of her own volition, and he had taken her, fed on her, like some animal, all-consuming, greedy. What was it about her that drew him towards her, again and again? Shame stabbed through him, freezing his heart, locking up his feelings in a deep vault of guilt—how could he have done this to her?

With a whispered curse, he rolled away from her and sprang to his feet, dragging on his braies, his boots. The curious heavy light from the sky shone down on the plane of his chest, the firm expanse of his belly. Katerina propped herself up on one elbow, her red-gold hair spilling out over the ground around her, trying to see the expression on his face. He dragged on his shirt, then his tunic, slinging his belt haphazardly around his waist.

Sitting up, wrapping her chemise around her naked body, Katerina hugged her knees. She watched his resentful, dissatisfied actions with a dismal, fading heart. What had she hoped for? That in the act of making love she would change him, make him desire her? Humiliation flooded through her veins; she had exposed herself to him, eager and vulnerable in her innocence, and now she would have to endure his disdain, his dismissal of her.

'Eager to leave?' Katerina said scathingly. Only her quick wit could protect her now. 'I knew you'd be like this.' She flinched at the savage blurt of her own words—she had made it sound as if she'd planned their love-making.

Her unexpected words astonished him. He stopped buckling his belt, staring down at her. 'Like what?'

Katerina hugged her knees. 'You've kissed me before and found me lacking, remember? So what did you expect when you made love to me? I'm still the same person.'

'Found you lacking?' he repeated dumbly. He had no idea what she was talking about.

'That's what I said. I'm under no misconception.'

She laughed, the sound brittle, self-conscious, the words gouging a foul taste in her mouth. 'I know I'm not to most men's taste.' Better for him to realise that he owed her nothing, was not responsible for her actions. She had been fully aware of what was about to happen, what *had* happened.

'Have you completely lost your wits, Katerina?' Fully dressed now, Lussac hunkered down, balancing beside her on the balls of his feet. He threw her a brief smile, but his eyes looked hollow, bleak.

She was waiting for him to turn his back on her, to stalk off, so this approach was unexpected. 'No,' she replied, doubt shredding her voice, 'but I know what I am.'

A few drops of rain splattered down at the field edge, spotting the dry earth. A sift of air lifted through the trees, gaining strength. 'And what is that?' he asked.

'Do I really have to say?' She arched one fine eyebrow in his direction. 'I'm too short, too thin, too wayward.' She drew a deep shaky breath, a fine blush seeping over her cheeks, smoothing her hands tremulously over her lap.

He was shaking his head. 'You have no idea, do you? My God, Katerina, you are beautiful, don't you realise?' She squinted up at him, not understanding. Lussac took a deep, unsteady breath, reaching up to cup her cheek in his warm, rough palm. 'I cannot keep my hands off you; it's me who should be apologising.'

'Why?' A warm, rosy glow swept through her frame; he thought she was beautiful. Hope fluttered, rising above her on fragile wings, suspended.

'I took advantage of you,' he murmured. His hand dropped and he stood up, the movement abrupt, awkward. 'It should never have happened.'

'But I don't understand…' Katerina clambered to her feet, his brutal words dashing her down once more. A vast sadness swept over her; she had been so certain he felt nothing for her, but here he was telling her he was attracted to her, yet he shouldn't have lain with her. In his last words, she had dared to hope, to dream that there might be something more to their lovemaking than a tumble in the grass. It seemed she might have dared too much. Her heart collapsed in on itself, shrouded in grief.

'Lussac, listen to me.' She thumped at his shoulder. 'I knew what I was doing…' The air around them had turned cold, the rain intensifying, gathering strength. Katerina shivered.

'You should have pushed me away.' The rich melodious timbre of his voice swept over her, condemned her.

'Why?' she cried out unhappily. The rain sluiced

over her face, hanging from her dark lashes, diamond drops. 'Why, when it was the most beautiful thing I have ever experienced in my life? Why would I push you away, Lussac? Why?'

Her simple speech knocked the breath from his lungs. He had never heard a woman speak thus, with such raw, blinding truth, such clarity. Did she honestly mean what she said? He stared at her forlorn figure through the slanting rain, the strengthening wind pinning gauzy folds to her perfect curves, to the body she had so willingly given to him. His heart twisted in shame. Every word she spoke merely strengthened the bonds between them, the stiffening ties that he had to break, had to cut loose from, if either of them were to survive at all.

'Because I can give you nothing more, Katerina.'

She heard the dullness in his tone, read the hollowness in his eyes. She stretched up her arm, cupping the chiselled plane of his jaw, her thumb stroking across his wet cheek. Against the roar of the rain, the wind, she caught his sharp intake of breath, before his hand snaked up, fingers snaring her narrow wrist, dragging her hand downwards, away.

'What happened to you, Lussac, to make you lose your heart?'

Chapter Fifteen

He told her nothing. As the rain flattened the grass around them, thick stalks splaying out like broken bones in disarray, the branches churning wildly at their backs, she had searched his impassive face for answers, found none. He had turned away from her, ordering her to dress, to hurry up, and she had run, staggered, her body still weak and shaken from their lovemaking, back beneath the shelter of the trees to fetch her clothes.

And now she followed him, broken-hearted, half-stumbling, as he forged across the fields in quick powerful strides, back towards the abbey. Tears ran openly down her face, mingled with the rain; she could taste the salt on her lips. She didn't care. He didn't want her; that much was obvious. He had told her she was beautiful, but that belief faded rapidly, faded with every step away from the river.

She felt used, discarded, but she only had herself to blame.

He stopped so violently at the abbey walls that she ran into the back of him, thumped heavily into the thick rope of his spine. She sprang away from the contact as if she had been burned.

'I...I had...' Unsure what to do, she twisted her head awkwardly in the direction of the castle, the tents, the canvas caving in precariously against the driving rain, wanting to be away from him, to slink away and lick her wounds in private.

'There's not much point in wasting any more time here,' he muttered savagely, raindrops sluicing down over his tanned, carved features. 'I have the writ and I have you, so we may as well start riding north. Go and fetch your things—a cloak if you have one.' Expression impassive, unreadable, he glanced up at the leaden sky. 'This weather is not going to let up.'

His words burned, scoured into her. She glared at him, arms locking across her chest. Is that how he viewed their lovemaking? As a 'waste of time'? It was as if he ground her into the mud with the heel of his boot, acting as if nothing had happened between them, as if, moments earlier, they had not been rolling together in the hot grass, breathing in the sweet, heady scent of each other's bodies, naked, abandoned. Her body shuddered, involuntarily, recalling the hard, sinewy imprint of his limbs upon her own. The delicious ecstasy.

'Go on,' he barked at her, as she failed to move. The rain poured down her face, dripping off her chin, the soft, downy lobes of her ears. Ears that he had touched his lips to. His eyes, chips of turquoise, focused on an insignificant spot over her head, willing the flames of desire that coursed his big frame to die down, fizzle out.

A squall of rain splattered heavily on to the cobbles beside them; water sloshed across the cobbles, darkening the toes of their boots. 'Why are you being like this?' Katerina flung at him, wanting to punch, to lash out at his solid, impenetrable chest, wanting to collapse to the ground and sob. 'Why are you being so cruel?'

He heard the sadness in her voice and hated her for it. Guilt crawled in his belly. He had taken her innocence, nay, robbed her of it, ruined her. 'Stop it, Katerina. I'm not worth it; I'm not worth crying over.' His gaze blazed down over her, over her sodden tunic that clasped lovingly to her slender curves, her rounded bosom.

'I'm not crying,' she spat out like a wounded kitten, blinking away the slashing rain that threatened to obscure her vision. She would not allow him to destroy, to wreck the beautiful memory of their lovemaking. By parcelling it up tight, and tucking it up deep into her heart, she would hold on to that, at least.

'This is who I am, Katerina.' His harsh tone barrelled into her. Didn't she realise that by pushing her away, he was doing her a favour? His blackened soul was no good for her. He would drag that bright, spirited light from her, douse it and pull her down to the cold, soulless level of his existence. He couldn't do that to her. He wouldn't do that to her. Better that she knew now what kind of man he was; better to remain aloof and cold to her, and suppress all feelings of desire towards her.

Katerina was shaking her head, spinning rain drops around her glowing hair, eyes wide and luminous. 'I don't believe you,' she whispered. 'I've seen a different kind of man.' A man who had helped her when she was down, caught by those horrible men. And who helped her again now, with the writ from the Queen. The rising whine of the wind forced him to lean down to catch her words. Above her head, a solitary crow, its wingtips frayed black against the lumpy, grey sky, struggled to remain airborne in the strengthening gusts of wind.

'It's the truth, Katerina. What do you think I'm going to do when we reach Longthorpe? Have a civilised dinner and chat with your father about your marriage? I'm going for other reasons, other selfish reasons, Katerina, you know that.'

'What reasons?' she asked in a small voice. 'You have never told me why you want to go to Longthorpe.'

Lussac circled her wrist with strong fingers, pushed her sleeve up her pale forearm, exposing the leather cuff. The etched silver discs glimmered in the dim light. 'Where do you think I found your family's cuff, Katerina?' His voice was raw.

She reeled back at the flick of savage desperation in his eyes, every fragile hair on her skin lifting in acknowledgement of his near, dynamic presence, responding to the sheer energy pouring from him in waves. Fighting to keep her breath steady, she held her frame perfectly still, bracing her legs astride, as if preparing for a blow. 'Tell me,' she whispered, heart thumping dangerously.

'My family home is…was on the borderlands between English-held Gascony and France.' Lussac sighed, pushing the wet hair out of his eyes, searching for the right way to tell her. 'There's constant fighting between the two sides; the King of France wants Gascony back as he feels that the English hold it unlawfully. My father's main job was to patrol the borderlands and keep the fighting under a modicum of control.' Lussac spoke in a monotone, his voice dull, emotionless. 'I was away, training as a knight in Paris, but due home on leave. A ceasefire was in operation, an agreement drawn up between my father and the English nobles, and to all intents and purposes it was working.' His eyes shuttered momentarily, dark lashes fanning his high cheekbones. 'But someone, some bastard English nobleman, broke that ceasefire and rode to my parent's castle one night.'

He paused, a muscle leaping in his jaw, eyes flaring like hot coals in his stern, rigid features. His hair stuck flat to his scalp, darkened by rain to ebony, emphasising the sculptural set of his head, the fine, chiselled bones of his face.

'What happened?' Katerina's wet fingers curled over his, her breath caught in her chest.

His fingers tightened on hers. 'They torched the place. My family—father, mother, sister—none of them had a chance. They died of smoke inhalation, locked in their chambers at the top of the castle. The fire died out before reaching them; it was the smoke that killed them.' He remembered his desperate rush up the stairs, round and round that dizzying stairwell, until he reached the bed-chambers.

'Locked in?' she murmured, horrified.

'Locked in,' he repeated grimly, a muscle tensing in his jaw. 'Whoever did this to them, this murderer, locked them into their rooms before starting the fire. He wanted them to die.'

'And the cuff?' she prompted in a small voice, a burning sadness gathering in the pit of her stomach. So that explained the haunted shadows in his eyes…the shuttering of his emotions…his coldness. He had lost so much.

'Clutched in my sister's hand. When she realised what was happening, when they were being locked in, she must have fought back and grabbed at whatever she could to reveal the murderer's identity.' His sister's fingers had been cold, rigid, as he peeled them back to reveal the leather cuff. Lussac's eyes pinned on Katerina's, waiting for her to make the connection. She would have to know, some time.

'Oh, my God, Lussac. I am so sorry.' Her fingers loosened from his and she wrapped both her arms around him without thinking, wanting to appease his hurt, to lessen his pain somehow. Her fingers laced at his spine, hugging him tight, hugging him against her. A gesture of comfort, of acknowledgement. Lussac reeled in shock at the close contact, the heat from her slim frame permeating the icy stiffness of his body. In trying to ward her away from him, he had only succeeded in pulling her closer.

'I am so sorry you had to lose your family in that way,' she mumbled deep against his chest. For a moment he allowed himself to soak up the warmth of her embrace, knowing he should shake her off, his arms moving with their own volition around her back. But what his mind suggested, his traitorous body dismissed, revelling in her delicate hold, the solid circle of her slim arms. Her touch flowed through him, easing his fractured heart, knitting the charred dregs of his soul.

He waited.

Her head knocked back suddenly from his chest, eyes wide, horrified. 'You think it was my father!'

He stared down at her, searching her face, the reddened curve of her bottom lip. His upper arms cradled her shoulders. 'Someone from your family was there, Katerina. And that someone murdered my family.'

'No….no…!' She staggered back at his blunt revelation, out, out of the hold of his arms, her face stricken, horrified. 'You think that my father…?' She clutched at her throat, her face pearly-white in the rain.

'Or your uncle,' he supplied. 'One of them, I suspect.'

'Lussac, it can't be true? Can it?' The words tumbled from her lips, erratic, anxious. She shivered, the soaking dampness beginning to crawl down her neck.

Lussac grimaced. This is what he wanted, wasn't it? To drive her away, before she became too involved, too entangled with his damaged soul? 'Believe it, Katerina. Someone in your family is responsible for their deaths. By travelling to Longthorpe, I'll discover who it is.'

Her body recoiled with the cruel punch of his speech, as if he had taken a weapon to her, and he hated it. Hated what he was doing to her with his words, wished he could have spared her the truth. But she had to know everything now.

'And whoever is responsible deserves to die, Katerina.' Screwing up his eyes against the driving rain, he glared at her slumped, wilting figure. 'Now do you understand? This is the kind of man I am.'

Blotches of colour high on her cheeks, Katerina turned and ran from him. Ran away from Lussac, his broad-shouldered silhouette like a statue in the cascading rain, staring after her as she slid and stumbled across the slippery cobbles, as she sought refuge beneath the makeshift security of canvas. All the tents were empty, deserted, the troupe having sought all the warmth and food that the monks could offer them in the great hall. She collapsed on to her knees on the coarse rug, pressing her hands over her eyes, horrified, distraught by Lussac's revelations. How could her family be involved? She couldn't explain it, couldn't work out how her family cuff had ended up in France. Every bone in her body screamed out to her that Lussac could not be capable of such a heinous crime, to kill someone in cold blood like that, but did she really know him at all? Her cheeks flamed with the vivid memory of their lovemaking, the hot sultry afternoon and the tenderness she had witnessed in his eyes—it seemed like a dream: a beautiful, magical vision, a chimera.

Breath clutched at her chest; she had read the pain in his eyes, seen the utter desolation, the tortured loss. What Lussac had suffered was truly horrific—what man wouldn't want revenge after such a hideous act? But surely he realised that killing another would not help him, wouldn't replace the family that he'd lost? He was a broken man, she could see that now, but a broken man who was capable of healing.

Hands dropping from her eyes, Katerina took a deep, shuddery breath. This afternoon had been a mistake, on his part, at least. He had made that clear in no uncertain terms; his treatment of her in the aftermath of their lovemaking had been brutal. But she would hold on to the memory, keep it close and secure. Whatever happened from now onwards, she would always have that, have a part of him to hold dear...and to love? The word whispered through her mind, suggestive, tantalising. She frowned.

Hurriedly, Katerina whipped off her soaking tunic and braies, dragging a creased gown from her satchel, shaking out the voluminous folds. She needed to make some effort to look presentable if she was to return home. Slipping the dress over her head, she winced as the movement stretched the taut skin over her injured shoulder. The round curving neckline of her faded blue underdress settled gracefully along the jutting line of her collarbone. The overdress was much looser, a darker blue with the sides hanging open to the hip to display the close fit of the gown beneath. Apart from two rows of tiny pearl buttons securing the tight-fitting sleeves, the gown was simple, with no decorative embroidery, sections of the hem sagged, threadbare.

Away from Lussac's devastating presence, she felt steadier in her mind, more able to concentrate.

She would ride with him back to her home and prove to him how wrong he was about her family, especially her father. She wasn't certain she could vouch for her uncle, couldn't think about him without a niggle of doubt, a lurch of fear at the possibility of what might have been, of how close she had come to being married off to him. Even now, she couldn't be certain that he would take any notice of the royal writ: he was as likely to rip it up as he was to obey it.

And Lussac? How would she be with him after what had happened between them? How could she cope in the grim light of his rejection? Her hands trembled as she closed up the drawstrings on her leather bag. It would be unbearable.

The stables of the abbey were an open-fronted affair: a length of wooden stalls butting up to a high wall behind. Chunky, hewn posts had been erected along the front to support the roof of sloping thatch which extended over the horses' stalls to cover an area of flat stone, providing more shelter for the animals. The numerous horses of the Queen's entourage packed the stables; the smell of jostling horseflesh, of dung and fresh hay, filled the air.

'Here, let me help you,' Waleran regarded Katerina with a worried frown. His skin stretched taut over sharp, jutting cheekbones. He pushed her fumbling fingers away from the rump of the grey palfrey and set to work attaching the small leather bag to the back of the saddle. The earlier rain had eased and a freshening breeze sifted into the stables, stirring the drifting mane of the mare, sneaking beneath the hem of Katerina's gown. Threads of loose hay danced across the tilting flagstones. 'Who's going with you?'

'Lussac, of course.' She hesitated, wondering whether she should tell him about Lussac's convictions regarding her family. What he planned to do. No, perhaps such things were better left unsaid. 'And Philippe, the Comte de Garsan. He's a good friend of Lussac's.' Her fingers played with the long trailing cords that swung from the hooded neckline of her cloak, twirling the plaited threads.

'Why, "Lussac, of course"?' Waleran's hands paused on the leather straps. 'Why couldn't the Queen send a posse of soldiers to accompany you?' She looked wretched, he thought, her face white and tired, purpling splotches of exhaustion dabbed beneath her eyes.

'Because it might take more than a posse of soldiers to convince my father and my uncle of the importance of the writ.' She raised her hand to the horse's nose, stroking the velvet softness. 'Lussac is more than capable of fulfilling that role.' As Waleran scowled, she frowned at the unspoken admiration in her own tone. Was that how she saw him, as her protector?

Waleran took a deep breath. 'What happened between you and him, Katerina? There's something going on, isn't there?' Jealousy surging through him, he gritted his teeth. He could be her friend, at least.

Her smoky eyes sheened with tears; she dashed them away, hurriedly, with the flat palm of her hand. 'Nothing happened, Waleran. Nothing of consequence, anyway.' She held herself rigid, tight, hardly breathing, trying to gain control of her unravelling emotions, searching for the anger, the resentment she wanted to feel, but instead finding only a crawling humiliation, crushed by his dismissal. He'd turned her into a mealy-mouthed, snivelling wreck and she hated him for it. *Stop it, stop this whining self-pity now,* she told herself severely. She was better than this.

'What happened?' demanded Waleran. What had that bastard done, to turn this happy, confident soul, his brave and fearless Katerina, into this bundle of dejected misery? He jerked savagely on the loosened strap, too hard, and the mare tossed her head up, eyes rolling wildly at the harsh treatment.

'I made a mistake, Waleran. A mistake that's best forgotten.' Although brittle, her voice had regained some composure. 'Let's not speak of it.' She grasped the reins hanging beneath the palfrey's chin, intending to lead the horse out into the bailey. 'It's time for me to go home.'

One glance at her stony expression told him not to pursue the subject. He could guess anyway: he knew. With a sinking heart, Waleran followed Katerina out into the breezy air, the horse's hooves clopping noisily across the greasy cobbles. She sprung from a standing position into the saddle, scissoring her legs across the horse's back.

'Astride?' Waleran teased in mock-horror, wanting to break the sombre mood between them. 'I'm not sure Queen Isabella would approve, if she caught you riding like that.' He busied himself by spreading the bulk of her cloak across the rump of the horse.

Nor my father either, Katerina thought. She tucked her gown down around her ankles, the blue linen falling in soft folds from her neat waist. For a brief moment, the haunted look left her eyes. 'It's the only way I know how,' she replied.

'The way I taught you,' Waleran said.

'Waleran, you will always be a true friend to me.' She leaned down, placing one hand on his shoulder, her bound, plaited hair shining like gold embroidery. 'I will come back, you know. After I've sorted things out with my father.'

'Nay, you won't. Once you have a taste of the high life again, you'll forget us all. '

'The high life would bore me rigid. Can you imagine me sitting in a woman's solar, embroidering all day?'

He laughed. 'You have a point. Mayhaps we will see you again, after all. We're sad to see you go. We all are.' He lifted his arms to give her a friendly hug and felt her pull back slightly, ligaments inflexible against the hard curve of his arms. For the hundredth time, he wished he had never declared his love for her. It had changed everything between them.

Chapter Sixteen

The trio of riders made good speed on their journey north-west. Lussac rode up front on his sleek muscled destrier, maintaining a fast-paced gait, while Philippe and Katerina rode behind. The earlier storm had cleared the air, the gusting wind driving the clouds away to the east, and now, even at this late hour of the afternoon, the sun shone fiercely, beating down on their necks, their faces. Katerina stared at the back of Lussac's head, miserable, heart clouded in grief. He had barely spoken two words to her since they had stood together in the slashing rain and he had told her what had happened to his family. It was if he had fenced himself off from her, shuttered down; as if, by revealing the truth about his family, he had nothing else to give.

But at least, now, Katerina understood. Understood the heartache, the pain that beat beneath his solid chest. The pain of losing everything.

She welcomed Philippe's congenial presence which acted like a balm, effectively soothing the icy tension strung like iron net between the two of them. Despite his portly stance, he demonstrated practised skill as a rider, sitting low and graceful in the saddle, and was happy to chat about this and that, whenever the horses slowed to a walk.

As the four o'clock bell rang out across the land, tolling sonorously, they had passed through the market town of Ditton, hazy in mist as the heat slowly sapped from the day. Now they followed a wide grassy drove, a man-made track banked high above the low-lying marshland. The landscape was flat, boggy, stretching into a shimmering horizon as far as the eye could see, a vast area thick with reeds and sedge, alive with the piercing call of the sparrow-hawk. Willows and alders hugged areas of visible water, drooping tendrils of thin leaves stirring the shallow pools; insects chirruped and whirred in meadows thick with flowers and grasses.

The narrowness of the drove forced their horses to walk. Seizing the opportunity, Philippe reached into the leather pouch dangling from his belt, extracting a large linen square. His sparse hair stuck chaotically to his scalp. 'Phew!' He glanced over at Katerina, strands of tawny hair floating about her flushed face, copper filaments glowing in the sun. 'I thought it was supposed to be autumn? Where did this heat come from?' He mopped his sweating face with the handkerchief, crumpling the used linen into a mass of creases.

'I'm feeling it, too.' Katerina made an effort to be friendly. But in truth she felt cold, numb, inside.

'Is the pace too fast for you? I can ask Lussac to slow down.' He nodded at the powerful, chainmail clad figure up ahead, shimmering, the silhouette blurring slightly in the heat haze.

She shook her head, violently. Her horse took advantage of the slow pace to crop at the lush, long grass of the drove, big teeth making loud, ripping noises as it tore at the vegetation.

'You're a fine horsewoman,' Philippe complimented her, his eye straying to the delectable flash of ankle on the stirrup. He grinned, his voice teasing. 'Even if you do insist on riding astride.'

Katerina adjusted her skirts so that the hem covered her slipper, smiling. Philippe was an easy companion, friendly and courteous, the ideal antidote to her lurching heart. She allowed herself to be distracted by his affable manner, welcomed it, for it drew her mind away from the man who rode up front, his manner grim and formidable. 'I'm so glad it was you who came with us,' she said, pulling on the bridle so that her palfrey walked in step beside Philippe's muscled destrier.

'I'm glad too,' Philippe replied. 'Anything to escape from the constant demands of that royal harridan.' He swivelled his head around, as if expecting to see the whole of the Queen's entourage approaching out of the hazy vista behind. 'No one said this campaign would be easy, but I'm convinced she makes it ten times more complicated.'

Katerina scarcely heard his words. Every step of their horses brought them closer to Longthorpe, closer to the inevitability of what Lussac planned to do. 'Has he told you?' She turned smoky eyes on Philippe. 'Has Lussac told you what he intends to do?'

'He plans to hand the writ to your father and tell him in no uncertain terms that any wedding to your uncle is null and void.'

Katerina raised her chin, feeling the warmth in the breeze that skittered across the land, bathing her face. 'Not that. The other thing.' She shivered, pulling her cloak more tautly around her shoulders.

'He's told you?' Philippe jerked his head back, grizzly blond eyebrows drawing together in surprise. 'Did he tell what happened? To his family?' He flicked his gaze towards Lussac, who had turned now, frowning at the distance between himself and his companions. Philippe and Katerina were lagging behind.

Below the drove, the stiff stakes of reed grass shifted, plumed heads riffling like purple feathers. 'Yes, yes, he did,' whispered Katerina. 'And I'm so sorry for it, my lord Garsan, so sad about what happened to him. But killing isn't the answer...'

'Philippe, please. You must call me Philippe. Katerina, you must speak to Lussac about this, talk to him.' He tried to pull the bulk of his hood away from his perspiring neck.

She laughed sourly, the sound breathy, truncated. 'Me? He wouldn't listen to me...' Her voice trailed off forlornly.

'Why ever not?'

'He scarce holds me in high regard, Philippe.' What could she say? That the man who rode up front, who was now riding back towards them, lay with me in the hot baking sun of an afternoon and made love to me so thoroughly that I forgot who I was, or who I had ever been. He loved me in such a way that I now cannot think straight, my senses rattled. I cannot bear it. I want to be with him, but he cannot stand the sight of me. I want to hate him, but all I can do is love him.

Love. The word knocked against the side of her brain like a bell, shocking, vivid and inexplicable. Was that what she truly felt towards him? Was it love?

A brimstone butterfly snagged her gaze; she followed its haphazard, illogical flight, the yellow wings glowing, sulphurous against the dull green reeds, her mind ripe with memories, crowded with questions. How could she put into words how she felt? For to speak of it would make it a reality and that would make it all the harder to bear.

'I think you are wrong, Katerina. I think he would listen to you.'

She shrugged her shoulders.

'For years he's been locked up in a circle of filthy, black guilt,' Philippe explained gently. 'He was due home on leave from the French court, but he stayed a while, dallying with friends. He was young, enjoying the life of a single man. He blames himself for not returning home earlier, for he feels if he had done so, then his family would still be alive. He would have been there to help them defend the castle against the English. He would have been able to save them.' Philippe squinted, his stubby blond lashes spiking against the baggy hollows beneath his eyes, his gaze travelling across the horizon. 'But for the first time since that terrible thing happened, I have seen a change in Lussac. We only landed a few days ago, but already there's something different about him.'

Excitement coiled slowly in Katerina's chest. What was he saying?

'In what way?' she spoke carefully. She was tempted to push the flicker of hope away.

Philippe shrugged his shoulders, grinned over at her. 'You're asking me, a man, to describe such a thing? It's only a feeling I have, a tiny shift in his behaviour.'

'It's nothing to do with me.'

'It has everything to do with you.'

'Come on, you two! Why are you lagging behind?' Lussac barked at them as he rode up at a fast gallop. His horse slid to a stop in front of them, snorting fitfully from rounded nostrils, enormous hooves carving great gashes in the dry earth. Despite wearing chainmail, Lussac's head was bare and fronds of his chestnut hair spiked wayward. Like Philippe, he was wearing the Queen's colours once more, the dark-blue tunic emblazoned with gold fleur-de-lys, which hugged his powerful shoulders and smoothed down over his lean, flat stomach, before the cloth split at mid-thigh. Gripping his bulky thigh muscles to control the horse, he swept his gaze immediately to Katerina.

Her small face was pale, features tight and closed. Her bound hair looked uncomfortable, as if it pulled too tight against her scalp. His fingers itched to release those glowing locks, to scatter those cruel long hairpins to the ground and allow the rose-scented tresses to spill over her shoulders, tumble down her spine. Her hair would be like cool silk against his fingers. He took a breath, feeling his lungs shudder with the effort. Dark smudges beneath her eyes mocked him; he had promised her a decent meal and a proper bed for the night at Bury St Edmunds, but what had he done instead? Propelled by his own guilt, he had whisked her away from the scene of the crime, the scene of *his* crime, when he had taken her innocence by a slow-flowing river.

She didn't deserve this; she didn't deserve him. Not after everything else she had been through.

'You need some rest,' he muttered in Katerina's direction. 'We need to find somewhere to stop.'

'What? Really?' Philippe piped up. 'I thought we would have a solid roof over our heads tonight. Surely Longthorpe cannot be that far away?' He glanced at Katerina, wanting her to supply the finer details, to fill in the blanks of the route.

'It isn't far, Lussac,' she agreed with Philippe, tucking a wayward strand of gilded hair behind her ear. The dropping sun highlighted the fine porcelain of her skin, the silver fire of her eyes. Sitting astride her horse, the skirt of her gown had gathered in soft folds around her legs, emphasising the rounded muscles of her thighs beneath.

'How far exactly?' he asked.

Katerina looked about her, trying to pinpoint any recognisable parts of the countryside. It had been so long since she had been home that the landscape now felt unfamiliar to her. Up ahead, a church spire loomed into view. Possibly the village at Hambridge? she wondered. 'About ten miles, I think,' she replied, finally.

'Ten miles!' Lussac narrowed his eyes on her; under his close scrutiny she shifted uncomfortably in the saddle. 'Have you any idea how long that will take us? We won't reach there before midnight, at least. Katerina, you need to sleep and to have something to eat… I can't even remember the last time you ate anything.

'Since when have you been so concerned about my well-being?' she flashed back at him, frowning, one thumb rubbing inadvertently along the reins.

Since I met you. Since I followed your darting, quicksilver figure through the forest on that very first day. Since I flipped you over on to your back and stared into your frightened, furious expression.

Lussac ducked his head, away from the vivid intensity of her haughty stare, scowling at the frothing black mane of his horse. 'You need something to eat, Katerina. So do I. I'm sure Philippe does as well.' He glanced over meaningfully at his friend. 'And I'm tired,' he added, for good measure.

Katerina stared at him, suspiciously.

'Ah, yes,' Philippe agreed, dampening down any thought of a comfortable bed for the night after reading the intention in Lussac's eyes. 'Ten miles is far too long to ride. We need to find a place to stop. In fact, my stomach is rumbling as we speak.'

Lussac was doing it for her, Katerina thought. He was doing it to be kind, nothing more, nothing less. And Philippe, bless his heart, was playing along for her benefit. She was certain neither of them were actually hungry. And Lussac couldn't have looked less tired if he tried. His long, lean body shed energy as he sat in the saddle, every muscle tense, alert, as if poised for action.

* * *

As the rosy hues of evening deepened to twilight, the sun sinking slowly towards the western horizon, Lussac rode towards a copse of beech, situated oddly on a shallow rise. 'This will do,' he called out across the flat expanse of field, indicating with his raised arm that Katerina and Philippe should join him. Behind the fiery colour of the beech leaves, a new moon, a narrow sliver against a dark-blue sky, rose gradually.

'Is it damp?' Philippe asked doubtfully, as he reined his horse in next to Lussac's under the trees and jumped down, thick boots sinking into the thick carpet of fallen leaves. He turned around, intending to help Katerina dismount, but she had jumped down already.

'No, but we need to build a shelter,' Lussac announced, his turquoise gaze trailing over Katerina's wan features, before switching back to Philippe.

She caught the look between the two men. 'There's no need to build anything on my account,' she announced, looking up at the sky. The vast dome of midnight blue was gradually filling with stars, tiny piercing diamonds of light. 'It's not going to rain tonight and it's not cold. I'll be fine with a blanket in front of a fire—you forget, I am used to this, sleeping outside.'

Sleeping outside, like a common vagrant. Lussac hated the thought of this delicate girl living rough, vulnerable to every kind of miscreant that happened along. He wanted her to be safe, in a stone-walled chamber, with a charcoal brazier burning snugly in the corner. He wanted to do that for her. To protect her from harm. But how could he do that when he had failed to protect his own family?

'We'll light a fire then,' he replied, agreeing with her. Katerina was right; she would be warm enough with a blanket. He moved around the space, collecting a few spindly sticks, a heap of dried moss to act as kindling, his graceful stride sweeping the deep waves of dark gold leaves in his wake. Katerina stood by her horse, unsure, feeling the animal's warm breath fan out over her shoulder as she watched him. He crouched down in front of the collected pile and took out a flint, striking a spark, holding it quickly within his curved hands to light the dry kindling. Immediately a flame took hold, growing fast, eating greedily into the dry sticks.

The firelight bathed the carved beauty of his face in an amber glow: the high cheekbones, clefted beneath with shadow, the curved upward flick of his eyebrows. He began to pile bigger pieces of wood on; lumpy, knobbled pieces covered in pale-green lichen sizzled and spat as he placed them over the flames in a criss-cross fashion.

'Here, I managed to filch some food from the monastery,' Philippe declared, bustling over from where he had been rummaging in his saddle-bags. 'Enough to fill our bellies, at least.' He spread a large woollen rug out beside the fire. 'Katerina, come and sit, please.'

She moved woodenly, stumbling through the drift of leaves, to sink down gratefully on to Philippe's rug. Across the flames, Lussac shifted his position, leaning against the tree trunk at his back, one arm resting on his upraised knee. His eyes glittered, searching her face.

'Have some bread, some cheese.' Philippe gestured across the spread of food that he'd laid out on the rug. 'Here…' He handed a parcel of food to Lussac.

'You seem to have filched quite a lot,' Lussac remarked drily, a smile touching the corners of his lips. His friend's ability to find food was renowned.

'At least enough for tonight and tomorrow morning as well,' Philippe announced proudly. 'And then once we reach Longthorpe, we might have a decent meal?' He raised his eyebrows in question towards Katerina.

She swallowed a knob of bread hurriedly, the doughy mass sticking to the sides of her gullet. 'I'm not entirely sure what will happen when we reach Longthorpe,' she admitted, an edge of doubt creeping into her voice. To her utter dismay, her hand shook as she reached out for a chunk of cheese and she drew her fingers back quickly, hoping no one had seen.

Lussac watched as Katerina snatched her hand back, hiding her trembling fingers in her lap. Something shifted within him, something deep and primeval. She was scared stiff of going home, frightened at what lay ahead.

'The Queen's writ carries a lot of weight,' Philippe commented benignly. 'I'm sure it won't be as bad as you think.' He munched contentedly on an apple.

Katerina filled her lungs with woody, moss-scented air. 'It will be if Lussac intends to kill a member of my family, Philippe. It will be very bad.' She glared pointedly at Lussac's sword, gleaming out from the cushion of leaves.

Philippe cleared his throat.

Caught in the silver magic of Katerina's eyes, snared by that silken net of glorious hair, Lussac jumped at her sharp words. They scoured into him, flaying his skin. He sprang up, moving swiftly over to his horse, guilt coursing over him in waves, black, churning waves. Lost in the enchantment of Katerina's beauty, he had forgotten, forgotten the iron-clad promise uttered over the fallen bodies of his family; now, his own words creaked and loosened, like the shedding of stiff, tight armour. Was it her? Had she done this to him?

'Lussac?' She was there, standing by him. A shimmering angel, his salvation. He wanted to reach out to her, and draw her in, draw on all her light, and warmth, and heart. 'I speak the truth, don't I? It's what you intend to do.'

Aye, it was what he had intended to do. Curious that his thoughts ran through his mind in the past tense. A spinning leaf, falling, brushed past her ear, landing on her shoulder. He flicked it away, waiting for the customary anger to rise in his gullet, the black bile of fury to rise up against her at her intrusive words, but strangely his heart felt light, lighter than it had in years. All he was aware of was Katerina, standing before him, her pearly white skin, dewy in the dusky evening, the pale flame of her hair.

'It's just that killing someone who you think is responsible is wrong,' she stumbled on, unnerved by his silence, trying to explain. 'And I'm not saying this because you think it might be my father, or my uncle, who did this. Killing for revenge does not help anyone.'

'It will help me.' The words lurched awkwardly from his mouth. Did he really believe what he was saying any more?

'Will it? It won't bring your family back.'

She heard the clutch of breath in his chest and wondered if she had dared too much. Reaching out, she laid a hand on his sleeve. 'Lussac, I can see how you lost your spirit; I can see how the loss of your family eats you up inside, but please, please, don't do this. You will never find your heart again if you do this.'

Held in her quiet, metallic gaze, Lussac was astounded by the forceful clarity of Katerina's speech, her boldness. No one had ever, ever spoken to him about his family like this. They wouldn't have dared. Only a few days ago, he would have struck out at anyone who said such things, but now, feeling the soft clutch of her fingers on his arm, the fires of revenge began to wither and die. His constricted heart slackened, then eased.

'Katerina…' He stumbled to find the correct words to explain, to tell her. Overhead, the breeze sifted through the branches, lifting them, rustling.

A shower of golden leaves burst down over them and over Philippe's seated figure poking industriously at the fire, pretending not to listen. 'I have lived with this thing for so long…and I am so close, so close to finding my family's murderer.' His voice was so low, she had to lean forwards to catch his words.

'I know…and I understand,' she said quietly. 'But do you have to kill him?'

He turned away from her, away from the sweet rose-scented fragrance of her skin, her limpid dove-grey eyes, and fumbled in the half-darkness for the straps on the back of his horse that held his blanket roll in place. This maid was turning the whole reason for him being in this country on its head. He felt unbalanced, topsy-turvy.

'But that's what I came here for, Katerina. If I step away from this, then I let my family down. They deserve more than that. Deserve more than a son who forgets and walks away,' he replied, hauling the thick blanket savagely from the back of the horse.

'Do you really think they would agree with what you are doing?' Katerina held her breath; she was taking a chance.

His mind reeled back: his mother, ebony hair falling in a shining plait over one shoulder, walking through the walled gardens of his home, drenched in sunlight, his sister skipping alongside, clutching her arm. He was walking behind, inhaling the fragrant scent of the roses, the swaying pine trees overhead. Arms linked, the pair of them, smiling, turned in unison, skirts swirling out, calling towards him, laughing. He couldn't recall the words. Deep in his heart, he knew the answer: no, they would not agree with what he was doing; both of them had an astounding capacity to forgive. His mother would even give chambers in the castle over to injured English soldiers, brought in from the battle-lines and left for dead by their own people. She would treat them and nurse them back to health.

With every fibre of his being, he wanted to tell Katerina that everything would be fine, but he could not. He would not lie to her, make false promises. She deserved more than that. He had lived with this *thing,* this pall of guilt, for too long; it was part of him now, part of his character. His fingers dug into the woollen blanket, held against his chest.

'A better person might give you the answer you want to hear, Katerina, but I am not that kind of man, do you understand?' His voice sounded hollow, echoing beneath the trees. The sky had darkened considerably, the only light emanating from the flickering flames of the fire. He sighed, running one hand through his hair, silky spikes standing on end. 'You're giving me qualities that I cannot live up to, setting the bar too high.'

'No—' she shook her head, eyes dark and twinkling '—no, I am not. You're a good man, Lussac. You're good and kind…and loving.' Her heart seized, clenched with a sear of desire. He had shown her so much, so much of the man he was capable of being. Her fingers drifted upwards, rested along the side of his jaw. Had she said enough?

Her words shot into his brain, like an arrow of fire. Did she really believe that, especially after what had happened between them? Did she really believe that he was a good man? 'Katerina, don't pin your hopes on me, please.' He shoved the blanket into her chest with such a force that she staggered back, dropping her hand from his cool skin to grasp at the bundle. 'Get some sleep. I can promise you nothing.'

Originally, Longthorpe Manor existed as a priory, thick walls of grey Barnack limestone built by the monks on the only piece of raised land for miles around. Over the years, the boggy ground around the fortified manor, with its three-storey, crenellated tower, had been gradually reclaimed with a series of hand-dug drainage channels. The resulting pastureland was rich, fertile, producing excellent crops, grain and root vegetables; the few poorer areas of soil with their thin, spindly grass were used for grazing sheep and cattle.

At first, Katerina could not be certain whether the darker patch on the horizon was her family home or not, but as the three of them plodded steadily northwards the next morning, frothy white clouds scudding across a turquoise sky, she began to discern familiar shapes: the solar tower with its wooden, conical roof and the gleam of slate from the lower building alongside which contained the main living quarters. The glass in the windows blazed in the sunlight, red, orange, as if they were on fire.

Her heart leapt, then plummeted, as she focused on Lussac's straight rigid back up ahead. After her dramatic plea last night, he had been quiet, rolling himself into his blanket and staring blankly into the golden flames. Had her impassioned speech meant anything to him? He had given her no clue. This morning, as they had cleared the camp, Philippe stamping out the charred embers with one great boot, he had been taciturn, mouth set in a grim line. She was glad of Philippe's chirpy presence as he was happy to chat and comment on just about everything, leaving her little time to brood.

She wondered how her father would react to her appearance. It had been over a year now—would he be happy to see her, or angry? He had changed so much after her mother had died, his character withering, folding in on itself, as if a significant part of him had followed her mother to the grave. His moods had become unpredictable, sometimes volatile, sometimes low and miserable, so that she had crept about the place not wishing to disturb him. With his brother, her uncle, who lived several miles away on another estate that belonged to the family, her father slipped into feeble subservience, placatory and subdued; she hated to see it and had begun to dread the impromptu visits from her uncle until the day she had overheard her father promise her in marriage to his brother. She had left the very next day.

Leading the way, Katerina navigated her horse off the grass drove on to a wide, stony track, shielded on one side by a stubby hawthorn hedge. The hour was still early, but the sun had risen enough to coat the top part of Katerina's body in a warm, fiery glow.

Lussac brought his horse alongside her own, matching her speed. 'How much further, Katerina?' He was so close to her that the lower part of his leg, encased in well-fitting woollen braies, brushed inadvertently against her upper thigh.

She flushed, the colour climbing rapidly across her fair skin. Tucking her chin in the air, she pointed. 'Look over there.' The edge of her cloak fell back, revealing a scarlet lining, patched and worn. Several threads hung from the seam that joined the lining and the outer wool fabric together. 'That is my home. That is Longthorpe.'

Lussac scrunched up his eyes in the direction she indicated. A faint haze of mist rose from the soaked, spongy ground, gathering, coalescing in slow trails, wisps of white floating two or three feet high, drifting. The details of the manor house emerged slowly, suspended on this thick cloud, like a magical dwelling from an enchanted land.

'My God!' breathed Philippe at their backs, as Katerina led the way across the raised causeway directly towards the gatehouse. Reeds rustled on either side of them, the top of the grasses barely reaching the level of the track. 'What an amazing sight! It's like a dream.'

But as Katerina neared the house, droplets of mist chill upon her face, she realised how wrong Philippe was. The manor looked nothing like the place she had left a year ago. The polished grey slates had fallen, shattered on the cobbles, leaving large, gaping holes in the roof; the window glass had cracked, or was missing completely and the wooden frames had warped and buckled with water damage. What had happened? Her father was normally so fastidious about maintenance; he had taken pride in his dedicated team of craftsmen devoted entirely to the upkeep of the buildings.

Katerina shook her head, puzzled. The climbing rose that her mother had planted by the entrance door had withered, leaves yellowing and spotted. One white rose, petals stained with brown, hung forlornly, jammed up against the crumbling mortar of the front wall. 'I don't know what's happened!' She turned to both men in dismay. 'This is not right—something is not right.' She bounced down from her horse, allowing the reins to trail over cobbles thick with weeds and moss. No stable-boy appeared.

'Katerina, wait!' Lussac dismounted quickly, strode over to her. 'You need to take care. Let me go in first, at least.'

She had reached the arched doorway, set into the gable end of the main house, before she stopped. 'But it's my father,' she blurted out, 'what can he do to me?'

'What hasn't he done, Katerina?' Lussac growled

down at her, eyes darkening to midnight blue. 'He has promised you in marriage to his brother, he has sent thugs halfway around the countryside to drag you back. I think that demands an element of caution on your part.'

She nodded her head, knowing Lussac's words made sense. Tears clustered, unbidden, in her eyes. What had happened to her beautiful home?

Pushing open the door with one hefty shoulder, Lussac drew his sword, the linear steel gleaming in the dim interior. He could feel Katerina at his back, almost touching him; his body warmed in acknowledgement of her closeness. A sound of splintering wood assailed them; shifting his head around to Katerina, Lussac raised strong eyebrows, silently asking for directions.

'That way,' whispered Katerina, pointing at an embroidered curtain hanging across a stone arch. 'The sound is coming from the great hall.'

She followed Lussac closely, standing on tiptoes to peep over his shoulder, anxious, afraid of what she might see. A man stood over by the vast stone fireplace, stooped, muttering, an axe in one hand, hacking randomly at what looked like the remains of a carved oak chair. The dull blade of the axe struck the polished wood repeatedly, obviously aiming to reduce the beautiful piece of furniture to a mass of serviceable firewood.

'Who is it?' Lussac hissed.

'My God, it's my father!' Katerina clutched at Lussac's arm, shock cascading in sharp rivulets through her veins, needles of fire. 'Please, don't do anything to him, don't harm him!' She stared up into Lussac's carved features, shadowed by the stone arch of the doorway, desperation pinned to her pale face. 'At least hear what he has to say for himself!'

Lussac tipped his head forwards in slow acknowledgement of her plea. With his body tense, rigid and acutely aware of the small delectable figure rolled into her blanket at his side, he had lain awake for most of the previous night, thinking about what Katerina had said. He had stared into the dying flames until his eyes scratched with tiredness. Her passionate words had released him, operating like a key on the final lock of his stiff, dried-up heart, releasing the last dregs of resentment. In truth, ever since he had met her, wilful and truculent in the forest, the radiant aura of her spirit had nurtured him, warmed him, gradually melting the frozen wasteland of his revenge. She had helped him; but what had he done for her? He had only taken from her, taken her physically; tormented her, forcing her to lead him to her family. It was as if a blindfold had dropped from his eyes; suddenly he could see clearly again. Everything was crystal bright, vivid.

Snared in his thoughts, Lussac failed to prevent Katerina from plunging forwards, his fingers holding fleetingly, then losing, the flying side of her cloak. She rushed over to her father, reaching out to grab his arm, to prevent the axe from doing more damage. 'Father! In God's name, Father, what are you doing?'

'Who are you? What are you doing here?' The man observed her through watery eyes, suspicious, cradling the axe against his chest like a friend. Lussac moved closer to Katerina, his gauntleted hands poised on his sword, ready to strike, to protect her. The man looked wild, demented. Philippe hovered near the curtained doorway, sweeping the chamber with his eyes, assessing the situation.

'It's me, Father, Katerina. Don't you recognise me?' Her heart sank at the sight of him. His hair, what was left of it, hung down in lank, greasy locks either side of his gaunt face, covering his ears. The knobbly ridge of his collar-bone poked up from beneath his tunic; he was too thin. His clothes were ripped and dirty, his leather boots warped with age.

Fingers roped with arthritis stretched out, touched the vital flame of her hair. 'Katerina,' the old man murmured. 'Is it really you?'

'What has happened to you? What's happened to this place?' Her eyes roamed around the hall; everything was missing, the tapestries, the shields and swords that had decorated the walls, all the silverware. There were no tables, or benches—had her father burned them all? Only the flagstones remained, stained with wine and ale, and the small pile of furniture clustered around the fireplace.

Her father began to shake, his eyes rounding with fear. 'You must leave, Katerina, go from here!' Without warning, he placed a hand on her shoulder, shoving roughly.

'Hey! None of that!' Lussac stepped in front of Katerina and pushed her father backwards with his muscled bulk, deftly removing the axe from his feeble grasp.

'No, no, you don't understand.' Katerina's father blinked up at Lussac, as if noticing his presence for the first time. 'You have to take her out of here— he will kill her when he sees her! He said that to me: "If I can't have her, then I will kill her!"'

'Who, who said that, Father?' Katerina placed one hand on Lussac's arm, skirting around him.

'Thomas.' He spat the name out.

'My uncle,' Katerina answered Lussac's questioning glance. 'The one I was supposed to marry.'

Chapter Seventeen

'Here, Father, let me help you to sit down.' Katerina caught the older man under the elbow, shocked at how little flesh cladded his spare frame, and steered him towards the last remaining chair by the fireplace. Crouching, Lussac poked at the fire, then placed more sticks in a criss-cross fashion on the feeble flames in an attempt to throw more warmth into the room.

'I don't understand,' Katerina said, kneeling on the floor beside her father's chair, chafing at his rough, worn hands. He scarcely seemed to notice her ministrations, eyes casting anxious glances towards the doorway as if expecting something. 'Why are you living like this? When I left, this place was beautiful—where have all the tapestries gone? The shields and swords from the walls?' Her voice rose with a note of wavering anxiety.

'It was because of you. When he couldn't find

you, he wanted something in recompense. I gave him money. Then, when the money ran out, I gave him pieces from the house.' He breathed heavily, focusing his grey gaze on his daughter. 'I did it to protect you, Katerina.'

Katerina thrust up from the floor, uncertain, confused by her father's words. 'But you and he sent those thugs after me anyway? How was that supposed to keep me safe?'

'I never sent anyone after you, Katerina. It was Thomas, all Thomas's idea. He wanted you back, so he could marry you.'

'Why did you promise me to him in the first place, Father? Surely then none of this would have happened?' She paced to and fro, her gown swishing against the stained flagstones. 'Why has your brother such a hold over you?' Rising to his feet, Lussac leaned against the fireplace, the turquoise velvet of his eyes observing her closely.

Her father jerked his head forlornly, shoulders hunched with the weight of his guilt. He threw a half-apologetic glance up at Lussac. 'Because I took the one thing in life that Thomas cared anything about,' he whispered. 'Your mother.' His pallid skin distended tautly over his cheekbones. 'Thomas loved your mother more than anything in the world; he intended to take her as his wife.

She was the only thing he wanted. But she chose me, Katerina. She loved me. And he's hated me ever since. He's been jealous of everything I've ever achieved in life: my marriage, and you, my beautiful daughter.'

'So that's why you constantly fight.' Katerina paused by her father's chair, sought to steady herself by placing one hand on the high chair back.

'Aye, we fought over her when she was alive, and, after she died, we fought over you. You look so much like her, he wanted to wed you instead. I had to make that promise to him, Katerina, despite knowing how wrong it was, because he said if he couldn't have you, he would kill you. It was the only way I could keep you alive.'

'Sweet Jesu,' murmured Lussac.

'I'm so sorry, Katerina.' Her father leaned back in the chair, sparse eyelashes shuttering over his watery eyes, exhausted by the whole proceedings. The loose, ragged sleeve of his tunic fell back, revealing the grey, drooping skin of his arm. Revealing a leather cuff.

The muscles in Katerina's knees faltered, sagged with relief as she spied the silver discs twinkling on her father's arm. All the pent-up worry, all the anxiety she held about her father's possible involvement with Lussac's family lifted away, a heavy weight removed. She swept around the chair, kneeling on the floor before her father, the long train of her cloak brushing over the rough leather of Lussac's boots, and grasped her father's arm. The leather around his wrist was well worn, silver discs glinting in the feeble light of the fire.

She arched her head up, meeting the turquoise strike of Lussac's eyes. 'Look!' she announced triumphantly. 'My father wears a cuff, *his* cuff. That means the one you have—' Her speech stuttered out so fast, her words tripped over each other.

'…belongs to your uncle,' Lussac finished the sentence for her.

Katerina rose to her feet, willowy, graceful, her eyes narrowing on Lussac. 'What will you do?'

'I will pay him a visit.'

'It won't do any good,' she whispered, a loop of amber hair falling across her forehead. It won't do *you* any good, she wanted to say. She wanted to protect him, protect him from the bad feelings that would persist, that would clag his heart if he followed his intentions. But she had said her piece, had told him how she felt. She could do no more.

'He lives out at Hambridge,' her father chipped in, catching onto the subject of the conversation, 'not above three miles from here.'

'I'll come with you,' Katerina said. Maybe there

was some way she could prevent what was about to happen. In truth, she didn't want to see him go.

Lussac's lean fingers touched the silken curl across her temple, smoothed it back. She caught the warm intoxicating smell of leather from the palm of his hand. Her eyelashes drifted down, fractionally, the thrill of his closeness dancing along her veins. The urge to lean into him, to press against the strong solidity of his frame, scythed through her—a lightning bolt of sensation. Her hands, hidden beneath her cloak, clenched tightly, her sole defence. She had to remain rigidly aloof, keep herself distant from him in mind as well as body, for it would only make it harder for her when he finally walked away.

'No, it is too dangerous for you.' Lussac's voice was a low, velvety timbre, a caress. She wanted to close her eyes and sink into the wonderful sound, be cradled by it; she cursed the weakness of her own body—why could she not remain immune to him? 'That man is too dangerous for you. I don't want you anywhere near him. Stay here with Philippe. I'll give him the writ, so he can show it to your father.' He glanced at the forlorn, shrunken figure in the chair. 'Although I suspect you'll have no need of it now.'

'But when…?' She stopped suddenly, aghast at

what she had been about to say. *When are you coming back?* She had no claim on this man, no hold over him. He was free to do whatever he wished. A raft of sadness crested through her, like a wave, dousing any hope she might have possessed. By obtaining the Queen's writ, he had helped her, but he held no feelings for her. He had made it clear that she was entirely lacking from a physical point of view.

'Take care,' he said, squeezing her hand briefly, before striding over to the doorway. Watching him go, her heart closed up with grief. He spoke to Philippe, who nodded and clapped him high on the shoulder.

And then he was gone.

'I think you should have gone with him, that's all.' Katerina clattered around the dismal kitchen, trying to find something for the three of them to eat. The state of the place appalled her. When her mother was alive, the kitchens had formed the hub of the home, a light, spacious room, filled with bustling servants, warmth and the delicious smell of food. Now, it was a dank cellar, thick stone walls sparkling with damp, a heap of cold, grey ash in the smoke-stained fireplace. The iron spit, the hooks that would have carried roasting meat and hams above the flames, now hung empty, dangling down from inside the chimney.

Philippe hoisted one hip on to the sturdy table in the middle of the room. A thick curve of hardened grease, speckled with dust, slicked across the table top behind him. 'It's more important that I stay here with you,' he said, his eyes following Katerina's rapid, darting movements around the room. The castle was so cold, she had kept her cloak on over the light-blue gown, the hood falling in soft gathers about her shoulders. 'Lussac can take care of himself.'

Her searching fingers touched a sealed jar of honey, pushed right to the back of a deep shelf. The image of Lussac's tall, broad-shouldered silhouette filling the arched doorway tormented her, drove into her soul like a knife. She wanted to weep, but instead gulped air, heart clutching in grief. He was gone. He didn't want her. She had to accept that and move on with her life.

'Here, look what I've found!' She pinned a semblance of a smile on her face, turned to Philippe, holding up the earthenware jar of honey like a trophy. 'We might not starve, after all.'

Arms folded across his belly, Philippe tilted his head to one side, studying the odd flare of colour in Katerina's white, drawn face, her wide, sad eyes.

'He is coming back, you know.' He eyed her curiously.

She lifted her shoulders, the healing skin on her shoulder puckering beneath her gown 'Why would he?' she blurted out. 'All he wants is recompense for his family, Philippe. All he wants is revenge.' Her voice echoed dully around the kitchen.

'Aye, he does,' Philippe agreed.

Her chin jerked up, her eyes a shrouded grey, lacklustre. 'So once he's achieved what he wants, he'll race back to France and forget.' Forget everything that ever happened, she thought forlornly. Forget the magical afternoon when we lay together, limbs entwined, by the cool rippling river. The kisses we shared. She thumped the jar down on the thick boards of the table, a discordant, crashing sound. 'Why would he come back here at all?' She almost spat the words out, her tone hectic.

'Because he wants something else as well—

A cry from above made them both jump up and race for the stairs that led up to the great hall, Philippe drawing his sword as he puffed up behind Katerina, following the bobbing train of her cloak. Together, they sprang through the curtained doorway at the top of the steps and into the dim light of the cavernous hall.

'It's Thomas, my uncle,' Katerina squeaked, her

eyes immediately alighting on a burly figure by the fireplace. She stopped, holding her arm across Philippe's torso, instinctively protective. An icy thread of fear sliced through her chest. 'Oh my God, Philippe, what's happened to Lussac?'

Stepping in front of Katerina, Philippe scanned the room. Two soldiers, dressed in the scarlet tunics of the Dauntsey family, stood by the door; another two flanked her uncle by the fire. Katerina's father cowered in the chair, his body bent and curved; he seemed to have shrunk.

'Well, well,' a harsh, guttural voice broke across the uneven flagstones. 'A little bird told me you had returned. But I refused to believe it until I saw you with my own eyes.'

'What have you done to him?' Katerina flew over the stone floor, closely followed by Philippe. 'Where is he?'

'He's right here, can't you see?' Her uncle swept a hand downwards, indicating her father. 'And from where I'm standing, he appears perfectly well.'

'No, not him!' Katerina shouted. Her voice rose to the high rafters of the great hall, hectic, panicky. Her limbs shook. 'Lussac. Lussac of Belbigny. The man who came to find you.' She closed her eyes momentarily. 'What's happened to him, Philippe?'

Keeping one eye fixed on Thomas, Philippe laid

a hand on her sleeve, reassuring her. 'Calm down, Katerina. Lussac will be fine; he always is,' he murmured quietly.

'Belbigny. Now there's a name I haven't heard in a while,' her uncle replied slowly. His narrow eyes were like slits, a muddy-brown colour, as they raked up and down Katerina's slim frame. 'Coming to find me, is he? I wondered if he might catch up with me eventually.'

'So it was you!' breathed Katerina. 'It was you, out in Gascony. It was you who slaughtered his family.'

'You talk about something that doesn't concern you,' her uncle said coldly, dismissing her accusations with a violent sweep of his hand. 'More importantly, what brings you back here? I must say, I'm delighted to see you, but I'm curious. You've managed successfully to evade all attempts to bring you home so far—so why come back now? After all this time?'

'Because you have no power over me any more, Uncle. No power over me, or my father. You cannot bully us any more about this ridiculous marriage. Philippe here has a writ, signed by the Queen of England herself, preventing your marriage to me.'

'Let me see this writ,' her uncle demanded. In contrast to her father, collapsed weakly into his chair, he looked impressively healthy, his face ruddy, his stomach padded out with the extra flesh of good eating. All at her father's expense, Katerina thought. She hated the husk of a man to which her father had been reduced.

Extracting the precious scroll slowly from his satchel, Philippe handed the parchment into Thomas's impatient, outstretched hand. Her uncle broke through the red-wax seal containing the imprint of the Queen's golden ring and unrolled the crackling parchment. His eyes moved swiftly over the document, his jowls sagging as he tilted his chin down. Lifting his eyes from the document, to everyone's surprise, he threw back his head and laughed. A cruel, metallic sound that ripped up to the rafters of the great hall.

'So do you see now, Uncle,' Katerina said urgently, as soon as his laughter had died away, 'that you must leave me alone, leave us alone.' She gestured towards the wan features of her father. 'There's nothing you can do; it's over.'

'If you think I'm going to take any notice of a piece of paper, you are seriously addled, my girl.' Her uncle tapped the side of his head, as if demonstrating her stupidity.

'But…but you'll be breaking the law!' she spluttered back at him. Fear slid down her gullet, her gaze moving to the curtained doorway, wishing, hoping that it would pull back, and Lussac would be there. She wanted him by her side. She wanted to know that he was safe.

'They won't give a damn, Katerina,' he snarled nastily. 'Do you really think the Queen cares about you? You're nothing to her. Do you think I care about what she has to say? Never. You will be my wife, Katerina, whether you like it or not.'

Katerina's world shifted, her mind hazing. In panic, she looked at Philippe, her expression shocked, questioning. Her father's head was in his hands; he wept quietly, the sound of his quiet, wretched tears breaking the tense silence in the hall.

In a trice, Philippe had grabbed her around the waist, brandishing his sword wildly at her uncle and his men. 'You...' he jabbed the point of the blade at Thomas '...you are going to let us walk out of here.' He backed away with Katerina, aiming for the smaller doorway at the opposite end of the hall.

'No chance.' Her uncle smiled slowly, his expression smug. 'Seize them,' he ordered his soldiers.

Katerina drummed her fists against the solid oak door, then sprang back, frustrated, stalking around the chamber like a fretful cat. They hadn't stood a chance against the overwhelming force of his soldiers, those big, burly henchman advancing swiftly on her uncle's orders, making a mockery of Philippe's brave attempt to extricate Katerina from the situation.

Philippe's sword had been struck away promptly, to spin in futile circles across the stone floor, a soldier hanging on each of his arms as they marched him away to some unknown prison. Grinning broadly, two other soldiers had approached Katerina, but she had refused to give them the satisfaction of fighting back; she had strode proudly after the lead soldier, following him up the spiral staircase to the third, and highest, floor of the solar tower. The key had rattled in the lock and the huge bolts were drawn across from the outside, securing her, trapping her.

She ceased pacing, placing her palms flat on the wide windowsill, tilting her body forwards to stare dismally out at the flat, flat landscape. Her fists balled against the gritty stone, tears of frustration hazing her eyes. Why was she even surprised by her uncle's behaviour? He was an evil man, tyrannical, a bully who considered himself above any laws. Obsessed with the idea of Katerina being his wife, he had never given up searching for her, and now she had walked right back into the whole messy business—and she had brought Lussac with her.

Lussac? Where was he? Anxiety coursed through her frame at the thought of him hurt, or injured somewhere. Or worse. She closed her eyes, tight shut, trying to block out that awful possibility. With him gone, it was like she had lost part of herself, like a leg, or an arm. The low timbre of his voice echoed continually in her head and she almost turned around, expecting to see him standing there. She missed him, but that didn't mean he was coming back. She hoped, beyond anything, that wherever he was, he was safe.

Her fingers picked idly at the loose mortar at the bottom of the window, beneath the glazing bars. Some of the lead-work that held the small, diamond glass panes in place had come away, creating a gap. Katerina glanced up. A pole had been secured across the whole window, carrying a heavy velvet curtain that swung back to one side. Now was not the time for self-pity, or to wait around for Lussac to come back and rescue her. She had become used to his strong, powerful presence at her side, had relished it, but, in truth, it had made her soft, vulnerable. She could take care of herself and would do well to remember that. Quickly, she shucked off her cloak, yanking the yards of cloth that formed her overdress over her head. The extra material would weigh her down, unbalance her. She needed to be as light as possible; the underdress, laced snugly at her waist and fitted tight to her arms, would have to suffice in this escapade.

Reaching up, she grabbed hold of the pole, lifting her knees and feet from the floor, so she could swing into the window space. Backwards and forwards she went, increasing her speed until the soles of her feet smashed into the weakened glass infill of the window and sent fragments of glass and little pieces of lead flying outwards. Balancing her toes on the sill, she briefly admired her handiwork, the substantial stone frame empty of glass, with a space big enough for her to squeeze through.

Crouching down on her hands and knees, she peered out through the gap. The warm breeze touched her face: fresh, invigorating after the musty stuffiness of the chamber. About five inches wide, the narrow ledge of decorative stone ran below the line of the windows, where she had known it would be. This ledge would be her escape route. She swung one leg out and her foot skimmed the ledge, then found a hold, followed quickly by her other foot. All she had to do was creep around this ledge to the western side of the tower, where her father had helpfully built an exterior staircase that led to the second floor. There, she would be able to jump down.

The gathered skirts of her gown billowed out in the drift of air; she burrowed her fingers into the chiselled stone above her head, finding handholds with practised efficiency. She felt no fear, being so high above the ground; her only instinct was to flee, to escape. Even now, her uncle might be priming and bribing the local priest in readiness for their marriage; once she was tied in matrimony, there would be no escape. It was now, or never.

As she inched herself along, hoping no soldiers would have the wit to look upwards at the tower, she peered into each window, helpfully set on a level with her upper body. Maybe Philippe had been put into one of these chambers; they were thought to be the most secure, after all. She passed one empty chamber, then another, until she came to the last window on this north-facing side. Thick iron bars had been secured into the stonework in front of the window and she reached for them, curling her hands around the substantial iron, resting for a moment. Her fingers ached with the effort of supporting her body weight, her nails coated with stone dust, but she knew she only had a little way to go; the staircase was around the next corner.

Philippe, slumped in a carved oak chair in the middle of the chamber, started in surprise as the shadow crossed his window. Levering himself from the chair, he strode over, eyes widening at the sight of Katerina, hanging by her hands from the iron bars outside his window. Fingers fumbling with the iron latch, he managed to open the casement by an inch or so. 'What are you doing?' he whispered, fiercely. 'Are you mad? How can you do such a thing?'

She shook her head sharply, dismissing his urgent questions. 'Where is Lussac? Where do you think he might be?'

Reaching out one hand through the bars, he touched her fingers, eyes flicking a warning. 'Keep your voice low, Katerina; there are soldiers outside my door.'

'But where is he?' she hissed.

'You must stop worrying, Katerina. He will be fine. He'll come back here when he fails to find your uncle.' A smile broke the fleshy planes of his face.

She tried, and failed, to gather some reassurance from his voice. As the light began to fall from the day, the wind strengthened at her back, pressing her skirts against the back of her legs. She would need to move soon, before her feet became numb.

'Can you get out of here?' she demanded, urgently. A small frown puckered her forehead as she assessed the space between the iron bars.

'It will be a miracle if you think I can squeeze through those!' He patted the round of his stomach where it bulged against his tunic. 'Listen, I have soldiers outside my door and your uncle is no doubt with your father. You have to save yourself, Katerina. You have to go and you have to go now.' His tone was stern, commanding.

She shook her head. 'But I want you to come with me.'

'Nay, you must find Lussac. He can't be far away. He will know what to do.' Her heart lurched pitifully, thrillingly, at the mention of his name, the man who permeated her every thought, who imbued her body and heart and brain with a continual, bubbling desire. She squeezed his hand, before continuing to move along the ledge. Rounding the corner on to the tower's west side, the stone warmed by the sun, she dropped down silently on to the outside steps, the flare of her skirts catching on the gritty stone. Within a few moments she was following a hedge-line northwards, one flat field after another, out of the sight-lines from the manor house, as the violet evening shadows stretched long and low over the land.

Chapter Eighteen

Katerina flung herself down on to the damp grass behind a scrubby hawthorn hedge. The dusky evening held the heat from the day; perspiration prickled along her spine, gathered beneath the crook of her knees. Plucking irritably at the sticking cloth of her gown, she tugged it away from her neck, relishing the air against her skin. She had tried, and failed, to run; the thick folds of material had wrapped round her legs, restricting her forward momentum. Her only option had been to resort to a purposeful stride along the high-banked droveway.

Now she sat with her legs drawn up, elbows resting on knees, trying to collect her breath, her exhausted, scrambled thoughts. The adrenalin that had pushed her on, had forced her to fight for her escape, leached away in the sudden stillness of her body, to be replaced by a consuming, strength-sapping fatigue. She hadn't eaten in hours. Her body craved food, liquid, something to replace the lost energy.

On the opposite side of the drove, in front of her, the land sank away into a limitless expanse of marshland, rustling with brittle, rust-coloured reeds, towards thick mist hovering on the horizon. A couple of black moorhens, beaks bright orange, dabbled about in the shallow water, glassy-blue in this limpid half-light of evening. Her sluggish brain struggled to work out where Lussac might be; he would have headed towards her uncle's estates, at Hambridge, but a curious reluctance plagued her, preventing her from starting in that direction. She bit her lip, not wishing to acknowledge the slick of fear that weakened her limbs, that sapped her strength. Her uncle and his thuggish soldiers would be roaming the countryside around the castle from the moment they discovered her disappearance. Hanging her head, she felt the hot prickle of tears in the corners of her eyes; she was simply not brave enough to head out there alone. 'Forgive me, Lussac,' she whispered at the empty land. At this point in time, she wasn't strong enough to go and find him. To save him from himself.

Picking up a loose stone from the track, she threw it across to the water, watching the concentric ripples widen out across the flat, reflective surface. Overhead, a flock of geese headed south, honking discordantly, flying in perfect arrow formation across the peach-tinted blush of sky. The combined beat of their wings was audible on the ground: a wheezy, feathered rhythm. Soon it would be dark; she needed to find a place to hide, with people who she could trust. Already, the wide, azure sky was deepening to purple; the tiny, winking pinprick of the evening star appeared on the horizon, a diamond on blue velvet.

The countryside around her was familiar territory, the tracks, pathways and hideouts mapped out in her brain from an early age. Here, she had run through the reeds with the other children, children from the village, children from the estates, screeching with laughter as they played tag and pushed each other into the water. The village. The people in the village would help her. Hauling herself up from her seated position, she stepped off the drove-way on to a narrow winding path through the reeds, her diminutive figure invisible within the bleached grass, rustling brightly.

Waleran's sister, Margrete, was astonished to see her, her mouth dropping open in a comical gape as she opened the cottage door. 'God in Heaven, is it you?' She reached forwards, pulling Katerina into her short, plump figure, hugging her tightly.

'Come in, come in.' She hustled Katerina into the cottage. 'Is Waleran with you?' She nudged her head out of the open door as if hoping to see her brother.

'No, I came alone, Margrete. It's a long story.'

'Come and sit by the fire. You look tired.' Margrete ushered her into the centre of the room, where a bundle of sticks burned merrily, the smoke rising up and out through a hole in the roof. The air was thick with the haze of smoke. Katerina nodded a greeting at the two children sitting cross-legged at the fire, Waleran's niece and nephew.

'Edith, Hugo, how are you?' She spoke gently to both children, conscious that they were regarding her with wide-eyed, wary interest. The boy smiled tentatively at her, but the girl drew back, hiding behind her older brother.

'I'm not sure they remember you.' Margrete bustled over with a mug of hot, steaming liquid. 'Here, drink this, and then you can tell me what's been happening.' She turned to the children, shooing them away with an impatient flick of her hands. 'Time for bed, you two.' Katerina sipped gratefully at the warm, sweet mead, watching the pair of them in their ragged clothes and bare, dirty feet scamper up the rickety ladder to the sleeping loft set above the main living quarters of the cottage.

'Waleran is in good health,' Katerina hastened to say, as Margrete shuffled her broad girth on to a three-legged stool opposite her.

Margrete let out a long sigh of relief, visibly collapsing. Her hands shook as she placed them squarely in her ample lap, smoothing her palms across her knees. 'Thank the Lord for that. When I saw you there, standing on the threshold...' She shook her head, the neat braiding of her black hair glinting in the firelight. 'I thought you had come to tell me the worst.' She lowered her voice. 'That's why I shuffled the children to bed; I thought you didn't want to say anything in front of them.'

Katerina placed her empty mug on the earth floor beside her, the taste of honey clinging to her lips. She reached across, took one of Margrete's cold hands within her own, the tight sleeves of her underdress straining across her shoulders. 'No, it's nothing like that.'

'But, Katerina, it's not safe for you here. I thought you vowed never to return. What is it?'

'I need some help.'

With no encouragement from his rider, Lussac's destrier gradually ambled to a stop, dropping its head to pluck noisily at the long grass at the side of the track. Mist rose across the unending marshland, a blanket of white, swirling droplets, landing on Lussac's face like a fine veil. He stared out across thick pillowing air, unseeing.

What was he doing?

He twisted around, seizing his water bottle strapped to the horse's rump. Pulling the stopper, he took a deep, long swig, wiping the spilled droplets from his mouth.

The only thing he could think about was Katerina. The only thing he could see was her slim, lithe body illuminated by the rosy fading sunlight, pleading with him, begging him to think again and not to kill. To forgive. She filled his brain, the delicate scent of her skin, the soft downy lobe of her ear. Her eyes had challenged him, sparking silver, and her words had rung as they rang again now, echoing bell-like in his ears. 'You're a good man, Lussac. You're good and kind…and loving.' His heart swelled at the memory.

Maybe she was right. Could he be that man again? Did he possess the capacity to forgive, like his mother and sister? A few days ago, he would have laughed in the face of anyone who dared suggest such a thing, but now?

Swinging his leg over the horse, he dismounted,

hearing the familiar creak of the saddle, the jangle of the bridle. The sounds barely touched his consciousness. Katerina was the only person who had succeeded in penetrating that ugly black fog of revenge, her luminous spirit shining through the thick layers of hatred. She had reached into him and touched his heart. She had given him hope. He hadn't realised it before, but he realised now. The diamond-grey glitter of her eyes had fixed on to his and asked him to let go, to move on. In truth, he had known since that point that his quest for revenge was futile, pointless, shrivelled up to a place where it was unrecognisable, rising and vanishing like thin smoke from a fire.

He wanted no more of it.

The only thing he wanted was Katerina.

Springing back into the saddle, startling his horse with the violent movement, he wrenched the reins around, a sear of joy in his heart. He had to go back to her. She had given him hope and he would seize it with both hands, with all of his heart. Turning his horse, he found that the mist had closed in behind him, tendrils of impenetrable white, clinging to his hair, his tunic. He wanted to shout out loud in frustration. He couldn't fight his way through this, back to Katerina's home, risking his horse's legs in some deep, muddy ditch if he lost his way. Through the shifting mist, he spotted a church spire and hoped it belonged to the village of Longthorpe. He would ask directions back to the manor from there.

Reaching the outskirts of the village, Lussac dropped from his destrier on to silent feet, leading his truculent animal towards the huddle of cottages, spires of smoke frilling up into the cold, twilight air. He hunched up his shoulders, rolling them forwards, trying to ease the tight, muscular tension that strained across his upper back, adjusting his heavy sword belt across the narrow breadth of his hips. From a long way off, a church bell tolled eight times, ringing out clearly across the quiet, sleeping land; it was a time when families closed their doors and gathered around the fire to eat, talk. At his back the moon rose, pale orange, streaked, up through a cloudless sky of midnight blue, promising a clear, brilliant night. The mist that had scuppered his earlier journey had disappeared.

He raised his fist to the door of the first cottage he came to, thumped hard. Inside he could hear chattering and laughing, sharply silenced at the sound of his fist. Cracking open the door, a man's wrinkled face appeared nervously in the narrow gap, eyeing up the tall knight dubiously. No, he'd never heard of Longthorpe Manor. Yes, this was Longthorpe village, but there was no manor. The door shut promptly in Lussac's face. He received the same answer from the next cottage, and the next, frightened peasants shaking their heads, shutting the door almost as soon as they'd finished their sentences. Standing in the middle of the deserted village, with a sense that he was being watched from all available windows, Lussac ran a frustrated hand through his hair. Was it possible that there were two villages with the same name? Had he come to the wrong one?

The door of the next cottage that he approached was opened, unusually, by a woman, a small, solid figure, amply clad with flesh.

'I'm looking for Longthorpe Manor.' Lussac sighed, already anticipating an answer in the negative. The rough-cut ends of the low thatch scratched at the top of his head; he took a step back to avoid the unpleasant sensation.

The woman stared at him, absorbing the details of his fine woollen tunic, the long legs, the intelligent sparkle of his eyes. For a moment he thought she might be dim-witted.

'I seek the Dauntsey family. Katerina of Dauntsey,' he tried again.

'What is your business with them?' the woman

answered pointedly. He sensed an immediate straightening of her spine, a tension through her body at the mention of Katerina's name. His blood began to beat faster.

'Do you know her?' Lussac demanded, dipping his head beneath the thatch, as if to shoulder his way into the building. The fragrance of something out of place, at odds with the damp, run-down cottage, tickled his memory: the smell of a fading rose, or another strong-scented flower that he couldn't identify.

'Stay back!' the woman warned, producing a fearsome-looking poker from behind her back. Cradling the makeshift weapon in front of her, she held her ground, but he could see the fear in her eyes.

Lussac rocked on the balls of his feet, holding his palms up flat to show that he meant no harm. 'Do you know her?' he repeated. His voice sounded hoarse, ragged.

'I knew her. I haven't seen her for some years,' the woman replied.

At the rear of the chamber, deep in the shadows, a door pushed inwards. An auburn fret of hair appeared, a slender figure in a faded blue gown hefting a bucket of water. Katerina. She straightened up. Saw him.

The bucket clattered to the floor, tipping, slopping water over the earth-packed floor, a dark stain. 'Oh, my God, Lussac!' she blurted out, wanting to wccp, wanting to laugh. 'You're alive!' Joy bubbled up at the sight of him, his big shoulders filling the doorway, sleek chestnut head bent slightly to avoid the low lintel. Each tiny link of his chainmail twinkled in the dim light from the fire, sparkling. She sprang forwards, arms outstretched, wrapping her slim arms about him, around the muscular cushion of his chest, the solid rope of his spine. All the pent-up tension, the anxiety she had carried with her from Longthorpe drained away; she breathed in the heady masculine scent of him, soaked up the comfort of his powerful frame. 'I was so afraid,' she mumbled out in a shuddery breath, the metallic thread of the fleur-de-lys on his tunic cool against her cheek, 'so afraid that something had happened to you! That you were dead!'

His roped arms curved around her, instinctively, supporting the slight sag of her body, feeling the small shudders ripple through her as he held her close. The scent of roses lifted from the warmth of her neck. Tilting his head, he studied the polished amber of her hair tucked against his shoulder, relishing the soft curves of her body pressed against his own. Desire flickered in the pit of his stomach, then ignited, streaking along his veins, wild, haphazard. He clenched his teeth, trying to regain some control. Her hair was different: released from the tight-braided coils pinned to the top of her head, the shining amber tresses now fell in two long plaits to her hips. 'No, I'm alive,' he said huskily, his smile crooked. 'Why wouldn't I be?'

From the centre of the chamber, Margrete watched her friend greet this tall, dark stranger with curiosity. It was obvious they knew each other, quite well it seemed, if Katerina's greeting was anything to go by. She stooped, picking up the fallen bucket, and disappeared out to the water pump at the back, reassured that her friend was in safe hands.

Katerina rested back against the link of his arms, a hectic flush colouring her pale cheeks. Tears gleamed across the mineral darkness of her eyes; he was surprised. Had she really been that worried for him? 'I'm sorry,' she said shakily, embarrassed by her behaviour, by her over-familiarity towards him. She stepped back abruptly, breaking his light hold at her back, biting her lip in shame. If she kept throwing herself into his arms like this, her heart would never survive when he was truly gone.

The steely iridescence of his eyes darkened. *She's*

remembering what I did to her, Lussac thought. *How I took her innocence. How can I ever hope that she will forgive me for that?*

Winding her arms about the front of her chest, she fought to keep her voice detached, unconcerned. 'I thought something awful had happened to you.' Her smile was brief, unsteady.

'I never even reached Hambridge,' he explained. 'I got hopelessly lost in the fog, lost my direction.' *And then fully realised the senselessness of my actions,* he thought. That the only thing that mattered in life was Katerina. How could he say such words to her when she eyed him so uneasily from the centre of the room, fractious energy peeling from her in waves?

'My uncle came to the castle,' she said, pulling at a loose thread that snaggled out from the waistband of her gown. Despair flashed across her face. 'He wouldn't have been—'

'What happened?' he cut across her speech. The flame from the tallow candle, set into a niche in the wall, jumped and flickered across the angular planes of his face.

'The writ's useless, Lussac.' She shrugged her shoulders, trying to recover some sense of equilibrium. 'He'll hunt me down until he finds me, just like before. I'm back where I started.' She stared blankly at the ground, shoulders hunched, features cloudy with fatigue.

Lussac read the fear in her eyes, the desperation, saw her belated attempts to cover them up. No, he wanted to say, no, you're not back where you started. Now, I am here, with you.

'No matter.' She lifted her head, grey eyes holding on to his. 'It's not your problem; I'm sure I'll think of something.'

'You need someone to look after you, to protect you,' he replied slowly, an inexplicable plan jumping into his mind. Would it work? He had to be careful; if he pushed too much, he risked losing her for ever.

'You mean, I need to find someone to marry?' Katerina replied sharply, toeing the ground with her leather boot. Her neat brows pulled together in a frown. 'I don't want to marry anyone,' she pronounced, haughtily. 'Besides, who would have me?'

I would. I would marry you. I would protect you, look after you.

'What about Waleran?' Lussac offered. His voice wobbled slightly; he cleared his throat. He had to make sure, make certain that she wished no other solution, other than the one he was about to suggest. 'He's your friend; you are close to him.'

'Close to him, but not in love with him.'

'Have you any other choice?' he asked.

A hard muscle quirked in his jaw and she ached to touch it, to smooth her fingers along his tanned cheek. 'Lussac, it wouldn't be fair to him! I couldn't do that to him, someone who I respect. It would ruin his life!' Her voice rose shakily. 'But, you're right, who else is there? Who else would put up with me?'

His throat went dry, his tongue cleaving to the roof of his mouth. 'Well, there's always me.' The words blundered out of him, awkward, jittery. His hands seemed to be in the wrong place, floating uselessly at his sides; he stuck his thumbs decisively in his sword belt, waiting. He shrugged his shoulders, playing down the offer; she could take it or leave it. It was of no consequence to him. Except that it was. Eyes of turquoise roamed her face, irises streaked with silver.

Stunned by his words, Katerina's mouth dropped open, smoky eyes widening. Had she heard him correctly? Her heart thumped rapidly, blood pulsing, picking up speed through her veins. 'Have you gone completely mad?' She stared at him, astounded. 'You would marry me, just to protect me from my uncle?' She smoothed her hand down the front of her skirts, slowly.

No, I would marry you because I love you.

'Of course,' he replied lightly, 'I forced you to return home, I got you into this mess. I never intended to wed anyway, given the kind of lifestyle that I lead. It makes no difference to me, either way. Look at it as a kind of business transaction.'

Her heat plummeted, sank. So that was it. That was how he saw her, as a business transaction, a burden for whom he felt responsible. How could she live with him, like that, together, and yet so apart, so distant? Would her spirit be able to bear such a thing? But then the thought of him walking away from her, maybe today, maybe tomorrow, never to see him again, seemed infinitely worse. Maybe marriage, albeit in name only, might be preferable.

She bit her lip, reddening the pink skin, twisting her fingers. 'Are you sure about this?' She scoured his face, looking for the jeer, the put-down, but could see only kindness in his eyes. He felt sorry for her, that was it, and realised he could help. Nothing more, nothing less.

He nodded. He had never been more certain of anything in his life.

Her mind scrambled, overwhelmed by his offer, overwhelmed with thoughts of what might be and what could never be. What could she do? He felt responsible for her, nothing more. Raising one hand shakily to her forehead, she tucked a shining strand of hair behind her ear. 'Lussac, I think you will regret this… I'm sure, I'm sure you will meet someone one day who you will want to marry…' her speech stuttered, faltered a little '…who you will love…' She stumbled to a halt.

I have already met her, he thought.

'Think about it,' he said. 'But at least wear this— as my betrothed, I can protect you.'

He delved inside the collar of his tunic, pulling out a ring on a silver chain. The gold circle spun in the air, catching the light. 'It was my mother's,' he explained, removing the ring from the necklace. Seizing her cold fingers, he slid the warm metal on to the fourth finger of her left hand.

'I…'An anguished look crossed her fine features, the words strangling in her throat. Her fingers clutched at her throat, at the rapid pulse that beat beneath her skin. The curving neckline of her gown puckered.

I'm moving too fast, thought Lussac, panic threading his chest. *She feels trapped already, hemmed in by my offer.* 'I've told you,' he said, deliberately keeping his voice blank, neutral, 'you're under no obligation to me. Wear this ring until you decide—then give it back to me if it's not what you want.' He shoved a hand through his thick, silky hair, sending the glossy strands awry. 'The ring means nothing, but others will take heed of it. It will keep you safe.'

She inclined her head shakily, praying that her swaying knees would keep her upright. 'I will tell you after we have fetched Philippe,' she whispered. 'I will tell you after that.'

He heard her words and wished the whole thing could have been different between them. Wished that he could have told her how much he loved her, how much he cared for her, to hear her shriek with joy, with happiness at the prospect of marrying him. But he saw the reticence in her stance, her agitation and embarrassment around him, and knew it could not be. She held no love for him, no respect. His only hope was that she would agree to his proposal. If that was the only way he could be near her, then so be it.

'Philippe?' He frowned. 'I thought he came with you?'

So that was it, she thought miserably, noting his dark eyes lifting to the attic space above the main chambers, searching the room for Philippe. Why had she even dared to hope that things might be different between them? She had to show him she was capable of picking herself up and starting again, capable of looking after herself. In that way he would not feel so obligated towards her.

'My uncle's men locked him, and me, in the tower at Longthorpe.' She threw him a meek, apologetic smile, 'I managed to escape, came here.' Her thumb nudged the unfamiliar metal on her ring finger, twisting it, pushing it back and forth across her skin. 'I was planning to go back later, when everyone was asleep, and help him.'

'On your own?'

'Margrete was going to ask a few men in the village to come with me,' she declared. 'It's not fair that Philippe was caught in the middle of all this.'

'Were you going to wait for me?'

'I had no idea where you were, Lussac. Or what had happened to you.... I couldn't leave Philippe locked up in the tower like that.' Patches of exhaustion reddened beneath her eyes.

He smiled down at her. 'You don't have to be so brave all the time, Katerina. Let others help you.' *Let me help you.* 'I think you should stay here, with your friend, and I will fetch him myself.'

Katerina was already shaking her head. 'The only way is across the marshes. The mist is too thick tonight; you'll never make it. You need someone who knows the route.'

'And I suppose that someone is you.' His eyes twinkled over her.

Katerina nodded.

She waited, restlessly, on the slight rise of the stony track while Lussac coerced his destrier into the lean-to shelter fixed to the side of the cottage, pushing one hand against the stubborn rump. The moon picked out the gleam of his hair, the diamond sharpness of his eyes as he settled the animal. The situation was hopeless: she had no idea how to be with him, how to behave or what to say to him. His ring winked on her finger, yet she had never felt more distant from him.

As Lussac approached, she flicked her skirts away and began marching off, her dancing step light and effortless across the loose gravel. Silently, he followed her, curbing his usual long strides to match her pace. His jewelled sword-hilt glinted, the silver blade wedged securely in a leather sheath that knocked occasionally against his leg as he walked.

Katerina shivered in the thin stuff of her gown. Since her escape from the tower at Longthorpe, she hadn't thought to borrow any extra clothes, no dress, or cloak, from Margrete; now she strode through the chill night air wearing only a chemise and her underdress of worn, shabby wool. Icy fingers of air crept beneath her skirts. All logic, all sense of practicality had vanished with the sheer unexpectedness of Lussac's proposal. Her senses were awry, shot to pieces; it was imperative to pull herself together if her heart were to survive at all.

Trailing her quick, purposeful gait, Lussac allowed himself to admire the seductive sway of her hips, the glittering plaits that bounced down the narrow indent of her back. In the moonlight, her hair faded to pale gold, a rich colour, incandescent. Her head was held high; he imagined her face set with a proud, scowling expression, her sweet, tip-tilted nose pointed up into the air, brooding over his proposal.

She stopped so abruptly he almost barrelled into her, twisting around decisively, glaring at him. He rocked back on his heels, keeping the distance between them. In a small copse of trees marking the end of the village, an owl hooted, the sound echoing eerily over the boundless sea of waving reeds to their left.

'What's the matter?' His breath punched out, a white mist dispersing.

'How can you do that?' she cried up to him, shivering, wiggling her toes within her boots, trying to keep them warm, to keep the circulation moving in her feet. 'How can you propose marriage like that?'

'I just did, didn't I? Isn't it the solution to your situation?'

'Yes! No!' Katerina stammered out incoherently, teeth beginning to chatter. Not like that! Not as some soulless agreement, she wanted to shout at him. Her head drooped. 'Lussac, I don't want you to throw your life away for me.' She hopped from one foot to the other; her feet seemed to be turning into blocks of ice. How could the temperature outside be so different from inside Margrete's cottage?

'I'm not,' he said bluntly, almost as if he hadn't heard her. He frowned down at her trembling frame, the way her arms crossed fiercely across her stomach, hands dug into her armpits to keep warm. 'Where's the other one?' he said, suddenly.

'Other one?' she repeated, puzzled. Hadn't they been discussing his proposal?

'Your other dress,' he said. 'Weren't you wearing a dark-blue gown over that thing? And your cloak, where's your cloak?'

She was shivering uncontrollably now, her slight frame racked with shudders. 'I had to leave them at Longthorpe,' she explained in a rush. 'And then I forgot to ask Margrete for something to wear.'

Forgot, because you were there. Because of what you asked me.

He was shaking his head at her. 'You're freezing. Here.' He swept the cloak from his shoulders, enveloped her in the fine warm wool, fastening the voluminous cloth deftly at her shoulder. His knuckles brushed her earlobe. 'There,' he said, 'at least you'll be a little warmer now.'

'Thank you,' she replied, stonily, annoyed at her own lack of self-preservation. The gathered wool of his cloak hugged her neck and shoulders, fell almost to her feet, shielding her from the cold, warming her. 'I don't know why you keep doing things like this for me, why you keep helping me. You hardly know me.'

His eyes deepened in intensity, sparkling over her. He adjusted the fall of his cloak, making sure it covered her properly. 'I disagree, Katerina. I know you.' The velvet timbre of his voice hurtled her back to the river, the flattened circle of grass, the delicious weight of his body slanted across her own. The breath snagged in her chest, knotting sharply; clapping one hand to her mouth, she staggered back, temporarily stalled. A ripe red flush stained her cheeks.

'My thoughts exactly,' he murmured.

'Yes—b-but,' she stammered out, 'a b-business

transaction, you said.' Memories of their intimacy shimmered between them, colouring the air, his raw, bleak gaze holding on to the smoky charcoal of her eyes.

If that was the only way he could be with her, then so be it, he thought. Strong, fingers grazed her chin, lifted her face to meet his. 'I'm sorry, Katerina. Sorry for everything. I should never have left you at the castle with Philippe.'

'You're not responsible for me, Lussac.'

I want to be. The silent admission seared through him, scorched his brain.

'Besides,' she continued, fighting to keep her tone even, neutral, despite the touch of his fingers lingering on her chin, 'you had other things on your mind.' Her voice lowered to a whisper.

'Hardly,' he interrupted her. 'If truth be told, any thoughts of revenge disappeared long before I left Longthorpe. It was pointless, me riding off to Hambridge like that. Stupid.'

'But you wanted to speak with my uncle...' Her voice trailed off.

'I changed my mind. You changed my mind, Katerina.' One side of his mouth quirked upwards, his fingers lacing with hers.

Her heart jumped, then plunged, beating faster, stronger under the light pressure of his hands, heat blossoming outwards from his rough palms. As if under a spell she swayed towards him, cleaving towards his muscular solidity. A moth to a flame, she thought, sadly, hopelessly. Unable to control herself around him, unable to hold her traitorous body in check.

He heard the truncated seize of her breath, felt the resisting brace of her muscles as she backed away. 'Forgive me,' he murmured, dropping his hands swiftly. Shame crawled through him. He had offered her a way out of her desperate circumstances, a life-line; he was in no position to abuse such a situation. He had to keep his hands away, his true feelings close to his heart, otherwise he might lose her for ever.

Stepping down from the village track, Katerina plunged down into the marsh, leading the way through the vast flatlands of rustling reeds on narrow, constantly dividing paths. Tall, bristling plumes waved madly above her head, feathers of bleached parchment in the glowing moonlight. The loose edges of his cloak, too big for her, billowed out, dark wings flapping. In the wake of her skittish pace, Lussac felt like an oaf, a great lumbering fool behind her, his marching stride heavy and purposeful.

Perched on its small bump of land, Longthorpe

Manor rose out of the shifting wreathes of mist, the tower black and angular against the silvery sky. Lussac reached out, caught Katerina's upper arm, curbing her fast stride. 'Where is Philippe?'

They were hidden in the mass of rushes, the muddy ground soggy and yielding beneath their leather boots. 'He's up there, second floor in the tower.' Katerina pointed out the dull glint of glass. 'But he has iron bars across the window; he cannot climb out that way.'

'Then how did you escape?' Lussac asked, not certain he wanted to hear her answer.

She smiled gently. The cloying air had spun her hair into delicate tendrils, framing her face like amber lace. 'There were no bars on my window; it was easy.' His fingers warmed her upper arm, heat travelling up to her shoulder, across her chest.

He glanced up at the crenellated edge at the top of the tower, marked the windows, the tremendous height from the ground, and knew that Katerina had climbed out. 'You fool!' he hissed. 'You could have been killed!'

'No, it was easy; you know what I can do,' she replied.

'I should have been here,' he murmured.

'You're here now.'

He acknowledged the softening of her voice; his

heart threaded with desire. His hand cradled the curve of her chin, his thumb drifting across the silken nap of her cheek, grazing the corner of her mouth, lustrous and pliable, then dropped away. 'Who do you think is in there?'

'My father, of course, and my uncle. And about half-a-dozen soldiers, at least two of them outside Philippe's chamber, and possibly one still sitting outside mine.' She laughed—an abrupt sound, disparaging. 'Fools, all of them.' Her eyes moved to his sword. 'Too many for us to fight, Lussac.' She paused. 'But I have a plan.'

He tilted his head to one side. A hard pulse knocked steadily at the base of his throat, surrounded by powerful, corded muscle. 'I'm listening.'

'I will climb up the outside of the tower to Philippe's window—' she began enthusiastically.

'Absolutely not!' he interrupted.

'And secure a rope to the bars,' she ploughed on, raising her voice against his objection. 'Then you will climb the rope and chop through the iron bars, and both of you will climb down.'

'And what do you suppose I chop through the iron bars with?' he questioned drily. 'My teeth?'

'Oh, I don't know,' she replied, frowning suddenly, looking about her, at the wind funnelling through the rushes, at the ground, as if the answer would helpfully materialise out of the air. 'Maybe…your sword?'

His expression was kind. 'Katerina, it's not going to work. The bars alone will defeat us. And I'm not having you climbing again, taking a risk like that. Is there no other way in, a way that would enable us to catch your uncle unawares?'

She thought for a moment. 'Well, there's always the kitchens, then up through the back stairs to the gallery. From there we can access the tower and bypass the main rooms on the ground floor.'

Lussac sighed with relief. He had no wish to remonstrate with her, nor belittle her considerable skill, but he had no wish to place her in danger either. 'Come with me, then,' he said, holding out his hand, 'and show me the way.' The shimmering moonlight flooded his face, throwing his long, spiky lashes into shadow on his cheek. 'And for God's sake, keep close by me,' he murmured as his hefty grip engulfed her slender fingers. 'That way I can keep you safe.'

Chapter Nineteen

Hugging the field hedges that ran up in rickety lines from the marshland, Katerina advanced on her home, aiming for a low huddle of buildings on the north side, Lussac behind her. A haze of cloud drifted across the moon, dulling the limpid brightness, shadowing their progress. Gaining the top of the gentle slope, she flattened herself against the mossy wall, reaching out for the circular handle, the ridged, cold metal pressing into the palm of her hand.

Strong fingers closed over hers. 'Let me go first,' Lussac murmured. Drawing his sword, steel rasping against the leather sheath, he turned the handle slowly, very, very slowly, nudging the door inwards with a faint squeak, the lightest protest from the rusty hinges. Damp, musty air flowed out from the darkened kitchens, the smell of rotting, fungal growth, of disuse and poverty.

Stepping down into the vast, cavernous space, Katerina picked out the huge fireplace, the jumble of pots and pans heaped up on the long trestle table in the middle of the room. Her heart lurched once more at the dismal state of the kitchens. 'My father has been living on next to nothing,' she said, trying to explain. 'I must go and find him, make sure he's all right.'

'No, stay with me,' Lussac replied sternly. 'We fetch Philippe first, then we find your father.'

'But my uncle was here…there's no telling what he might do!'

He held up one hand, hard callouses ridging the base of each finger. 'If your father has managed to exist without you for this long, then a little longer won't matter. How do we reach the tower from here?'

Biting her lip doubtfully, she showed him the narrow arched doorway in the corner of the kitchen that would take them to the gallery on the second floor. Her father had seemed so broken, so forlorn when she had seen him earlier. Silently, she prayed that he would keep himself safe until she, until they, could reach him. Lussac squeezed up the tight spiral staircase, the rough steps tilting and uneven.

The wooden gallery spanned the length of the

great hall along one side, suspended on chunky joists of silvered oak. Carved wooden palings, set at intervals, formed a banister to stop people falling into the space below. The high vantage point, on a level with the hefty chandeliers hanging from the rafted ceiling, afforded a bird's eye view of any activity below. As soon as he emerged into the space, Lussac crouched instinctively, sliding his back down against the bumpy, white-plastered wall, and, at his side, Katerina did the same.

'I'll see if anyone's there,' she whispered in Lussac's ear. Her warm breath brushed the sweet spot beneath his earlobe, tickling his neck, her lips tantalisingly close. If he had turned his face in that instant, his mouth would have been on hers. His fingers tightened around his sword hilt as he fought the urge to catch her in his arms, to take her mouth against his own. Desire sliced through him, a cutting zig-zag, tearing through his limbs. Taking a deep steadying breath, he watched her crawl to the edge of the gallery, her movements graceful, controlled, like a cat, skirts, his cloak, slipping behind, the gathered fabric following her across the planked floor. Peeping through, Katerina saw the stone mantelpiece of the fireplace and the destroyed chairs strewn across the flagstones like broken bones, starkly visible in the pool of moon-light piercing down from the upper windows.

Carefully, she crept back to Lussac, twisting her body so that she sat on the floor next to him. 'There's nobody there,' she whispered. 'My father isn't there…' Her voice tilted, tipped with anxiety. 'Where could he be, Lussac? Where is he?'

'He's probably tucked up in bed, fast asleep.' Lussac reassured her. Truthfully, he didn't care much about where her father was, after the way that man had treated his own daughter.

Another staircase spiralled up from the far end of the gallery leading to the upper floors of the tower where Philippe was imprisoned. With one shoulder braced against the central post that ran the vertical length of the stairwell, Lussac moved up slowly, sword outstretched and poised before him, the tip winking dully in the faint light from the narrow windows: open arrow-slits designed for defence. Katerina matched her pace with Lussac's, keeping level with him.

Lussac stopped, one powerful arm flinging out in front of Katerina, stalling her neat steps. The thick sinews in his forearm tensed against the soft muscles of her stomach. 'Katerina,' he said, exasperated, 'you have to stay behind me, remember. I am armed, you are not.'

She nodded, retreating down one step. 'Sorry,' she whispered. 'I forgot…I'm so used to doing things on my own.'

'We're in this together, Katerina, but, like it or not, you must heed my command.'

We're in this together. The words reverberated around her head and, for a moment, she forgot what they were doing and why they were both there, crowded together in delicious proximity on the shadowed stair. Her heart swelled with a delicious fulfilment, a hazy, rose-fringed chimera of her future dangling before her mind's eye; she would cling to that vision when reality came crashing down about her. And it would come. He would leave and she would be alone again.

Unless. Unless she agreed to his proposal. She picked unconsciously with her thumbnail at the heavy gold ring on her finger.

Lussac rounded the corner, his sharp, piercing gaze touching the dusty floorboards, the vaulted, cobwebbed ceilings. The landing was deserted. No soldiers in scarlet tunics. Nobody. With quick, skilful fingers, he shot the bolts on Philippe's door, turned the hefty key, helpfully left in the lock, and shoved the door inwards.

At the noise, Philippe staggered upwards from the chair he was sitting in, face pouchy with sleep, staring at the pair of them in consternation, as if he couldn't work out who they were.

'Philippe!' Lussac strode across the room, gripped his friend in a hug.

'Thank God!' Philippe blustered, his eyes switching between Katerina hovering in the door and Lussac at his side. 'Katerina found you!'

'The other way round,' Lussac replied, shortly. 'I found her.'

'Well, I'm very glad to see you, however you came to be here.' Philippe smiled. He picked up his cloak, laid across the hard oak chair. 'Let's get out of this place.'

'Lussac, please let me go and find my father,' Katerina said, as the two men walked towards her. 'I'll go to his bedchamber, see if he's there.'

'Not without me you don't,' Lussac said sternly.

Katerina's father slept in a chamber on the floor below. The door stood open, leaning in crazily, the iron hinge wrenched from the splintered oak frame. Inside, the tattered curtains around the four-poster bed drooped down in loose, ripped folds, the patterned silk torn and ripped. Shards of an earthenware jug and bowl, used for washing, littered the floor in rough, jagged pieces. By the window, a chair lay on its back, one leg broken, jutting outwards at an odd angle. The window glass was cracked.

'Is my father there? What has happened?' Katerina hopped about behind Lussac's broad back as he filled the doorway, blocking her view of the chamber. She pulled frantically at his shoulder, trying to sneak beneath the burly rope of his arm. 'Let me in, Lussac, please!' The panic rose in her voice and her eyes widened, huge discs of pewter. Lussac turned his head slowly, caught Philippe's eye over Katerina's head, sending a silent command. Philippe took hold of Katerina's arm, restraining her gently. 'It's better if you stay here,' he said. 'Let Lussac go in.'

Katerina's father sprawled across the floor on the other side of the bed, out of sight of the door. A pale yellowish colour spread across his face, his lips tinged with grey. Placing two fingers to the artery in his neck, Lussac confirmed what he already knew: the man's heart had stopped. Katerina's father was dead. A huge, wrought-iron candlestick rested in his lap, stained with blood.

Against the wall, jammed between an elm coffer and an unlit charcoal brazier, another man lay, chin pressed hard against his chest. The colour of his face, ghost white, suggested he was dead as well, blood seeping from a substantial gash on his hairline. The red liquid trickled down past his shuttered eyes, to the corner of his mouth, dripping slowly from his chin. Lussac hunkered down by this man, reaching forwards to feel for a pulse.

'He's dead, isn't he?' Katerina cried out, distraught, twisting herself out of Philippe's hold with a savage wrench. She burst into the chamber. 'Oh, my God!' Her eyes alighted immediately on her father, collapsed by the bed.

'Keep her out of here!' Pivoting angrily in his crouched position, Lussac roared at Philippe, who trailed in apologetically after Katerina.

A glint of steel behind Lussac's head caught Katerina's eye. The glint of a blade.

'Lussac!' she screamed, springing towards him, her body flying almost horizontally through the air to wrap the heft of his shoulders in her lissom arms, to roll him away from the blade, the deadly point of the blade carried in her uncle's hand. Her slight weight cannoned into Lussac, caught him by surprise, unbalancing his superior strength to knock him away. The blade, originally intended for Lussac, pierced the fabric of her cloak and gown instead, driving into the flesh beneath.

'Oh!' she gasped, as the knife rattled away, spinning across the floor. The breath left her uncle's lungs for the last time, and he sagged back, lifeless.

Intense pain ripped through her, tearing into the layers of muscle at her side, sapping her strength. She reeled away from Lussac sitting up, her head dipping and swaying with shock. She pressed one hand firmly to her flank, blood flowing through her fingers. A horrible, sickening nausea roiled in her belly.

'Why, in Heaven's name, did you do that?' Kneeling before her, Lussac stared at her, totally perplexed.

'You were in danger,' she replied in a clipped, tight voice. Was it her imagination, or did his voice boom very loud in her ears? She screwed up her eyes, trying to focus on his face, to quell the rage of sickness flooding her gut.

'No, I was not,' he countered softly. 'But both these men are dead. I'm sorry, Katerina.'

She pointed at the man slumped against the wall, delicate fingers trembling in the half-light. 'Not dead, Lussac,' she declared, voice shaky. 'That man, my uncle, is still alive.' She watched as Philippe stepped over to him, pulled back his eyelids, checked his pulse.

'He is most definitely dead,' Philippe said.

A sob of panic rose in her chest. Why wouldn't they believe her? 'He tried to stab you, Lussac,' she explained. Her head felt like it was slowly detaching from her body; her fingertips were numb. The lean contours of Lussac's face receded, his features becoming indistinct as the dark, frilling edges of unconsciousness threatened to claim her. She clung to the turquoise radiance of his eyes, willing herself to remain upright, to focus. 'I saw the blade,' she stuttered out. Lussac was looking at her as if she had gone mad. Head swimming, she searched the floor for the knife, spotted its feral gleam. 'There! Look, there!'

Philippe picked it up, handed it to Lussac.

'This knife has blood on it, Katerina,' Lussac said, puzzled. 'And he never touched me.' He stared at her. In the gloom of the room, her face seemed very, very white, unnaturally white, her eyes huge, burning orbs of mineral darkness. A slick of perspiration sparkled on her forehead.

'What's the matter with you?' he said slowly, suddenly noticing her awkward stance, the hand clamped to her side. His heart lurched, then plummeted. 'Christ in Heaven, Katerina, please tell me you didn't do what I think you did!' He scrambled over to her, gently pulling her hand away from her side to see the dark, tell-tale stain of blood. 'No, you stupid, stupid girl! You took the blade instead of me!'

'I couldn't let him kill you,' she muttered, her

whole body beginning to shake. She reached out through the misty haze, trying to touch his blurred features, to bring him back into focus. The last thing she saw was the stricken look on his face as she collapsed forwards into his arms.

'Philippe…fetch a light! Now!' Terror surged through him, a sour, metallic taste in his mouth. Bundling Katerina's limp form up against his chest, he carried her swiftly down the spiral steps, his shoulders and elbows knocking painfully against the rough stone walls in his haste to reach the ground floor. In his arms, she groaned fitfully, head lolling on his shoulder, the silken rust of her hair soft, tickling his neck; against his hand clamped around her waist, beneath his cloak, her blood pumped steadily, seeping through his fingers.

'Drag that table near the fireplace!' he bellowed at Philippe who puffed up behind him. Adjusting Katerina's weight so he could support her with one arm, he swept the table of useless detritus: a jumble of forgotten pewter plates, a dirty wooden spoon, a stained, ripped tablecloth—all went crashing to the flagstones in noisy cacophony, a jangling crash reverberating around the huge shadowy hall. He laid Katerina down carefully, supporting her head, shock flicking through him at the waxen gleam of her complexion, keeping one large hand pressed firmly against the wound. He refused to entertain the thought that she would die. She would not, could not die. He pushed the vile thoughts away, stamped on them, clenching his fists as if ready to fight.

'Light! Philippe, come on!' Urgency laced his voice, splitting his control. 'Stop fiddling about with that fire!'

Philippe, noticing a small gleam in the ashes of the fireplace, had blown the glowing sparks to life, and now fed the rising flames with the pieces of splintered furniture strewn around the hearth. Hunkered down, he thrust a torch into the flames, setting it alight. 'I need the fire, Lussac, in order to light the torch,' he explained patiently, coming over to the table, holding the burning, spitting brand aloft. Light flooded over Katerina's prone form, her gown twisted around her legs, one hand hanging limply off the edge of the table. The edges of the cloak fell away, either side of her. 'You need to calm down, Lussac, otherwise you'll be no use to her.'

Ignoring him, Lussac tore at the side of Katerina's underdress, her chemise, ripping open the seams to expose her pale, silken flesh.

'She won't thank you for that.' Philippe stared at the trailing threads in dismay. 'It will be a devil to mend.'

'What do you suggest I do?' Lussac bellowed at him. 'Undress her properly? It's too slow! I need to stop this bleeding now!'

Picking up the discarded tablecloth from the floor, Philippe shook it out, then passed it to Lussac. 'Here, this will help pad the wound.'

Lussac glanced at the stained tablecloth, scowling. 'No, too dirty,' he muttered, yanking his tunic, then his chainmail hauberk over his head, swiftly followed by his shirt. He rolled the fabric into a makeshift pad to press against the gash in Katerina's side. By alternately pressing and dabbing, he managed to soak up a significant amount of blood; to his relief, the constant flow seemed to be abating.

'Hold the light higher, Philippe, I can't see properly.'

With the torch held close, both men bent over Katerina, trying to gauge the extent of the damage. She stirred once or twice, head moving restlessly from side to side. Mouth set in a grim line, Lussac held on to her shoulder, stopping her falling from the table. From the torn seams of her garments, Katerina's wound gleamed, now reduced to a gaping, blood-filled line about the length of a man's thumb.

'What do you think?' Lussac murmured.

'Lussac?' Katerina whispered through cracked, dry lips. She shifted her head, resting her gaze on the two men at her side.

In that single, ecstatic moment, Lussac closed his eyes, savouring the tide of relief that flooded his limbs. For the very first time in his life, his knees weakened. He leaned over her, the rippling musculature of his bare chest glowing in the torchlight, absorbing the wonderful sight of her silver eyes, the fragile tilt of her smile.

'You're alive!' he said, stupidly. His hand cupped her cheek, thumb gently caressing.

Katerina smiled faintly, wincing with pain. Her side ached; she tried to lever herself up into a sitting position, but he held her down easily, palm spread across her chest. She flushed at the close contact, his fingers hard up against the curve of her breast.

'No, stay down for a bit. I need to bind the wound, otherwise it might start bleeding again.' His voice was gruff, but his heart soared with joy.

'What happened, Lussac? My father, is he...is he...?' The sentence choked off in her throat, her speech truncated. Dizziness swept through her,

threatened to take her down into the depths of unconsciousness once more. Gritting her teeth, she
clutched the table edge for support, willing herself
to remain awake, alert.

'Do you remember what happened?'

'Aye, I do. The knife in my uncle's hands. I saw
the knife.'

'And I didn't believe you. I thought the man was
dead.' He shook his head at his own foolishness.
'It was a stupid mistake; I should have checked.'

'At least he didn't harm you,' she said.

'No, but he harmed you! You took the blade that
was meant for me! It was such a dangerous, risky
thing to do! I can look after myself but you—'
his voice was raw, bleak '—you could have been
killed.' He pushed one hand through his hair, twisting the silken strands chaotically. 'Why, Katerina,
what on earth made you do it?'

*Because I love you. Because I love you and I
couldn't bear to see you hurt.* She chewed on her
lip. 'It was instinctive,' she muttered. 'I would have
done the same if it had been Philippe.' She lifted
her arm and crooked it over her eyes, blocking out
the searching intensity of Lussac's gaze. Her head
swam, befuddling logic. She found it impossible
to marshal her thoughts into any sense of order;
in her present, debilitated state, her mind was un-

trustworthy, floating on a cushion of unstable air. It would be better to remain silent rather than blurt out something she would later come to regret.

Reaching for one of the strips of white linen that Philippe had ripped into bandages, Lussac opened his mouth as if to disagree. Philippe frowned at him sharply, shaking his head. Partially hidden by her upraised arm, Katerina's face was chalk-white. Tresses of amber hair, dislodged from their braids, spilled out across the pale-grey planks. 'Not now,' Philippe said. 'You need to bind her up, not interrogate her. There'll be time enough, later on.'

Lussac nodded. His friend was right. With deft, practised movements he began to bind up Katerina's wound, lifting her gently. Philippe helped him, guiding the linen strips around her waist, beneath the loose folds of her gown. In silence, together, the two men worked over her, as they had worked over injured soldiers in their many battles before this time. Katerina lay back, sweat prickling her brow as her body tensed with pain. Lussac knotted the final strip into the smooth hollow of her waist, folding the splayed edges of the cloak together across the ripped devastation of her gown.

'We can't stay here,' she heard Lussac announce through her haze of exhaustion. Philippe muttered something in response, which she failed to catch. 'No, the village; she has friends there.'

At first, Katerina wasn't certain where she was. Opening her eyes, she encountered solid blackness, the atmosphere thick and close with the breath of many sleeping bodies. Above her head, she could just make out rough-hewn roof supports stretched into an apex. Margrete's cottage... Of course! She lay on the sleeping platform, a heaped mound of straw cushioning her back and hips, the fragrant smell of dried grass scenting the air. Her right flank throbbed incessantly, painfully, and an arid dryness scratched her throat; she needed a drink. Lifting her fingers, she moved them experimentally to her side, discovering the tight bindings around her waist, recalling the horrific events of the previous evening: her father, collapsed against the bed; her uncle, making one last stab for victory and...Lussac.

She twisted her head to the right, heart leaping with delicious shock. Somehow she had known he had been there all along. His long, lean body stretched out beside her, his broad chest rising and falling steadily with the deep, even breathing of a satisfying sleep. A coarse linen tunic covered his upper body, the fabric creased and worn; he must have borrowed it. His face was in profile, the sculptured indent of his cheek turned towards her. Her fingers itched to trail across those fine hewn contours, to smooth over the broad chest and hug him close. She heard the balanced sigh of his breath as he turned his head.

Dark lashes spiked open; his eyes twinkled at her, immediately focusing. 'Awake?' he murmured, his hand extending around her shoulder. 'How do you feel?'

'I feel sad,' she whispered across the darkness. 'Sad about what has happened.' Head pillowed in the straw, she licked her lips, craving liquid.

'Here.' Lussac lifted his leather water bottle. Reaching an arm beneath her narrow back, he helped her to sit up. She felt too weak to argue, to resist, bracing her body against the solid comfort of his chest. He pulled out the cork stopper from the bottle, handed the vessel to her.

He cleared his throat. 'I am sorry about your father, Katerina.'

She took a long cool drink, licking the stray drops from her lips, replaced the stopper and shook her head. 'I hadn't seen him for so long— and now this.' The bronze-coloured sift of her hair rested against the curve of his neck. On the other side of the platform, two small bodies slept soundly, alongside Margrete. 'I had a chance, a small chance to make things right again. What do you think happened?'

'I think there was a fight,' Lussac said gently. 'Two men at their wits' end with each other.'

Tears gathered in her eyes, spilled over, tracking a silvery gleam across her cheeks. 'What a waste, Lussac. Such a stupid, pointless waste of both their lives.'

He shifted around, bringing both hands up to clasp the sides of her face as she sobbed. Tears splashed on to her hands. His breath was warm across her skin, the generous curve of his mouth inches from her own. 'Shh,' he hushed her, low voice vibrating silkily across the darkness. 'Don't wake the children.'

She traced the fine contour of his upper lip, the quirk of muscle in his cheek. His hands moved upwards, pushing through her hair, the pads of his fingers cool against her scalp. Desire rushed through her, unbidden, relentless. She swayed towards him, her lips grazing the corner of his mouth. A butterfly touch. Her heartbeat tripped, then gathered speed, galloping haphazardly. Warnings flashed in her brain; she ignored them, stamped down viciously on them, unwilling to listen to the anxious chatterings of censure. Right now, she craved his touch, his kiss. She needed him.

He groaned, every nerve-ending in his body arcing with delight, clamouring for more, for her sweet touch. His hands looped behind her head, winching her closer, slewing his mouth more firmly across her lips. Passion sliced through his gut, hard, visceral; blood pumping furiously through his veins, hurtling, unstoppable. His hand swept down, across her shoulder, holding her tight beneath her arm. She shuddered as his thumb moved in a wide sweep across her breast, sending a fresh volley of desire rushing through her body, before recoiling suddenly at the jab of agony in her side. His hand had inadvertently strayed across the tight wrap of bandages.

'Christ, I forgot.' Breath punched from Lussac's lungs in short sharp bursts. He ran a distracted hand through his hair.

Her cheeks were bright, flame-red, irises huge, dilated with desire. The unexpected slice of pain jolted her senses, thumped her down into cold, clear reality once more. Shame washed over her at her wanton behaviour—what must he think of her? Her relatives lay dead in the castle, yet all she could do was think of the two of them together, their bodies linked, coupled for ever. Why did she persist in wanting him, in lusting after him? Surely she realised it would make it harder in the end?

'I started it.' Her half-smile was wan, apologetic.

'Yes, you did.' He smiled, relishing the race of blood through his heart. 'But I didn't mind.'

The tantalising warmth of his speech, his devastating smile, twisted at the strings of her heart. It would be their last kiss, a keepsake with which to remember him. Now she had to work at building her resistance, armouring herself against his deadly enchantment, the magic that he wove around her, for if she didn't, then her heart would surely break. She dropped her gaze to her hands, lying quietly in her lap, palms turned upright. The gold ring winked up at her in the half-light. His ring. His compassion, his sense of duty, of obligation, had offered her a way out when she had no place left to turn. But now the bars of her cage had been lifted. She had to let him go. To keep him at her side under false pretences, and watch him endure a life of misery with a woman for whom he held no love—that, she could not do.

'You do realise you are free now, Lussac,' she said, her heart folding in on itself, quietly, sadly. 'With both my father and my uncle dead, I have no need of your protection, your name.' She slipped the gold band from her finger, placed the shining metal into his palm. 'This belongs to you.'

So cold, so polite, after the heated intensity of their kiss. Hope flared, then spluttered, a feeble flame about to be snuffed out. The words tumbled from her mouth like shards of ice, each one driving deep into his heart. The heart that she had healed, had knitted back together with her soft, lucid ways, her limpid smile. She had mended him and put his damaged body back together, piece by piece. And now, it was about to be shredded apart, torn, all over again. He wanted to throw the ring back at her, stuff the warm metal back on her finger, force her to wear it. He wanted to shake her, to yell at her—*I want you to keep this, I want you to be with me!*

But she had to come to him willingly. He would not, could not force her. If he did that, he was no better than her uncle.

Katerina took a deep, shuddery breath. It was over. Hitching the torn sides of her gown together, she curled her body away from him, away from temptation, knowing that she was about to face an even greater loss than her father's death. Her head lolled against the mound of hay and she dragged the coarse woollen blanket across her back and shoulders, cocooning herself, closing her eyes. She couldn't bear to watch him walk away.

Chapter Twenty

When Katerina woke again, brilliant sunshine streaming through the crooked window set low into the attic eaves, the space beside her was empty. A numbness stole through her limbs, a creeping, debilitating despair, as she blinked at the dip in the straw where his body had lain. Birds twittered and chirruped outside, muffled by the thick cob wall: the indignant single note of a blackbird; the harsh guttural croaking of a raven. Lying prone, she angled her head; the sleeping spaces on the other side were also empty. Margrete and the children were obviously up and out. The temptation to lie there and succumb to the sweet oblivion of sleep once more, to forget, was so powerful that it threatened to overwhelm her. She had given Lussac his freedom and he had taken it, willingly. Had she made a dreadful mistake, by not telling him how she felt about him? She bit at her lip, choking back a welling sob, heart seizing with grief. She had lost him.

Planting her hands firmly in the drift of scented straw, she raised herself on to all fours, head reeling slightly. Her wound felt stiff and sore, but the tight bandaging made it feel more comfortable. Bleary-eyed from sleep, she crawled over to the open edge of the platform, peering down into the ground floor of the cottage.

Sunlight flooded in through the open doorway, illuminating the space; a pulse of fresh air breezed in, touching Katerina's face. Below, Margrete was stirring something in a round black pot, suspended on an iron chain over the fire. Steam billowed upwards; Margrete put a hand to her forehead, smoothing hair away from her hot, flushed face. Her raven hair was smooth, sleek, fashioned into two braided knots over each ear, a central parting revealing her scalp's white flesh. The wide curving neckline of her simply cut gown hugged her ample bosom, the russet-coloured fabric gathered in at the waist with a plaited girdle.

'Margrete,' Katerina called down.

'Oh, my Lord, Katerina, you're awake!' Margrete jumped, pressing one hand to her mouth. 'You gave me a start, you really did!' She placed the long-handled wooden spoon on a trestle behind her, her plump frame bustling to the foot of the ladder. 'Do you think you can climb down? Lussac told me what happened yesterday.'

Katerina's throat closed up with sadness at the mention of his name, nails digging into the soft skin of her palms. Was this how it was going to be? Was this how she would react any time anyone spoke his name? Surely it would become easier, with time. If it were to be like this, every single day for the rest of her life, then how would she ever endure it?

'Katerina? Shall I help you?' Margrete's strident voice budged through her thoughts.

'What? No, I can manage, thank you.' Turning around, she made her way down, feet sure and nimble in her stockings.

'I am so sorry about your father,' Margrete said, when Katerina reached the bottom of the ladder. Her lips pressed together, mouth turning down in a gesture of sympathy. 'I know you were hoping to sort things out with him.'

Katerina shook her head, tears welling up in the corner of her eyes. Margrete patted her hand. 'We'll talk about it later. Right now you look like you need something to eat.' She headed over to a collection of covered earthenware pots in the corner of the room and began rattling through them, lifting various lids and banging them down ahead.

Katerina licked her lips; her mouth was dry, her stomach roiling. The faintest suggestion of a headache tightened her brow, threatening. Sidling over to the open doorway, she inhaled the fresh, invigorating air. Her ripped gown gaped open, revealing the white bandages; she clutched at the ruined material in irritation, holding the edges together. 'Were you here when Lussac and Philippe returned last night, Margrete?'

Busy loading a wooden platter with an assortment of food, Margrete paused, a sprinkle of freckles standing out in her tanned skin. 'I certainly was. There was a tremendous knocking on the door, like the devil himself had arrived. Edith and Hugo, they were terrified, poor little things, huddled together up there on the sleeping platform. And then that man of yours strode in, with you half-dead, bundled in his arms, closely followed by the other one.'

That man of yours. Margrete obviously had no idea. Katerina tipped her chin in the air, fighting the desolation that knifed through her. 'The other one,' she repeated. 'Philippe, you mean.'

'Aye, that's his name. He slept down here last

night, by the fire. But Lussac, he insisted on carrying you up the ladder, sleeping next to you.'

Katerina's head swam and she clutched at the split oak door frame for support, wriggling her toes against the packed earth floor to keep her balance.

'He wouldn't let me touch you. He carried you all the way from Longthorpe,' Margrete continued, her voice brimming with admiration. Glancing at Katerina's pale, stricken face, she hurried to push a three-legged stool nearer to the fire. 'Here...' she handed Katerina a plate brimming with bread, cheese and cold meats '...come and eat now. You're looking a bit peaky.'

Stumbling towards the stool, Katerina sat down abruptly, accepting the food from Margrete. Two bread rolls, a hunk of crumbling cheese and a couple of thick slabs of meat, edged in white, viscous fat, wobbled precariously on the plate in her lap.

Picking up her spoon again, Margrete resumed her stirring. The pot bubbled and boiled frantically, great globs of liquid rising and falling on the greasy surface. 'He's handsome too, Katerina. Tall and strong, like my Peter used to be, God rest his soul.' She crossed herself. 'You're lucky to have found someone like—'

'He's not "my man", Margrete,' Katerina interrupted sadly. The smell of the cheese rose to her nostrils, acrid and pungent. 'He was only being kind, bringing me back here.'

'Kind? Are you mad, Katerina? Of course, I agree, he's kind, but that man adores you! It's written all over him, the way he acts around you, the way he looks at you...'

'Nay, Margrete, you have it wrong.' Katerina licked her lips, trying to rid her mouth of its sour taste. She stared bleakly down at the food on the plate, her throat closing up, knowing she was unable to eat it. 'He's gone, Margrete. He's gone and he's never coming back!' Her voice rose, pitching forwards into a shuddering sob. She stuffed her fist in her mouth, hating herself for this outpouring of emotion, trying to stop the rapid onslaught of misery, of grief.

Margrete's spoon stilled. She frowned. 'Why, no, Katerina, he's... Katerina, what's wrong? What's the matter?'

The plate sprung from Katerina's lap, the contents scattering across the floor as she staggered upwards, bolting for the open door. Outside, the sun beat down on the top of her head, lurid, glaring. The air hummed, colours intense, vivid. She ran for the orchards at the rear of the village, gasping, oblivious to the interested stares from the few villagers going about their daily chores. Brambles, thick, over-arching branches set with vicious thorns, tore at her skirts as she stumbled onwards, panting, half-collapsing against the stunted trunk of an apple tree. Dew soaked her stockinged feet. One hand braced against the tree, she pulled the balmy autumn air deep into her lungs, the scent of fermenting fruit. Disturbed by her sudden arrival, a raft of bright butterflies, feasting on the fallen apples, rose as a fluttering group, wings red, white and black. Raising her head, she stared at them listlessly, seeing only the wavering greyness of a bleak future ahead. A future without him.

Margrete puffed up, bosom heaving with the exertion of running. 'Katerina, are you all right? Did I say something to offend you?'

Katerina threw her a wobbly smile. 'No, of course you didn't. I needed to get out for a moment…all that talk of…' Her voice trailed off, unable to form his name. 'Of what has happened,' she finished lamely.

'Grief can show itself in many ways, Katerina.' Margrete looped her arm through Katerina's and the two women began to walk back to the cottage, skirts swishing through the long grass. 'It's only right that you should feel sad.' The rounded flank of Margrete's hip bumped companionably against hers. 'But at least now you have someone to take care of you, someone to love you through all of this.'

Katerina turned furious eyes on her friend. 'Will you stop talking about him like this! Like I mean something to him! He's gone, and there's an end to it.'

Margrete placed one hand on her arm. 'But he's not gone, Katerina. You ran out before I had a chance to explain. He and Philippe have gone to Longthorpe to...to bury your father.'

'I can't believe he's still here,' Katerina whispered, eyes widening with astonishment. 'Are you telling me the truth?'

'It's the truth, Katerina. That man is not going anywhere.'

Katerina fidgeted restlessly on the low stool, Margrete standing behind, clucking fretfully over the tangled hair. With an ivory comb, she pulled the tines slowly through the washed tresses, deep creases appearing on her brow whenever she encountered a particularly difficult knot. Water dripped from the curling ends, scattering dark spots on the floor.

'Bundle it up, Margrete, please.' Katerina twisted around, pleading with her. 'I need to find him, speak with him.' Her heart skipped, dancing with a thrilling beat. Fate had dealt her a second chance, a chance to tell him how she truly felt. If he pushed her words back in her face, rejected her, then so be it. She had to talk to him, tell him the truth. If she didn't, she would regret it for ever.

'There!' Margrete pronounced proudly, casting a triumphant eye over her friend's finished hair, the two thick plaits wound and pinned neatly at the nape of her neck.

Katerina rose from the stool, facing her friend. 'I'll go to the end of the village, wait for him there.'

'I'm not sure…'Margrete replied doubtfully, suddenly reaching behind her to release her apron strings. 'I'll come with you.'

'No, please, let me go alone. It's hardly strenuous. I'll wait at the edge of the marshes, I won't go any further, I promise.'

'Well…'

'Please, Margrete.' A sense of desperation rose in her chest. She picked fractiously at the frayed cuff of the gown Margrete had loaned to her: pale lilac linen, with an underdress of a darker violet colour. Her own ripped gown lay in the corner, a jumble of bloodstained rags, discarded remnants of a harrowing night.

Her friend nodded. 'I understand,' she said, 'but, please, please take care. If anything should happen to you...' Her oval eyes, liquid brown, widened dramatically in her sunburned face at the thought of encountering Lussac's wrath.

'Thank you,' Katerina said. She stepped out into the strong light, sun bathing her face, breathing a sigh of relief. Sometimes, Margrete's constant ministrations could be a little overbearing. Her body lightened, released, and she stretched out her arms wide, feeling the corresponding pull in her muscles.

Outside, Margrete's two children played around the cottage with another child who she didn't recognise, their screams of joy thrilling the balmy air. Seeing her appear, they stopped their game and scampered over, bare feet skipping across the stony ground. 'Where are you going, Katerina? Can we come too?'

Katerina bent down, ignoring the hot, stretched feeling in her side and hugged them both. 'Not this time, I'm afraid. This is something I must do alone.' Straightening up, she ruffled the thick brown hair on their heads, in turn. 'I'll be back soon and then we'll be able to walk together.'

She strode out along the track, the track that she had walked along with Lussac on the previous evening, heart threaded with stuttering unease. Her whole future was held in the fragile balance of the words she was about to say. The fields to her right were alive with the sound of insects, whirring and buzzing in between the ripening grass, the dusty seed-heads. The sky formed a wide bowl of pale blue above her head, hazed by a few white wisps of cloud. It was a perfect day, a perfect late summer's day.

She willed her skittering heart to settle, to cease rearing upwards in renewed waves of rattling panic. Clutching her hands across her belly, she knotted her fingers, trying to kindle some inner strength, a thickened layer of fortitude, for the conversation that lay ahead. A conversation that she had to have, and had to endure, whatever the consequences. She would take this chance, this risk.

She reached to place on the track where the narrow muddy trail led south to Longthorpe. Lussac would return this way, retracing his steps across the marsh. Behind her, the expanse of good pasture fields had ended in a copse of pollarded willows, trunks poking out at crazy angles from the spongy ground. The trailing willow branches whispered in the breeze.

'Katerina?'

Her heart seized. She turned, slowly, pivoting on the ball of her foot. Lussac stood below her in the tall rushes, his big-shouldered body framed by the rustling, waving grass. He was so beautiful, she thought, the polished shine of his hair fringing his tanned forehead, the expression on his strong, lean features expectant, curious, meeting the mineral sparkle of her eyes.

'I thought you would still be sleeping.' The husky melody of his voice reached up to her. 'What are you doing here?'

'I came to find you.' Anxiety jerked her speech, hobbled it; she chewed on her bottom lip. 'I wanted to see you, to speak with you…alone.' Her eyes flicked nervously to the swaying rushes, searching for a sign of Philippe. Her voice sounded weak, thready; she cleared her throat, swallowing down the dryness.

'He's a long way behind me,' Lussac interpreted her look, the curve of his mouth turning upwards into a smile. In one powerful stride, he leaped up the bank and on to the road where she stood, linking strong fingers with her own.

Her spirit quailed beneath his touch. 'I know what you did today. My father. I wanted to thank you.' No, no! she berated herself, that wasn't what she wanted to say at all. 'I wanted to thank you before…' she hesitated '…before you left. You've done so much for me…' In her agitation, the words stumbled out from her, tripping over each other, blurting fitfully. 'Everything...' she clutched about for words '...the marriage proposal...that was kind of you.'

'I'm not sure it was prompted by kindness,' he said.

'You asked me out of a sense of duty.' She attempted to explain his actions.

'No.'

'You forced me to return home; you felt responsible. It was to be a business transaction, you said.' Her speech scuttled out of her, carried on a wave of apprehension.

'I lied.'

The breeze, sifting through the willows, stirred the loose gathers of her gown, wrapping them around Lussac's legs, lovingly. Violet silk against tan-coloured braies. Above their heads, a swallow danced, a curved black V shape barrelling chaotically through the rising air.

'What do you mean?' she whispered slowly. Hope flickered in her chest.

'I asked you to marry me, Katerina, because I love you.' His eyes locked on to hers, held steady. 'Did you not realise? I would have done anything to keep you at my side.'

'Love...?' Had she heard him correctly?

He threw her a soft smile, fingers circling her slender wrists. 'Yes, Katerina, I love you. I want to live with you, lie with you, have children with you.' His eyes glittered over her, turquoise. 'When I first met you, I was a shattered man living a semblance of a life. Nothing mattered to me, no one. I was eaten alive, consumed by a cold, black-hearted revenge. I had one goal and one goal only: to kill the man who had slaughtered my family. I thought that killing would solve everything, but I was mistaken. It was you, Katerina, you have made life bearable again, with your bright courage, your beauty and your unerring ability to find the good in me.'

'You want to marry me?' she spluttered out, clinging to his fingers. 'Truly?'

'Will you?' She caught the slightest note of hesitation in his voice, the doubt.

Her heart soared with delight. 'Oh, Lussac, yes, yes!' she almost shouted, tears welling up, threatening to fall. 'I can scarce believe what you are saying!'

'Believe it, Katerina, for I speak the truth,' he replied solemnly. 'I love you and there's not a thing you can do about it.'

'I have always loved you, Lussac, from the moment I first met you.'

He smoothed one hand across the shining bronze of her hair, chuckling. 'What, even when I caught you in the forest? When I chased you up that tree?'

'Well, maybe not quite at that moment,' Katerina admitted, throwing him a shy smile. Tears spilled freely down her cheeks as she stared at him in wonderment, at this man who loved her, who had openly declared his love for her. As if in a dream, she touched his face, the lean slant of his cheek, the silky drift of his hair, her heart overflowing with pure happiness. Raising herself on tiptoes, she brushed his lips with hers, a fleeting exquisite touch, before he gathered her to him and bound her mouth in a kiss that would tie them together, for ever.

* * * * *

Discover more romance at

www.millsandboon.co.uk

- ❤ WIN great prizes in our exclusive competitions

- ❤ BUY new titles before they hit the shops

- ❤ BROWSE new books and REVIEW your favourites

- ❤ SAVE on new books with the Mills & Boon® Bookclub™

- ❤ DISCOVER new authors

PLUS, to chat about your favourite reads, get the latest news and find special offers:

- Find us on facebook.com/millsandboon
- Follow us on twitter.com/millsandboonuk
- ❤ Sign up to our newsletter at millsandboon.co.uk